MATTIE

SINGLE DADS OF GAYNOR BEACH

ELOUISE EAST

MATTIE

Three single dads looking for love that is right before their eyes.

Mattie's life is as perfect as it could be without a partner. The one person he wants is oblivious, but he doesn't want to rock the boat and change how things are. When his life irrevocably changes by the appearance of a baby on his doorstep, he calls in his best friend to help. After all, Jordan had a child of his own; he knows what to do. Right?

Jordan's life is as perfect as it could be minus a lover or two. His best friend, Mattie, is amazing; his ex is amicable, which is great as they have an eight-year-old son together; and he loves his job. Helping Mattie with his newfound daughter is a dream come true, and their bond grows into more with this new dynamic, but why does it feel incomplete?

Bray's life is as perfect as it could be while withholding himself from the truth. He's retired military, loves being outside, and when it comes to children, has a heart the size of all the oceans put together. He creates wooden toys for the children's hospital, and when Jordan comes asking for help for his son's new hobby, he can't say no. Throw in Mattie and his beautiful daughter, and it's more than he can resist.

But merging three separate lives into one cohesive family is harder than it seems.

Mattie is an MMM romance in the Single Dads of Gaynor Beach series. It follows a shy lingerie shop owner, a wild but adventurous lifeguard, and a rough and ready woodworker as they work their way through the trials of a new triad relationship.

AUTHOR NOTE

If you would like to see any potential triggers for this book
and any other books I've written, please go to this link on my
website: https://elouiseeast.com/triggers

CHAPTER 1

MATTIE

MATTIE EVANS SHIELDED HIS FACE AS WATER DROPLETS SPLASHED him. "Mind my book!" he grumbled as his best friend shook his hair some more. He turned the book face down to protect the pages. "You're an asshole."

Jordan Storm squinted at him, his mouth curved at the corners while his sun-tanned skin gleamed in the sunshine. "How else am I supposed to get dry?"

"Use a towel like normal people do. Just because you live in the water doesn't mean I want to."

"You should swim more often."

A shiver went down Mattie's spine, and he shook his head. "No way. Paddling, yes, but swimming? I'm good, thanks."

Jordan waved his hand dismissively before planting both on his hips and studying their surroundings. "I still can't understand why you love boats but hate being in the water."

Mattie wasn't upset by his distracted best friend—after all, he was a lifeguard and needed to be alert at all times while he worked. Mattie peered at the vast ocean laid out before him, past the umbrella shielding him from the lobster-inducing effects the sun sometimes had on him, and considered his answer. Again.

"I don't care for the unexpected," he said in the end. It was true. He loved being organized and prepared, and planning for every eventuality was his preference for anything, work or personal life. Surprises threw his balance off. But the truth was, it was the ghost stories that had him.

Ever since Gaynor Beach's founding father and first Mayor's wife died in a sailing accident on the rocks of Willis Point five years after the founding of the city, there had been stories told of a woman walking on those very rocks and a boat that could be seen whenever it was foggy. And after seeing something on the rocks near the lighthouse himself as a child that he couldn't explain, he had stayed away from the ocean. Swimming in a pool was fine, but the ocean was a whole other ballgame. Except for paddling because his feet were still firmly on land with that.

"That I can testify to," Jordan said. "Are you still staying until the end of my shift?"

Mattie nodded. "Sure. I have plenty of pages left to get through."

Jordan threw his head back and laughed. "I would need to do a double shift for you to finish that book."

Dropping his head, he tried to stop himself from smiling. "So?"

"I'm not doing that. You can finish it at home. You still have the rest of the day."

Since it was Sunday, he had the day off work because his shop was closed. Lovely in Lace was a lingerie shop for people of all kinds who wanted something decadent and pretty to cover themselves with. Despite the nature of his business, it had been a tremendous hit with the residents, all the way from Oakdale's working class to Willis Cove's wealthier constituents, from the moment he'd opened it twelve years ago.

"Are you cooking dinner?" Mattie asked.

Jordan chuckled. "If I didn't, we'd starve. We'll drop by Sea Breeze to grab something tasty on the way home. You can buy." He took off, jogging back to his colleagues, and Mattie sighed.

"It's a good job his cooking is worth it," he mumbled, bringing his book back up now the chance of ruination was gone.

Three hours later, he packed his belongings, shrugging on a loose T-shirt, and headed for Jordan. His best friend clapped hands with another lifeguard and slid his arm around Mattie's shoulder.

"Ready for home?" he asked.

Mattie tried to ignore the heat burning through the fabric of his T-shirt from Jordan's arm, which had nothing to do with the sun and everything to do with Mattie's fantasies about his best friend. Fantasies he'd kept secret since they'd first become friends ten years ago when Jordan entered his shop to buy a gift for his cousin.

"Good afternoon. Let me know if you need any help," Mattie said to the new customer. He was always unfailingly polite, even to those who looked down on him despite wanting what he sold.

"I will, thanks."

The guy was maybe early twenties, maybe a little older, but he was definitely what Mattie described as a beach bum. His skin was tanned to a golden hue from the sun—no fake tan could ever get that good of a result—his hair had lightened in places, giving a shimmer to some strands depending on how the light caught it, and his face was full of masculine beauty.

Mattie blinked and turned away, not wanting to creep on the guy when he might buy something. He monitored him from the corner of his eye, though, interested in what he was looking for.

There was no rhyme or reason to what he inspected. Sometimes, it was stockings and suspenders. Sometimes, it was a lace teddy. Then he moved to the corsets. Mattie wanted to ask if there was something specific he was looking for but didn't want to intrude. Luckily for him, the guy came over.

"Hey, I'm looking for something for a guy." His eyes twinkled as he spoke. "He's quite muscular, but I want something that would fit him but not rip."

Mattie nodded. "Okay." He moved from behind the counter and headed for the corsets. "When you say muscular, are you talking Dwayne Johnson muscular or Chris Hemsworth?"

The guy squinted. "Dwayne Johnson."

"Okay." Mattie looked through the selection and chose two options that could work, depending on his actual size. "No matter what you pick, you can get a refund if it doesn't fit, as long as it's not ripped. But this would probably be the best idea. The corsets are versatile in that they can be loosened or tightened as needed."

The guy threw his head back and laughed. "Perfect. He'll die over this."

Mattie frowned. "Sorry?"

The guy waved his hand. "It's a gag gift for my cousin's bachelor party. He'll look amazing in it." He chuckled again.

Mattie pursed his lips and looked at the ceiling, counting to ten. Then he faced the guy again. "These clothes are not for gag gifts. They are exquisitely designed items for those who wish to explore a different side to their appearance. They are not to be laughed at or ridiculed because someone is wearing them." He put the corsets back. "I'd like you to leave now."

The guy's eyebrows rose, and he pressed his lips together. He rubbed at his forehead and nodded. "Understood."

Then he turned around and left, not even slamming the door behind him. Mattie exhaled heavily, willing his heart rate to calm. He wasn't one for shows of temper, but when someone mocked his livelihood, he wasn't having it. Let the guy get his kicks elsewhere.

He put it out of his mind as much as he could until the following day, when the guy came in again.

Mattie stood up. "I thought I told you —"

The guy held up some flowers. "I come bearing an apology gift."

Mattie's mouth gaped, and he couldn't think of what to say.

"I'm really sorry about yesterday. You had every right to go off on me about it. I didn't think how my actions would be construed, and I am truly sorry."

He handed the flowers over, and Mattie stared at them, rather than the man who had apologised for his behaviour. The first man Mattie had ever known to do so.

"Um, thank you."

The guy held out his hand. "I'm Jordan Storm."

Mattie shook his hand, inhaling when a spark pinched his palm. "Mattie Evans."

"I told my boyfriend about what I did, and he gave me a talking to as well. Sometimes, I don't think before I act, and it doesn't go well."

Mattie chuckled. "I understand."

SOMEHOW, JORDAN HAD WORMED HIS WAY INTO MATTIE'S LIFE like he belonged there. And Mattie had fallen harder and harder for the funny, easygoing, amazing person Jordan truly was. Those feelings had never left.

"Lead the way," he said, instead of grabbing Jordan's nape and pulling him in for a kiss. He cleared his throat and dragged his bag to his shoulder, dislodging Jordan's arm.

They jumped onto the bus after picking up the fish and headed for Mattie's house. Whenever they got together, it was always at Mattie's home because Jordan shared a house with roommates. He'd offered Jordan his spare bedroom several times, but he'd refused without offering a reason.

By the time Jordan was elbow-deep in cooking, Mattie was showered and dressed and sat at the table, pretending to read his book when, in fact, he was watching his best friend move around his kitchen like he owned the place. And what Mattie wouldn't give for that to be true.

"Cody is asking if you're coming camping with us next weekend," Jordan said.

Mattie glared at him. "You know my answer to that."

Jordan chuckled. "Yes, but I told him I'd ask. He's only eight. He doesn't understand why you don't enjoy camping."

"Explain that not everyone likes the same things."

"I have. But because he enjoys it so much, he doesn't understand how you can't."

A shudder ran down his spine. "And I don't understand how you both can enjoy it so much."

Jordan's mouth stretched into a smile. "It's the outdoors, Mattie! Fresh air, cool breeze, no noise pollution. It's great."

"I can do that by opening the window and putting my headphones on."

"Pfft. You need to get out more."

"And we have had this conversation how many times over the years?"

"Too many," they said in unison and laughed.

"I know Cody wants me to come," Mattie continued, "but the idea of sleeping out in a tent in the middle of a forest is not at all appealing."

Jordan snorted. "No. Burying your head in a book in a corner of a room is so much better."

Mattie looked around for something to throw at him, but all he had was his book, and he wasn't throwing that anywhere. "Shut up. It's okay to be different."

Jordan held up his hands and then plated their food. The lemon and herb scent was divine. This was the reason he didn't mind paying for the food. If Jordan kept cooking, he would keep paying.

"How is Cody doing now?"

Cody was Jordan's son with his ex-partner, Ash. They had

been together for around five years before deciding to arrange a surrogate for them. Unfortunately, their relationship didn't work out, and when Cody was three, they split amicably. They shared custody of him with Jordan working his lifeguard shifts around Ash's Home Health Aide job, which, as far as Mattie was concerned, was damn good of him. The end of that relationship was something Mattie could've jumped on, but he couldn't find the courage.

Jordan finished his mouthful and put his fork down, crossing his arms and leaning on the table. "He's better now we've spoken to his teacher. Although Cody said he'd told the teacher, the teacher denied knowing about it. We didn't bring that up with Cody because it could've been that the teacher wanted to pretend he didn't know. But anyway, Cody doesn't seem to have had a problem with that kid since. We're monitoring it, though."

"I'm glad they at least seemed to do something. That kid should never have bullied Cody in the first place."

Jordan resumed eating with a grin. "You are a fierce uncle, to be sure. I wouldn't like to get on your wrong side when it comes to Cody."

"Definitely! He's an amazing kid, and Uncle Mattie is happy to babysit anytime. Unless it involves camping," he added when Jordan opened his mouth. His best friend snapped his mouth shut again, and Mattie chuckled. "You're too transparent."

They finished their meal, and Jordan checked his watch. "I have to go. Cody will wear a hole in the carpet, waiting for me to pick him up."

Mattie smiled. "Have fun and be safe."

Jordan hugged him as he always did and headed for the door. "Sorry for leaving the dishes!" he called back.

"No, you're not!" Mattie shook his head. Jordan knew he enjoyed doing it himself because everything got put back where it was supposed to be rather than where Jordan thought it should go. That was one thing about not having Jordan living with him. At least he could keep his stuff where he wanted it.

When he finished, he grabbed his book, checked everything was locked up, and headed up the stairs to bed. He changed into his pajamas, even though it was still fairly early, and climbed into bed. Tucking the duvet around his hips, he reached for his book and lost himself in the story once more. As much as he wanted to, he wasn't going to get it finished that night, but he wanted to see them at least past their troubles.

An unexpected sex scene jumped into the story, and fuck, it was hot. Mattie swallowed hard as the author described what one character did to the other, and his cock responded as images bombarded him. His mind automatically pasted his and Jordan's faces over the characters, and Mattie's blood heated. He licked his lips, eyes glued to the page as his free hand wrapped around his dick.

The characters had been watching TV, and one had reached across and palmed the other's cock. Within seconds, their clothing had been opened and pushed aside, and the bottom had straddled the top's legs, backwards, and sank down on him. He braced himself on the top's knees and bounced.

Mattie could just imagine doing that to Jordan when he least expected it, and his orgasm barrelled through him. He closed his eyes and finished the scene in his head. He rested his head back against the headboard as his body cooled.

"Fucking hell, Mattie. Grow a pair."

He put the book on his bedside table and cleaned himself up, grabbing a new pair of pajamas. This time, when he settled into bed, he didn't reach for the book. He rolled to his side, turned the lamp off, and stared into the darkness. His brain conjured up more images of Jordan, playing with Cody, teasing Mattie, rescuing people in the ocean, the wet T-shirt competition they did one year. There were ten years' worth of memories, and yet, he couldn't bring himself to ask Jordan if he wanted more than friendship. Yes, Mattie had other friends if his relationship with Jordan suffered for his question, but Jordan was Jordan. No one could replace him.

One day, Mattie would get the courage to ask Jordan that all important question.

Will you go out with me?

CHAPTER 2

JORDAN

JORDAN SPENT THE FIRST PART OF THE WEEK FERRYING HIS SON back and forth from school on his way to work, and by the end of the week, he was as ready for their camping trip as Cody was.

He pulled up to his ex's house and switched off the engine. The moment he stepped out of the car he had borrowed from his parents for the weekend, he heard Cody's shout, and he laughed. The little guy must've been watching out of the window. The front door flung open, and his rambunctious eight-year-old ran down the path and into his arms. It was the best feeling in the world.

"Hey, bud. How're you doing?"

"Great! I got all my spellings right today."

Jordan hugged him again and then ruffled his hair. "Good job." Cody had trouble with spellings and times tables, but he was getting better. The school was great at helping the kids with schoolwork without the kids even realising they were doing it. He glanced at the door as Ash exited, carrying Cody's bags. His ex was a handsome guy, ten years older than him, but still looking good. "Hey. How're things?"

Ash smiled, though Jordan swore the lines were deeper on his face. "Good. Busy."

Jordan understood that. With Ash's job as a Home Health Aide, he was attending to patients day and night, depending on his shift pattern, and the hours could be horrendously long some days. It had never been something that had affected their relationship when they'd been together because Jordan had known from the beginning what Ash did, and he didn't expect him to change his job for him.

Their problem had been that they just hadn't seen each other. They were like ships passing in the night, to borrow a phrase his father liked. When Ash came home from work and went to bed, Jordan was getting up. Then when Ash woke, Jordan was heading out to work or bed himself. It was neither of their faults, but it hadn't worked for them. Their split, however emotional, had been a mutual agreement.

Jordan still loved Ash, and always would, but they weren't right for each other.

He turned to Cody. "Are you ready?"

Cody nodded. "Is Mattie coming?" His voice was so hopeful, but Jordan shook his head. "Is it bad that I want to kidnap him and take him, anyway?"

Jordan threw his head back, laughter booming from him. "I don't think he'd appreciate that."

Ash chuckled. "He definitely wouldn't. Have a good time, Cody. Not too many marshmallows this time, huh?" He raised his eyebrows and stared at his son.

Cody bit his lip. "I'll try?"

Jordan doubted he meant it as a question, but when Ash shook his head and smiled, Cody hugged him and scrambled into the car. Jordan grabbed bags and put them into the trunk. Before he climbed back into the car, Ash said his name.

Ash slid his hands into his pockets, something he always did when he had something serious to say, and Jordan braced himself. "We always said we would be honest and upfront with each other." Jordan nodded. "I've met someone."

Jordan grinned. "That's great!"

Ash raised his eyebrows. "It is?"

Jordan squinted at him. Was there something wrong with finding someone else? "Of course it is. You've been alone for a while. I'm happy for you. Does Cody know?"

Ash shook his head. "I wanted to wait a bit before I said anything to him. You know, in case it fizzles out."

"Understandable. I don't think you'll have any problems. He'll probably see it as someone else to wrap around his fingers."

Ash chuckled. "Yeah, probably. Anyway, sorry to drop it on you before you go, but I wanted you to know in case Cody had seen or heard something and I hadn't realized."

"Thanks. Have a good weekend. Get some rest, yeah? You look tired."

Ash snorted. "Thanks…I think."

Jordan winked and climbed into the car. "Ready?" he asked Cody.

"Set? Go!"

Chuckling at his son's regular reply, he waved at Ash and headed for the campsite they always used. It wasn't far away, just up Route 5, to the north of Gaynor Beach, where the land was covered with trees. It was the perfect getaway, but also close to home should they need to go back. He'd promised Cody they would go somewhere else to explore when he was a little older, but neither of them cared. They loved their home away from home.

"So, what have you got to tell me that you haven't already told me this week?" Jordan asked.

Cody fiddled with the radio. "Erm, I don't know. Did I tell you about the basketball competition we did?"

"Nope."

Cody described what they'd done the previous day and

then continued about his favorite TV show while Jordan navigated the roads. When they made the turn for the campsite, Cody went quiet and stared around them as he always did. He'd once told Jordan that he enjoyed looking around and seeing what he could see before he got to their spot, so Jordan stayed quiet for him.

He stopped the car and looked around. Apart from their breathing, there was silence. He climbed out and stood still. Pure silence. Cody settled beside him, and Jordan closed his eyes and breathed. He couldn't understand why Mattie didn't like camping, either. It was so peaceful.

"Right. Tent."

They set to work, getting the tent set up, the firewood collected, and the pot hanging from their makeshift stand so they could cook their dinner. It was a good hour and a half before they were done, but it was worth it. The warm August air meant they wouldn't need the fire for heat, but it was part of the experience. He tugged Cody to him and took a selfie, shooting it off to Ash and Mattie to show them they'd arrived safely.

Mattie replied immediately.

MATTIE: BE SAFE.

JORDAN SMILED. MATTIE WAS A WORRIER, WHICH IS WHY JORDAN sent updates regularly to him. The one and only time he hadn't, Mattie had gone off like a rocket when he'd got back. That was something he didn't want to experience again.

He tipped some soup into the pot for their dinner and settled beside Cody to wait for it to warm. His son held a stick and was peeling off the outer part, using his fingernails to dig into the softer part of the wood.

"What are you making?" he asked.

Cody didn't look up. "School has started doing woodwork with us, and I really enjoy it. If I had a knife, this would be called whittling. It's where you slice off layers of the wood and make it into something else. A teacher showed us a pencil he had made entirely from wood that had been shaped into a bear. It looked amazing. Obviously, the ink wasn't wood, but it was fantastic."

Jordan picked up on the excitement Cody felt. "Is this something you want to continue with?"

Cody glanced at him. "If I could, that would be great. I know things can be expensive, though."

Jordan ruffled his son's hair again. "We won't say no until we look into it. How does that sound?"

"Really?" His eyes lit up.

"Really. When we get back, I'll do some research—you can do some, too—and we'll compare notes. Even if we start you off with something small. Like whittling. I'm sure we can make it work."

With how excited Cody looked, Jordan was going to make sure it happened.

———

Their two-night stay at the campsite went far too quickly for them both, but real life intruded. Ash wasn't working for the next four days, so Cody would stay with him until Thursday evening, when Ash would drop him off with Jordan.

In the meantime, Jordan had work to do.

Before his shift started on Monday, he researched woodworking and then wished he hadn't. There were so many options, he couldn't decide what was right or wrong. So, he changed his search terms and tried to find someone who could give him some pointers. He started with a couple of carpenters he knew in passing. Chris and Mike were part of

Smithson Construction, and although they gave him plenty of information, they suggested speaking to someone who specialised in whittling. The guy's name was Bray, and he made wooden toys for the children's part of the hospital.

Unable to visit the guy straight away, Jordan nipped into Nice Buns to grab some deliciousness that was baked goods and headed for Lovely in Lace.

"I'm looking for a gag gift for my friend," he called, leaning his elbows on the counter and grinning at his best friend.

Mattie's eyes lit up, and he tilted his head. "I'm sorry, but I don't allow such moronic behaviour in my shop. Please leave immediately."

Jordan chuckled and glanced around. "Slow day?"

Mattie stood and leaned his hip against the counter, crossing his arms. "Actually, no. It's only just slowed down. I got a delivery of the new stock, so everyone wants a piece. I'm ready for lunch, though."

Lifting the bag from where it had been near his hip, he held out his offering. "Nice Buns?" Mattie groaned and grabbed for the bag, but Jordan held it out of his reach. "Now, now."

Mattie threw his hands in the air and then to his hips. "What? I'm hungry!"

"Yes, you are. Very *hangry*."

"I'll show you *hangry* if you don't feed me."

Jordan smiled and lifted up the cookie he knew Mattie would kill for. Sure as the sun came up in the east, Mattie's eyes and mouth widened. Without pausing, he held the cookie to Mattie's mouth. His best friend closed his mouth around it and groaned, his eyelids fluttering as they fell shut.

Jordan's heart rate increased, his eyes stuck on the sight before him. Mattie's eyes stayed closed as he bit off a piece, moaning as he chewed, and Jordan froze. His cock thickened behind his shorts, and he swallowed, but he couldn't look away. When Mattie opened his eyes again, searching for more, Jordan—who was a glutton for punishment it seemed—held it out again, and they repeated their previous exercise. Crumbs covered Mattie's lips, and as he licked it away, Jordan licked his own lips.

"Excuse me?"

Jordan dropped the cookie as they were interrupted by a customer that he hadn't heard enter. He cleared his throat and diverted his gaze—and his hip—towards the counter, picking up the remains of the cookie and placing it on the paper wrapper.

Mattie finished chewing. "I'm sorry. It's lunchtime," he said with a small chuckle. "How can I help?"

While Mattie dealt with his customer, Jordan took out the glazed donut he'd bought for himself and devoured it as slowly as humanly possible to give himself time to calm the fuck down. What the hell had that been? Mattie was his best friend, but he groaned like he was being reamed, and Jordan's brain couldn't distinguish between the two, apparently. He drank the coffee he'd also brought and tried to ignore his body.

By the time Mattie had finished with the customer and they'd paid and left, Jordan was under control.

"Thanks for the cookie," Mattie said and picked it up.

Oh, hell no. Jordan smiled, shaky though it seemed, and picked up his coffee, walking backwards. "That one's yours. I have to go. Work." He bumped into something and barely stopped it from cascading to the floor. Stepping away slowly, as if the items were just waiting for him to get outside of reach before falling, he headed for the door. "See you later!"

He slipped through the exit and leaned against the wall, breathing like he'd just run a marathon. What the ever-loving hell was wrong with him?

Wiping his forehead, he sipped his coffee as he strode for the beach. It wasn't far from Mattie's shop, and as the sun was shining, he pushed all inappropriate thoughts to one side and focused on the day ahead. He had four hours of lifeguard duties to attend to before finishing his shift by completing the relevant activity reports for the day. It was often a lot of standing around and watching, dealing with visitors who were a little rowdy, and giving medical aid should someone need it, but he loved it. When he wasn't a lifeguard on the beach, during the winter, he did it at swimming pools and also did swimming lessons for people. He spent most of his time around the water. There was just something about it that fed his soul.

If he had time after his shift, he might see about finding this Bray guy. He would hopefully be able to give him some advice on what to buy and where to get it from.

Throwing his empty coffee cup in the bin, he jogged the rest of the way to the lifeguard station, signing in for his shift and heading for his tower. Helen was already there, arms crossed and staring out at sea.

"Hey," he said as he climbed the steps.

"Hey, yourself." She smiled. "How was the camping trip?"

"Awesome as always." He leaned against the railing. "Didn't you have your parents over this weekend?"

Helen shuddered. "Yes. First time meeting Greg. It didn't go well."

Jordan raised his eyebrows. "Why not?"

"Greg burnt the chicken and set the smoke alarms off. He then put it on the side to deal with later while he tried to find something else to cook, and the dogs got to it."

"Oh, my god." Jordan tried to not laugh.

"That was only the beginning, but I can't say anymore because it's just…oh, god. Let's just say my parents are happy they live five hours away."

"Oh, poor Greg. I bet he was mortified."

"He was. More so because we turned up just as the dog

tore the chicken to shreds and dragged it across the kitchen floor."

Jordan covered his mouth with his hands, but he couldn't stop the laughter. "I'm so sorry."

Helen grinned and shook her head. "It's fine. Afterwards, Greg and I laughed about it, but at the time…"

"Well, if it helps distract you, I'm trying to find someone who can explain to me about woodworking so I can help Cody do it."

They spent the rest of their hours together, trying to one-up each other with stories. Jordan wasn't sure who'd won by the time they'd finished, but his sides ached from laughing.

Then he remembered he was supposed to be cooking for Mattie the following day. How was he going to face him after what happened that afternoon?

CHAPTER 3
BRAY

Retired Sergeant First Class Bray Rushden palmed the basswood block and his whittling knife and settled into his chair. He already knew what the little wooden block would become. He just had to make it. There was a sweet seven-year-old girl who loved bears sleeping at the hospital awaiting the results of the many tests they had put her through, and he wanted to do something special for her. Creating a little wooden bear wouldn't take him much time at all.

When he'd finally retired from the US Army, he'd been at a loss as to what to do. With his two sons all grown up and moved out and his ex-wife moved on, he had nothing waiting for him whenever he came home. Instead of becoming the couch potato he'd seen some of his friends touting, he took up fishing, running and, when he'd visited the hospital and seen the state of the available toys for the children, woodworking. He enjoyed working with his hands, and it would keep him out of trouble.

What had started as a hobby had become even more than he'd expected. His weekly visits to the hospital to bring new toys had evolved into specific toys for specific children that they could take with them wherever they went. Hence the bear.

He'd just started carving the initial shape when a knock sounded. He gritted his teeth and rolled his shoulders as he put the wood down. Who the heck was bothering him at home? Everyone who mattered had a key to let themselves in.

He flung open the door, and the guy on the other side jumped about two feet in the air.

"Holy—" The guy exhaled. "You scared me." Bray just glared at him. "Okay. Um, I was told that you were a good person to speak to about woodwork. My son has been doing some at a school and he wants to continue, but I know nothing about it, and I wondered if you could give me some pointers on what to buy and anything else you think a clueless guy like me might need to know."

The verbal barrage of information sank into Bray's head with years of experience in making split-second decisions. So why he didn't shut the door in the guy's face, he didn't know. He didn't want to help someone else because it meant he'd have to interact with them. The reason he'd chosen solitary hobbies was because he wasn't a people person.

At all.

"Um, is that...something you can do?" the guy added.

Bray sighed and left the door open, pivoting and taking his seat once again. The door remained open and the guy on the other side of it.

"Get in here," Bray said, a little more gruffly than he'd intended.

"Yes, sir."

The guy stepped over the threshold and into Bray's sanctuary, but instead of feeling overwhelmed, he was just aware. Overly aware.

"What's your name?"

"Jordan Storm..."

Bray raised one eyebrow at the guy's trailing off instead of saying "sir" again. Bray wouldn't have minded.

"What do you know about woodworking?" he asked.

Jordan avoided his gaze by looking around. "Nothing."

Bray sighed. He put down the soon-to-be-a-bear and stood. "Follow me." He moved towards the back of the house where he kept his tools, but he felt the hesitation in Jordan. "If I was going to kill you, I would've done it when you first interrupted my morning."

"Understood."

Tentative footsteps followed him, and Bray led the way into the room. To uneducated eyes, it could easily have looked like a torture chamber, but every tool was for a specific use. He focused on the smaller tools he used for whittling, rather than the larger ones that he used for bigger pieces of woodwork he rarely made.

"Okay. You ready for a lesson?" Bray asked.

Jordan nodded. "Oh, hold on." He grabbed his phone from his pocket. "I need to make notes." He pressed a few times on the screen. "Okay, ready."

Bray opened his mouth to start, but a thought crossed his mind. "How old is your son?"

Jordan smiled, and Bray blinked as if the sun had just come out. "He's called Cody, and he's eight. He started whittling at school—"

"School. Yeah, you said. I know which school you mean. Well, in that case, you need these."

He pulled several things forward and let Jordan take a photo of them, which he then annotated with the names of them. After explaining the basics of it to him, Bray saw the slightly glazed expression in his eyes and sighed.

"You might be better getting him some lessons."

Jordan brightened. "Oh, that's a great idea! How much do you charge?"

For the first time in a long time, Bray's mouth flapped, but no sound came out.

"And what days do you teach? He's just gone back to school, so it'll have to be after or on the weekends."

Finally, Bray's senses returned, and he held up his hands. "Hold on. I said nothing about lessons."

Jordan narrowed his eyes. "Yes, you did."

Bray shook his head. "No, I didn't."

"You specifically said that I might be better off getting him some lessons."

"Yes, but I never said I did them."

Jordan's shoulders lowered. "Oh. Sorry. I thought that's what you meant." He sighed. "Do you know someone who does? I'm so out of my depth here, it's not even funny anymore."

Bray scratched his chin. "Can you do Thursdays?" *What the hell am I doing?*

Jordan stared at him, eyes gradually lightening until they were as bright as they had been at the beginning of their conversation. "Really? Yes. Definitely. Thursdays are good." He visibly calmed himself and met Bray's gaze once more. "Thank you. I appreciate it more than you know."

Bray raked his fingers across his close-cut hair and raised an eyebrow. "By how enthusiastic you were, I have an inkling."

Jordan covered his eyes with his hand and groaned. "Sorry. I just really want this for him. He had a rough time last year with bullying, and although it's supposedly sorted, he's a little anxious." He covered his mouth this time. "Oh, my god. You don't need to know all this. I'm sorry. Thank you for your time."

He shuffled back the way they'd come, and Bray followed, surprisingly charmed by the guy's runaway mouth. He would bet his savings that he got himself into trouble many times with it.

When they reached the front door, Jordan let himself out, and then quickly turned back as he reached the bottom step.

"I forgot to ask. What time on Thursdays?"

"Would four o'clock work?"

Jordan nodded and grinned. "It would." He spun around and jogged to his car, waving before he climbed in.

Bray stared after him. There was a reason he chose a house on the outskirts of Gaynor Beach. Conway Heights might be closest to his old military base, but it was also quieter than most others, especially this far out. Usually, he would've heard the car arrive, but he'd been lost in his thoughts. He was losing his touch.

And now he had agreed to teach an eight-year-old how to whittle. He sighed and headed inside. What the hell had he done? His earlier words were no less effective that time around. He didn't need the income. He didn't want the company. So why had he agreed?

It had nothing to do with the sparkling amber-coloured eyes, the wind-blown ash blond hair, or the frantic ramblings falling from those full lips. No, nothing at all to do with those things.

It had been far too long since he'd allowed his thoughts to go in that direction. His ex-wife had pretended she didn't know he was bisexual, and the Army definitely announced nothing of the sort, so he'd pushed his attraction to men right down into the bottom of his lockbox, never to think of. Men had turned his eye. Of course they had. But they had been more of a passing glance, which was easily ignored. Jordan, however…

Bray sighed and settled back into his chair. He had a bear to make.

When his phone rang, he glanced at the clock. He smiled.

"Hey, Ma."

"Bray, sweetheart. How have you been this week?"

His mother's croaky, cigarette-strained voice soothed his

soul in ways nothing else could. His father had passed away three years ago from a heart attack, and although they were close, they had nothing on him and his mother. He would move heaven and earth for her.

"Ah, same old." His mind brought Jordan's face front and center, but Bray didn't mention him yet. No doubt she would get it out of him, anyway. She was a damn mind reader.

"Did you finish the train for Ryan?"

Bray smiled. "Yes, I did. It's already in his hand, too."

Paula cooed. "I'm so glad he liked it. Although, I haven't heard of anyone yet who hasn't liked what you've made them."

"It's easy when you know how. As I've said before, I might as well do something useful with my time."

"Mmhmm." Paula inhaled, and Bray closed his eyes, imagining exactly what she looked like as she reclined in her armchair and chain-smoked far too many smokes. As much as he would love for her to stop for the good of her health, she wouldn't, and it was her choice at the end of the day.

"Have you seen much of the gruesome twosome?"

She laughed. "One of these days, you'll slip up and say that to their faces."

The gruesome twosome were his two aunts, who were as potty-mouthed and filter-free as every soldier and sailor in the Army and the Navy put together. Loretta and Maggie were twins and five years younger than his mother, but they didn't act as any older person Bray knew did. The three of them were as thick as thieves and had been arrested just as many times.

"I saw them earlier today. They had been out last night, and they popped by on their way home."

Bray chuckled. Loretta and Maggie defied every "older person" generalization anyone could make. They were out partying with the kids in their twenties, and no one seemed to give a shit. He worried about their safety when he heard some of their stories, but then he reminded himself that they beat four Army Sergeants in an arm wrestle. He truly didn't have to worry about them, but he did. Their entire family was Army through and through.

"And what about Roscoe?" Bray asked.

"Ah, he's still hanging on. I swear this dog's waiting until I'm gone before he goes. We'll both wither into a crinkled heap before we agree to depart this world."

Bray snorted. "You're both too stubborn."

"Ain't that the truth." She inhaled again. "So, what're you up to? Someone taken your fancy yet?"

She always knew, even if she couched it as a general question. He'd even checked his entire house for cameras and bugs because he wouldn't put it past her to keep tabs on him, but he'd found nothing.

"Not really." The moment he'd said the words, he winced.

She jumped straight on his word choice. "That means someone has caught your eye. Who is he?"

"How do you know it's a he?"

"Are you going to deny it?" she asked with a laugh.

Bray sighed and gave in to the inevitable. He explained his earlier visitor, and how he hadn't planned on offering lessons, but had somehow found himself agreeing to it.

Paula chuckled and coughed, and Bray waited for her to stop hacking up a lung before she continued. "It sounds like he's perfect for you?"

"How do you get that from just what I've told you?"

Paula tutted. "You have good instincts, Bray. If you didn't think he was worth your time, you would've stood your ground and kicked him out of the door."

She wasn't wrong.

"I know nothing about him."

"So find out. Or are your joints all rusty now that you've retired?"

Bray burst out laughing. "I would call you a witch, but I know better."

"That better have been a witch, my boy, or we'll be having words."

"Trust me, Ma, you're definitely a witch."

"I've never denied otherwise."

They finished the call after more gossip from the mills of San Francisco, and Bray smiled. His mother might have had him when she was thirty years old, but she didn't act like the seventy-five-year-old woman she actually was. He was grateful she had so much to live for because he couldn't imagine life without her.

He rose and headed for the kitchen when a scratching sounded at his door. He shook his head and opened it. "You should stop coming here. I know you get fed already. You'll end up having to roll around if you eat much more."

Despite his words, he reached for the tins of cat food he'd begun buying when the black cat had first started coming around. Initially, he'd had no idea that they belonged to anyone because there hadn't been a collar, but he soon realized she had taken him for a mug when Smudge's owner came around to see if Bray had seen her—Smudge because she had a white patch on her nose as if there was a smudge of something on it.

While Smudge ate her fill, Bray made his dinner and repeatedly pushed thoughts of Jordan aside. And then, when that didn't work, he just let the images come.

Jordan was athletically built and tanned, so Bray thought he must do manual labour outside of some sort because it was a suntan, not anything else. He was shorter than Bray was, but not by too much, maybe three inches. He'd fit perfectly under Bray's chin. Not that he would do that. He had a son, and therefore, Bray assumed there was a mother somewhere, too. Perhaps a wife or girlfriend. Maybe a boyfriend.

And although he wouldn't do anything about his attraction to Jordan until he knew more about him, it didn't stop his mind from churning out erotic dreams all night long. By the time he woke, Bray was harder than a diamond and had the sweat-soaked covers to prove it. After throwing them in the washing machine, he stared through his kitchen window while he drank his coffee and cursed Jordan to hell.

He had never had such a visceral reaction to anyone as he had to him, and he wasn't sure what to do about it. Being comfortable in his skin only worked for a certain amount of time, and when, or rather if, he got any part of Jordan, he probably wouldn't know what to do with him. There was no one he could ask for advice, either. All his military buddies would laugh him back into the desert at his questions—not because of his orientation—and his mother and his aunts would give him far too much information.

No. This one, he was going to have to navigate blind.

CHAPTER 4

MATTIE

Earlier that day, Jordan had flounced into his store as if he'd won the lottery. Mattie had barely understood what he'd been saying, but he figured out the gist of it. When he raced out of the store again after dropping all the information on him, Mattie just stared after him and chuckled. He'd get a calmer version of his best friend's info dump when they met again for dinner. Jordan had offered to cook again, and despite Mattie offering to pay for them to eat out instead, Jordan had shaken his head. Far be it for him to argue.

He finished work earlier than Jordan did, so he made his way home alone and tidied up the living room. It wasn't untidy, but Mattie had thoughts circling his head since Jordan brought him a cookie the previous day. He hadn't meant to groan so much when he'd eaten it, but he'd been so hungry. And then, when Jordan had reacted to it, Mattie had done it again. Then the customer had interrupted, and the moment had passed. Unfortunately. All evening, night and that day he'd been wondering if he should say something to him about it, or if he should try to kiss him, or if he should just leave it alone. He was inclined to leave it alone, as he always did, but that way of thinking had been when he had no signs that

Jordan was interested. What had changed yesterday? He had no idea.

So, he was between a rock and a hard place as things stood, and he couldn't decide which way to go. If he did something, it might ruin their friendship. If he didn't, they would continue in their current pattern. Neither path seemed to have a bright light at the end.

Which was why he was still tidying when Jordan turned up.

"Honey, I'm home!"

The usual greeting had another meaning to it that night, and Mattie's voice stuck in his throat. Jordan stopped in the doorway with his eyebrows raised, and Mattie just stared.

"Everything okay?" he asked. Mattie nodded. "Am I still cooking?"

Mattie nodded again, but his manners won out. "If you still want to."

"Of course." Jordan grinned and disappeared, and Mattie found he could breathe again.

What the hell was he going to do?

Breathing deeply, he centred himself as much as he could and entered the kitchen. Jordan was already preparing, so Mattie went to his usual perch at the table and returned to their earlier conversation.

"So, you've found someone to help Cody with his woodworking?"

Jordan nodded. "Yes! At first, it felt like he was going to bite my head off, but then he offered lessons." He paused. "Well, I thought he did."

Mattie frowned. "I thought you said he had a lesson on Thursday."

"He does." Jordan sighed and resumed his chopping. "He mentioned lessons first, and I assumed he meant he could do them, so I said yes. But then he said he didn't do lessons, and I said that he'd said he did. We argued a bit, and then he agreed to do lessons on a Thursday. So, I'm not sure if he does do lessons and didn't want me to know, or if he didn't, but decided to do them for me." He shrugged. "I'm a little unclear."

Mattie couldn't help it. He laughed. "Trust you to work someone around to offering lessons when it's not something they do. You could sell milk to a cow farmer."

Jordan snorted. "Not true." He glanced over his shoulder and laughed some more. "Okay, maybe true."

"It's good that Cody has something. Have you told him yet?"

Jordan shook his head. "I won't hear the end of it if I do, so I'm going to tell him when I pick him up from school on Thursday."

"Good idea. I'm sure Ash appreciates not having his ear bent every minute."

Mattie fisted his hands as he tried to segue into what happened yesterday. "So, um, when you brought the food yesterday, we kind of got interrupted…"

Jordan froze and then continued. "Uh-huh."

Mattie swallowed. "I don't want what I'm going to say to ruin anything, but it kind of felt like something was happening." Silence. "Between us." Silence. "Before we were interrupted." He tried to calm his breathing so he didn't hyperventilate. This was way outside his comfort zone, and he was already regretting it. "Never mind. I'm just going to—"

As he stood to leave on some lame excuse of needing to clean something, Jordan slammed down whatever he'd been holding and stalked over to him.

"I'm sorry in advance."

Jordan palmed his cheeks and kissed him, giving him no recourse, no time to think things through, no time to reconsider. It was exactly what Mattie had needed.

And so was the damn kiss.

His eyes fell shut, and his hands gripped Jordan's wrists, needing something to hold on to. His lips were warm, demanding, and Mattie let himself go. He kissed him back, sliding his arms around Jordan to dig his nails into his back. Their mouths met and left, met and left. Their breathing increased, gasping breaths to grab what little oxygen they could before they lost themselves in the kiss again. Jordan's hands left his cheeks, sliding around his neck and holding him closer, gripping the back of his head to keep him steady.

When Jordan's tongue slid inside his mouth, Mattie almost melted as heat bombarded him. Jordan held him steady, licking every inch of his mouth, and then pulled back. Mattie wouldn't let him go, though. Not completely.

Their gazes met, and he saw the answering heat in Jordan's eyes. Mattie's mouth twitched into a smile a second before he went in for more. He couldn't get enough. He breathed through his nose as their tongues dueled, each leaning back as the other dominated the kiss for a few seconds before the other took over again.

Jordan's hands cupped his nape, his thumbs caressing the side of his face as he gentled the kiss once more. He dropped another kiss on Mattie's lips. And another. Then stared into his eyes.

"That answers that," he murmured.

"Huh?"

Jordan smiled and brushed his thumb across Mattie's lips. "I said that answers that."

Mattie blinked, still not quite with it after such a mind-blowing kiss. "What answers what?"

"If yesterday was a one-off boner or a regular thing."

Mattie snorted, closing his eyes and nuzzling his cheek into Jordan's hand. "And which was it?" he whispered.

Jordan didn't answer. Instead, he fused their lips again, kissing him harder than anyone had ever kissed him before. His hands lowered to Jordan's ass, and he palmed them, grinding their groins together. Jordan groaned and pushed Mattie backwards. He hit the wall, and Jordan increased his efforts to make him lose his head. Both heads.

Hands roamed. Chests, asses, backs, shoulders. Every inch of them was explored by the other until Jordan rested their foreheads together and panted into the space between them.

"That was…"

"Amazing?" Mattie finished.

"And unexpected."

That pulled him up short. "Unexpected in a good or bad way?"

Jordan shook his head and sighed, pressing his hips into Mattie's. "Does that feel like it's a bad way?"

Mattie's mouth curved on one side, and he lowered his eyes. He'd seen this side of Jordan before, but not aimed in his direction. Jordan thumbed his chin, bringing his gaze back up again.

"Talk to me, Mattie."

"Can we talk after dinner?"

Jordan squinted his eyes at him. "Delaying tactic. I see what you're doing. But okay. I'll let you get inside your head for a little while, but after dinner, we're talking about this." He waved a finger between the two of them. "Because while this is unexpected, it's not unwanted. Remember that distinction."

Jordan dropped another kiss on his lips and then stepped back, adjusting his trousers as he went back to cooking. Mattie stood where they had been for a few moments and settled back at the table. He had a problem. All those endings he envisaged while he tidied up? He never anticipated it being reciprocal. He never imagined Jordan wanting him in return. Even though he'd caught the boner in question the previous day, it had never occurred to him that Jordan was interested. He'd been with Ash before, and they weren't the same.

"Stop thinking so hard. Tell me about work or the book you're reading or something. The quiet is making me nervous."

That made two of them. "Work was—oh, yeah! I had a customer come in asking for sex toys."

Jordan stared at him. "Seriously?"

Mattie nodded. "When I explained, he said that he knew what I sold and assumed it meant I had sex toys, too." He huffed. "As if you had to be into that to be able to wear something pretty."

"You're not?"

"Not what?"

"Into that?"

Mattie's mouth went dry. "Well, I never said I wasn't. I just meant—"

Jordan chuckled. "Don't get yourself in a knot. I'm kidding. Kind of. This is a conversation for later. I just like getting you flustered." He winked, and Mattie swooned.

"You're an asshole sometimes. You know that?"

Jordan tutted. "I said we'd get into that later. Mr Impatient already wants to know about asses and holes. What am I going to do with you?"

Mattie spluttered, palming his burning cheeks. "Change the subject."

"I was trying to. Anything else happen at work?"

"Nope."

"How far have you gotten into your book now?" Jordan put the dish into the oven and set the timer, mesmerising Mattie with his movements. "Mattie?" He looked at him. "Book?"

"Um, nearly at the end now."

"I'm surprised you haven't finished it already."

Mattie cleared his throat and stared at the table. "Well, something kept distracting me," he muttered.

"We've got ten minutes until the enchiladas are done. What do you want to do?"

Kiss more? Mattie swallowed. "Choose a movie for after dinner?"

Jordan threw his head back, chuckling as if he'd known where Mattie's thoughts had gone. "Lead the way."

They were arguing over the merits of Vin Diesel's *Pitch Black* series when the timer went off. Jordan disappeared into the kitchen, which gave Mattie time to put his choice on pause. Entering the kitchen, his stomach growled.

"And that's my cue to feed you." Jordan placed a plate in front of him. "Eat up."

The spicy scent tickled his nose, and he dug in straight away. Why Jordan hadn't become a chef instead of a lifeguard, he did not know. He'd have made a fortune hiring out his services privately. Mattie paused with his fork halfway to his mouth as thoughts of other things he could make a fortune doing that hopefully they would soon be doing themselves. Unpaid. Mattie closed his eyes and shook his head, resuming eating once he'd pushed those thoughts aside. He didn't miss the smirk Jordan sent him, but he ignored it.

"What was the guy like? The woodworker?" Mattie asked.

Jordan tilted his head, looking off to the side. "Military. Closely cropped hair, muscles for miles, tall, sturdy."

Mattie's heart thumped. Exactly what Jordan usually went for in a guy. He drank some water, trying to swallow the food in his mouth that had turned to dust. "Uh-huh."

"Yeah. He was a real grump when he first answered the door. I was ready to race back to my car when he stared me down like I was prey and he was a fox waiting to attack."

Mattie grinned. "A fox?"

Jordan shrugged. "A wolf was too obvious." He shovelled more food in.

They finished dinner with a more mundane conversation. Undoubtedly, Jordan's way of trying to get him to relax before they talked. It didn't work, though Mattie was good to pretend. But when the dishes were done to Mattie's specifications, Jordan grabbed his hand and led him into the living room. He tucked himself into the corner of the sofa and tugged Mattie down beside him. Then he pulled Mattie into his chest and wrapped an arm around him.

That was new.

"Now, you'll be able to talk without having to face me," Jordan said.

Mattie's shoulders relaxed instantly. He didn't have to worry about what he was going to say because Jordan would still be there. Even if that kiss was the only thing they ever had, it would be okay.

Jordan pressed play, grunting when his second choice came up, and Mattie hid a smile. "Okay, Mattie. Talk to me."

Mattie took a deep breath and then another before he let go of his ten-year-old secret.

"I've wanted to be with you since the day after we met."

Jordan tightened his hold and pressed his lips to his head. "Why didn't you ever tell me?"

Mattie snorted. "Well, for starters, you were with Ash when we met, and then you had a kid."

"What about when we split up?"

"You tell me. When would've been a good time to say, 'Oh, are you over him yet because I want a turn?'"

Jordan hummed. "We've been apart for five years now. Did you think I still wanted to be with him?"

"No, I knew you didn't, but..."

When he didn't continue, Jordan nudged him. "But what?"

"I don't look like the men you usually go for. I'm not muscular. I'm not tall. I'm not...big. I couldn't compete with them."

"Oh, Mattie. You don't need to compete with them. You

are your own person, and you need to be confident in what you can offer someone."

"Oh, yeah? What's that?"

"Your love. Your commitment. Your loyalty. Your friendship within the relationship. Your organisational skills." Jordan chuckled, and Mattie rolled his eyes. "You have so much to give. It doesn't matter what you think you look like because I see you." Jordan cupped his cheek and turned him to face him. "I'm just sorry it took me so long to see what we could be together." He dropped a kiss on his lips. "I was never that bright." He winked.

Mattie laughed. "I think I can forgive you. Although there might be a price."

Jordan squinted. "What price is that?"

"Will you stay over tonight? Just to sleep. Next to each other."

Jordan smiled. "I can do that."

He lowered his head and claimed Mattie's mouth in a fierce, brain-cell-reducing kiss that turned him to jelly.

"I might have to borrow some clothes in the morning."

"I can do that." He repeated Jordan's words and faced the TV. "Besides, I think you have several clothes you've left here at some point."

"Even better. Oh, you've not seen my yellow tank, have you? I've put it somewhere and can't for the life of me remember where. I've not seen it for months."

Mattie shook his head. "Nope. Can't remember seeing it."

He was a big, fat liar. That tank top lived in his bedside table because Mattie loved it. He'd never said a word about it, but he'd never give it back unless he had no option. It was his now.

CHAPTER 5

JORDAN

Jordan woke, wrapped around his best friend, and it put an instant smile on his face. He hadn't wanted to rush into a physical relationship, not because he didn't like Mattie that way, but because they were already so close, he wanted to make it special. And giving Mattie his undivided attention after such a good night's sleep was the best plan ever.

He moved his hand ever so slightly up and down Mattie's body, hoping to lure him slowly into wakefulness. Express permission was required before he went any further than that because he refused to let Mattie have regrets after they'd slept together. Despite Jordan having only come around to the idea a couple of days ago, it felt right to him. Like putting on his favorite pair of trainers. They just fit perfectly. He wanted that for them.

Mattie fidgeted in his sleep and sighed, and Jordan's hand grew a little bolder, teasing him out of his slumber.

"Mmm." Mattie leaned back into him.

Jordan could see his eyelids trying to lift, but sleep was trying to pull him back under. He nibbled softly on his ear, sucking the lobe into his mouth. Mattie pushed his ass into Jordan's groin, and Jordan's breath caught in a hiss.

He heard a car engine, which wasn't unusual in the neighbourhood, but it was at that time of the morning, and when it cut out, he thought nothing more of it. Someone had probably come back from their night shift. He refocused on Mattie again and enticed him from his sleep.

"Good morning," he murmured, pressing a kiss onto Mattie's cheek. "How are you?"

"Eager to wake up like this every morning," he mumbled.

Jordan smiled, slightly distracted again when he heard a car again. Then he mentally slapped himself. What did it matter?

His hand slid up to cup Mattie's cheek, and he brought their faces together. "Question. Morning breath kisses, yes or no?"

Mattie smiled. "Yes."

"Good answer."

He lowered his head and kissed him. And kissed him. And kissed him. He stole every molecule of air from his lungs and gave every bit of his own before he pulled back.

"I want to wake like this every morning, too."

A baby cried, and Jordan tensed. He turned his head towards the window. Plenty of people had babies around there, but it sounded extremely close.

"Does your neighbour have a kid now?"

Mattie shook his head. "None of them do. Although one is pregnant, but she's not far enough along to have had it yet."

The cry sounded again, and Jordan understood the tone. They were unhappy.

"Sorry. It's none of my business." He turned back to Mattie. "Where were we?"

Mattie shook his head. "You wouldn't be the person I know if you weren't concerned about a crying baby. Check out the window. Maybe someone's just having a bad day."

Jordan climbed from the bed and peered through the curtains. He couldn't see anyone, but the crying was a little louder still. "I'm going to have a look out front. I won't be long."

Mattie got up. "I'll come with you."

They jogged down the stairs, and the wailing sounds increased in fervour.

"Someone really isn't happy," he murmured.

Mattie opened the front door, which set the crying to screeching levels, and then froze in the doorway.

"What is it?" Jordan asked, peering over Mattie's shoulder.

There, in a car seat, was a baby, kicking their legs and waving their arms to match the anger in their voice. Jordan pushed past Mattie, who still hadn't moved.

"Hey, you. What's all this noise about?" He crouched down and rocked the seat a little, noticing several bags behind the seat and a pushchair. There was also an envelope. He picked it up, saw Mattie's name, and reached behind him to give it to him.

Mattie was still frozen.

"Mattie," he said.

Mattie blinked and grabbed at what Jordan held out. He stared at it for a moment before tearing it open and reading aloud.

MATTIE,

I'm sorry to be the bearer of bad news, but Dionne passed away in childbirth. I can't look after her. It's too difficult to see her face when all I can see is my sister. Please don't contact me. I won't take her back. I'm signing all rights over to you as her father. Yes, you are her father. She fell pregnant but didn't want to bug you about it. She had planned to tell you after the birth, but there were complications. Her name is Ama. I'm sorry to drop this on you, but I need to grieve, and I can't do that when Ama is there every day. I wish you well.

Rhia.

JORDAN STARED AT MATTIE TO SEE HOW THE NEWS HAD FALLEN, but the man just stared at the letter as if it was going to bite him. So, Jordan took charge. He grabbed the car seat and a bag and manoeuvred it into the house.

"Grab those bags, would you?"

This wasn't quite how he'd envisioned spending the morning, but who could resist such adorable cherub cheeks as this princess had? Besides, keeping her outside in this weather was unkind. Whoever Rhia was had a lot to answer for.

He placed the car seat on the floor in the kitchen and rifled through the bags. He plucked out a bottle, some ready-to-use formula milk, and a bottle warmer someone had kindly put in. He highly expected there would be pretty much every-thing this little baby would need to stay indefinitely, except for a crib. Making bottles was something he'd loved doing when Cody was little, and it wasn't something he forgot how to do. He set it all up and got the bottle of milk warming for her.

Then he faced Mattie, who stood just inside the kitchen door, staring at the baby. It looked like he was going to need to take charge while it sunk in for the new dad.

"Hey, Princess Ama. Come to Uncle Jordan." He unbuckled her and lifted her free, cuddling her to his chest and inhaling that scent only babies had. She cried a little more, but as he bounced her, she settled and rested her head on his chest. "Check the milk for me." No answer. He glanced over. "Mattie?" Mattie blinked at him. "Check the milk."

Mattie seemed to pull himself from his stupor and put the letter he'd still been gripping on the table. He checked the milk, shaking his head, but still no words.

Jordan stepped closer to him, putting Ama between them.

"It'll be fine, Mattie. No matter what, we'll figure it out. Okay?"

Mattie nodded and checked the milk again. "It's ready."

"Would you like to do the honours?" Jordan asked. Mattie licked his lips, seemingly ready to decline, so Jordan enticed him. "Oh, that's it. You can't remember how. No problem. I'll show you." He passed Ama over to him, giving him no choice but to take her, and then he pushed him towards a chair until he sat down. "You hold her like this…"

He moved Mattie's arm, but Mattie said, "Enough. I know what to do."

Manoeuvring Ama into the crook of his arm, he took the bottle and rubbed the teat against her lips. As babies were prone to do, she opened her mouth, and Mattie slipped it in. Ama started drinking, and she stared up at her dad.

Mattie having a baby was not a surprise in some ways. He was bisexual, after all, but he'd never mentioned seeing anyone. Jordan didn't want to pry, but eventually, he would ask; it was an impossibility of him keeping quiet. Mattie had not looked shocked by who had written the letter, so that was something interesting. At least to Jordan.

"What am I going to do?" Mattie mumbled, his eyes on his daughter, though the question was for Jordan.

"You'll be a dad."

"What if she's not mine?"

There was no way on this earth that Ama wasn't Mattie's daughter. She was the spitting image of him, except for the eyes. "Then you get a test to be sure. But do you really need one?"

Mattie shook his head. "Can someone just hand over a baby and say, 'You take care of them?' Doesn't there have to be social workers or something involved?"

"Probably. We'll need to let them know." Jordan stood and emptied all the bags onto the table. "Although…" He picked up a folder and took out the contents. "That makes things easier. You're listed on her birth certificate."

"Is that allowed? I thought you had to be present to have your name on it?"

Jordan shrugged. "I've no idea, but your name is here." He turned it around so Mattie could see it.

Mattie sighed. "How the hell can I be a dad, Jordan? I have work."

"Take her with you. I bet anything that she'll bring more customers to your shop than ever before. Nosy neighbours will have the gossip ring working overtime already. You just wait."

Jordan hated that what he said was true, but it was inevitable. With any town, there were always the busybodies who needed to know everything and insisted everyone else knew it as well. It wouldn't take long at all for this information to be handed to them—if it hadn't already. Ama surely screamed loud enough to make someone take interest before they'd gone out to her, despite how early in the morning it had been.

He glanced at the clock. "I'll make breakfast. What do you fancy?"

"I'm not hungry."

"You need to eat, Mattie. I know your brain is going around in circles at the minute, but you still need to eat. You don't have long before you have to be at the shop, and we need to get things prepared for Ama."

Mattie peered up at him. "You don't have to go to work yet, do you? Could you have her to begin with and then bring her to the shop before you go to work?"

Jordan smiled and leaned down to peck his cheek. "I would love to look after this angel."

"Thanks." Mattie sighed. "I'm not copping out on my duties, but I want to get the shop opened and make some room for her. I'm going to need some stuff."

"You just open your shop. I'll grab a crib you can use at the shop and maybe a baby carrier so you can walk around holding her. I'll order a cot for her, too."

"You don't have to do all that—"

"I don't mind. With how your brain is right now, you'd end up ordering the wrong stuff, anyway."

Mattie pursed his lips. "Hey!" Ama stopped sucking and scrunched her face as if she was going to cry. Mattie leaned close. "Hey, sweetie. Are you still hungry?" He teased her mouth with the teat again, and after a second's hesitation, she latched on again.

Jordan smiled, seeing the Mattie he remembered from when Cody was little reappear. He focused on getting breakfast ready. French toast sounded good. He watched Mattie and Ama from the corners of his eyes, when he picked her up to wind her, when he laid her back down for some more milk. His eyes were constantly on her, which was a good sign.

He wondered about the mother. The letter had said she'd died in childbirth. Had there been complications with the birth, or had it been something else? Ama looked healthy, so it didn't seem to have affected her unless there were some development delays they hadn't been made aware of or that hadn't shown themselves yet. It was possible.

He placed a plate in front of Mattie and reached for Ama. "Eat. You haven't got long."

"Yes, sir."

Jordan smirked at him. "Save that for later."

Mattie gaped at him, and Jordan chuckled. Ama waved her hands and tried to grab his chin. He caught her little fist. "What? What are you after, little miss?" Using the baby voice understood by all parents and children. He kissed her hand. "You're going to break hearts all over this town."

Mattie ate his breakfast quietly, and Jordan understood where he was coming from. When they'd woken that morning, he'd had plans involving being horizontal for an hour or so, not playing with an adorable…wet girl.

"Uh-oh. Someone's needs changing. Shall Uncle Jordan see to your diaper, sweetie?" He stood, putting her on his shoulder, and grabbed the things he needed from the items they had left. Plenty of diapers, thankfully. At least they hadn't left her with nothing but the clothes on her back.

He knelt on the floor and changed her diaper—he hadn't forgotten how—and then dressed her again. When he stood, Mattie waited for him.

"Thank you, Jordan."

Jordan bit his lip. "For what?"

"For making this easy. For not freaking out like I was. For bringing me back down to earth." He brushed a finger over Ama's cheek. "For being willing to help. Mom and Dad are going to freak out."

"So is Lia."

Mattie chuckled. "Lia will not believe a thing. My sister is a menace. She'll have Ama dressed in tutus and crowns in seconds."

"And why would that be a bad thing?" Jordan squinted at him, amused.

Mattie rolled his eyes and wagged his finger. "Don't go getting any ideas."

"Wouldn't dream of calling your parents for a visit."

"Don't. Not yet."

Jordan kissed his cheek. "You're going to have to do it soon because you might need the childcare."

Mattie exhaled. "True. But give me a couple of days. I'm sure they'll hear before then, but I just need to…adapt."

"Just like any new parent." Jordan kissed him on the lips this time. "Go get ready for work."

"I like that you kiss me whenever you want to."

"I like that I *can* kiss you whenever I want to."

Mattie shook his head, looking at both him and Ama. "How did I get to be so lucky?" He disappeared up the stairs.

If he was already thinking about being lucky and including Ama in it, then he was already in love with the child. And so was Jordan. But she wasn't his. Only as an uncle. He'd always wished Cody hadn't been an only child, but there was no bringing another child into a relationship that wasn't working. Maybe Cody could have a cousin instead.

He stared down at Ama, her eyelids getting heavier and heavier. She truly was adorable.

CHAPTER 6

BRAY

Bray wasn't prone to listening to gossip, but when the gossipmongers were both excited and appalled by the story of a baby being left on someone's doorstep, it was hard not to have an opinion. Whoever had done that needed a serious talking to. Who left a baby on a doorstep where not only could anyone snatch them, but where they could get seriously ill from dehydration if they hadn't been found in time? Especially in California's August weather.

He hadn't been told the story, but he would've been hard-pressed to miss the loud conversations as he worked his way through the grocery store. He must've heard a version of the story six times, at least, during his half an hour visit.

He pushed it aside on the drive home. He had friends to meet this afternoon, and then he had to be back in time to tutor an eight-year-old on whittling. Shaking his head for the dozenth time about what he'd managed to get himself into, he parked the car and unloaded his groceries. Once he'd put them away and he'd chugged a glass of water, he climbed back into his car and headed to West Beach, where he was meeting Dante, Freer and Radar for a late lunch.

Parking was a bitch because of the time of day, but he'd

arrived early for that specific reason. Once he had, he still had over half an hour before he had to meet them, so he went for a stroll on the busy beach. He preferred it when it was quiet, but he would never complain about being near the ocean. His mother had once remarked that he'd shocked her when he'd chosen to join the Army and not the Navy with how much he loved water, but he'd explained that he felt more kinship to the Army. He couldn't explain it further than that. And he didn't regret a minute.

Well, he regretted one thing. Not all of his team made it home. But it was the way of the military world.

He removed his shoes and socks and rolled up his trousers. As he wandered down the beach, his feet immersed in the water, he breathed the pain away. He'd almost reached the pier before he realized it and turned back the way he came. He paid more attention to his surroundings that time— not that he hadn't been aware of everything around him, but he'd learnt to push aside what wasn't necessary—and as he strolled towards a lifeguard tower, he spied someone he recognised. But they'd not noticed him.

He continued past without bringing attention to himself, but his mind was on the sweat-slicked skin of the lifeguard, laughing with some beachgoers. Jordan. So that was how he got his tanned skin. He sat on the edge of the beach and brushed off the sand as much as he could before he pulled his socks and shoes back on. Then he leaned his elbows on his knees and stared at the tower, though he couldn't see Jordan. He assumed his son was at school, with it being a Thursday. Was there someone waiting for him to finish work?

Hands slammed down on his shoulders, and despite his heart tripling in rhythm, he didn't react in any way. He'd learnt that what would've been an okay reaction in Afghanistan didn't work back home. Grabbing his friend by the throat and slamming him to the floor in front of him was not a good idea.

And yes, it was Freer. Because he always did it.

"One of these days, I won't stifle my reaction to you," Bray said, the threat clear in his voice.

Freer chuckled, the booming sound bringing looks their way. There was no mistaking that they were military, and reactions were usually either moving away from them or ogling them. Bray didn't care for either version, but he let them have their worries or fantasies. None of his team would ever hurt anyone that didn't deserve it.

"You wouldn't do a thing while we're out in the wild, Pack," Freer said, settling beside him on the bench.

"Doesn't mean he wouldn't retaliate when you're alone," Radar said, leaning against the nearby waist-height wall and crossing his arms. His usual pose.

Bray waited for the inevitable response from the third member of their group, and he wasn't disappointed.

"He has more control than you do, Radar," Dante said.

Each of his men was identifiable by their charms. Dante, named for his good looks and a nod towards the TV horror show, *Dante's Cove,* which he'd admitted to watching once. The name had never left him and never would. As his second-in-command, he had proven time and again to be intelligent and resourceful, but also laid-back, which helped with unifying the team.

Radar was the more serious of them. His eyes would continuously scan the area. Always. Hence his name. No matter what you asked him, he could tell you everything about their surroundings in a millisecond.

Freer, on the other hand, was the joker. The one who drove the rest up the wall, around the ceiling and back down again. His name came from his training days. From the story he told, he and his buddies were talking, and he'd wanted to be in the Army to be "free-er" from his family. As in, less restricted from his extremely close-knit, hovering family. No one had believed him that freer was a word, and so his nickname was born.

Bray had been branded "Pack" because he'd once calmed a pack of dogs in Afghanistan that had been hell-bent on tearing his first team to shreds. He never introduced himself with the name, but all his military friends and colleagues called him it.

"I'm hungry," Freer said, jumping up. "Let's eat."

They wandered through the tourists and locals, working their way to Let's Talk Tacos, the best taco place in Gaynor Beach. This was a regular haunt for them, and as soon as they entered, the host grinned and waved them through. Nico Cruz owned Let's Talk Tacos, but he also worked as the host because he believed in keeping things simple within the business—no point employing people when he could do the job himself.

As they took a seat, Nico said, "Welcome back. Are you having your usual today?"

Dante, Freer and Radar nodded, but Bray held up his hand. "Everything the same for me, but minus the beer this time." He could've heard a pin drop when his friends fell silent, and he rolled his shoulders. "I have something to do this afternoon. I need a clear head."

Nico nodded. "Good for you. I'll be right back with your orders." He clapped Bray on the shoulder and left, leaving Bray's friends staring at him.

"Oh, shut the fuck up," he muttered.

"You meeting a 'friend?'" Freer said, waggling his eyebrows.

Bray ignored him and changed the subject. "How's your family, Dante?"

Dante's sister had given birth to a boy three months ago, and from the updates Dante had given him, he was growing fast.

"God, he's a chunk for sure. Molly was pleased to inform me that Odin has a hearty appetite."

Bray chuckled. "I remember it well. Is she getting any more sleep yet?"

Dante shook his head. "He doesn't like sleeping, apparently."

"A soldier in the making," Freer said with a laugh.

Bray leaned forward, linking his fingers and staring at his second-in-command. "And what about Milo?"

Dante had recently come out to them all, making Bray wish he'd done the same so he could offer more support than he currently did.

Dante exhaled. "It's complicated."

"Don't let him fuck you up, man," Freer said. "No one is worth that."

"Some people are," Radar said as Nico brought their food and drinks.

The scent of freshly cooked tacos filled Bray's nostrils, and his stomach growled. "Thanks, Nico. I needed this."

"My pleasure, as always." Nico smiled and left.

"What's complicated about it?" Freer asked, and Bray shook his head. They were all used to him having no filter or boundaries.

Dante's face coloured, and Bray stared at him, having not seen such an expression before. Dante cleared his throat. "Um, he likes…" He exhaled.

"Tacos *and* hotdogs?" Freer said.

"Whips and floggers?" Radar supplied.

"Howling at the moon?" Freer added, ending with a howl of his own.

Radar nudged him. "No, that's just you." Freer laughed and shoved him back, dislodging Radar's hold on his taco. "Hey, watch out! This food ain't for wasting."

"Enough," Bray said, and they both subsided. He focused

on Dante. "You don't have to tell us, Dante. Just let us know if you need help with anything."

"He enjoys wearing lingerie," Dante blurted.

It took a few seconds for the words to register, but then—as Bray had expected a second before it happened—Freer burst out laughing. Dante clenched his fists and stared at his food. Bray grabbed Freer's jaw, silencing him with a look. He let him go, and Freer nodded, knowing he'd gone too far.

"And what's your opinion on it?" Bray asked. "Because that's the only other opinion that matters."

Dante worked his jaw. "I..." He sighed and shook his head. "I like it. I just don't know what to... What do I buy? I could figure out what to buy for a woman, but for a guy...?" He shrugged. "There are...bits on a guy that aren't there on a woman. How do I know?"

Bray inhaled. There had never been any topic they couldn't discuss, and he would not start now, but hell if he had an answer. "Have you looked at...items? Like on the internet?"

Dante nodded. "I have no idea. I know I should ask him, but I want it to be a surprise. To show him I accept it all."

Radar reached past him and held his phone in front of Dante. "Go here. I've heard good things about him. The owner caters for all people, no matter who. He's got excellent reviews, too."

Dante took the phone and peered at the screen. "Lovely in Lace? Sounds more feminine."

Radar shook his head. "My brother's friend goes there for his boyfriend. He says the guy..." Radar took the phone back and scrolled, "Mattie is very informative and if he doesn't have it, he knows how to get it."

"I never realized there was a place like that here," Freer said.

"It's Gaynor Beach. We're eclectic." Bray shrugged. "I fully believe if you can't find it here, you won't find it anywhere."

They laughed, dispersing the serious tone. "But yeah. Start there. If he can't help, let me know. We'll figure it out."

"Thanks, Pack."

"Anytime."

Bray had no idea what he could do if this Mattie guy couldn't help, but he'd figure it out. He always did.

"Let's visit after we've finished," Radar said. "We have plenty of time."

Freer's eyes widened, and Bray couldn't resist. "Definitely. Maybe we can open Freer's eyes to the joys of lingerie."

"You're not getting me in any."

Bray laughed at Freer's expression. "You never know, Freer, you might find something you like the look of."

They shot the shit for the next hour, paid the bill and headed down the street towards Lovely in Lace. Bray could honestly say he had never expected to be visiting a lingerie shop with his teammates, but if they got through their tours, they could do this, too.

The shop was in Gaynor Village. A deceptively small front, which, when they entered, opened up into something much larger and filled with every imaginable outfit.

And the incessant crying of a baby.

Bray heard soothing sounds coming from someone, so he ignored the noise and followed his men around. Several items caught his eye. He already knew he liked his partners in lingerie, though he'd never seen a man in it in person, only in photos. Several of which filled the walls above them.

He glanced towards the other side of the shop, where the baby continued to vocalise their upset. Unable to resist, he wandered away from his friends and towards the noise. The crying stopped for a second and then restarted louder than ever.

"I know. I know. I'm sorry. I don't know what's wrong, sweetheart," a voice crooned.

Bray stepped out from the racks of clothing and saw a

slender guy with more than a five o'clock shadow rocking a little girl in his arms. That little girl was the source of the noise.

"It sounds like she has wind," Bray said before he realized he was going to say anything.

The guy spun around to face him, eyes wide. "Oh! You startled me."

"Sorry," Bray said. He nodded to her. "She sounds unhappy."

The guy sighed, continuing to bounce and rock the baby. "She is. I don't know what else to do. I fed her a little while ago, but she won't burp. I've exhausted my limited knowledge." He pressed his lips to the girl's head, and when he pulled back, his lips trembled.

Bray stepped closer and held out his arms. "Can I try?"

The guy narrowed his eyes. "I don't know you."

Bray stood to attention and saluted. "Sergeant First Class Bray Rushden at your service."

The guy's arrestingly blue eyes widened again. "Military," he breathed. He glanced at the baby, who was still crying despite having her eyes closed and her head resting on the guy's chest. "He can't be too bad, can he?" he mumbled to her. He glanced back up at him. "Stay where I can see you."

"Understood."

Bray reached for the little girl, turning her to face his chest and cupped her diaper, allowing her to crunch her legs up beneath her. He bounced and rubbed his hand in circles on her back a few times before patting firmly, repeating the actions several times. When she bellowed a very unladylike burp, the other guy sighed, his shoulders lowering.

"How did you do that?"

Bray smiled. "Years of practice. I have twins who are now twenty years old." The baby's cries slowed but didn't disappear altogether. He kept up the motion while he asked, "What's her name?"

"Ama." The guy's cheeks flushed. "And I'm Mattie. I own…" He waved his hand around. He sighed again. "I wouldn't usually bring her to work, but I haven't found a childcare solution yet, and my best friend, who's helping me, is at work now. I'm…" He chuckled without humor. "I'm out of my depth."

"If you don't mind me asking, where is your…partner? Couldn't they help?"

"Well, my partner…actually, my partner is my best friend, but he isn't the father. I am. Well, so I'm told. I haven't got the results of the DNA test yet, so I'm not certain. But as I said, I'm still trying to figure out the whole dad thing. It's, um, a lot."

Bray let him talk. So, this is the baby who was left on the doorstep. He held her a little tighter, inhaling the baby scent he'd never forget. Her father was struggling, he could see that, but he was still doing an amazing job, having had this thrown at him at short notice.

"I know you don't know me from Adam, but if you need anything, please let me know. I'm retired military. I have hours to spare."

Mattie shook his head. "No, I can't ask that. I'll figure it out. I will. I just need…"

"A break."

Mattie slumped. "Is it that obvious?"

Bray smiled. "Tell you what? My friend needs some help to choose something for his boyfriend. He's a little unsure, and he doesn't want to ask his partner because he wants it to be a surprise. If you can help him, I'll sit here with this beautiful girl and give you a breather."

Mattie shoved his hands in his pockets, and his lower lip trembled again. "Are you sure?"

"Perfectly."

"Thank you." Mattie shuffled from behind the counter.

"Sit wherever you want. If anyone comes up to the counter, tell them I'll be back in a minute."

"We'll be fine, won't we, princess?" he said to the now-sleeping baby. He settled into the chair, getting himself as comfortable as he could, and watched as his teammates got a lesson in lingerie.

CHAPTER 7

MATTIE

Mattie had no idea why he'd agreed to leave Ama with a stranger, but there was something about the guy that just… felt safe. He glanced back again, seeing the way he held Mattie's daughter—god, that was still a weird thing to think about—and then focused on his customers.

"Hey," he said. "Your friend said you needed some help to find something for your boyfriend?" He wasn't sure which one he was talking to, so he glanced at them all.

The one on the right pointed at the guy in the center. "Dante."

Mattie focused on him. "So what does he like?" The guy just stared at him, and Mattie withheld a chuckle. "Okay. Let's start simple. What's his favorite colour?"

"Blue."

"Does he already have anything…?"

Dante cleared his throat. "I assume so. He told me he liked to wear…lingerie, but I've not seen him in it yet."

Mattie nodded. "All right. This way." He led him to a rack that held lacy pants. He heard a chuckle behind him and faced the guy's friends. "I think Bray needs you two."

"Where did he go off to?" the one who pointed to Dante originally asked, craning his neck.

"He's helping me," Mattie said. "You'll find him at the checkout."

They disappeared after slapping Dante on the back. He sighed. "Thanks for that. They're good friends, but they don't leave things alone."

Mattie shrugged. "It's not easy when you don't know what to expect or look for." He pointed at the underwear. "If you're unsure what he likes at the moment, the best idea would be to start with something small. Not all guys like the full…for want of a better word, feminine look with the tops or corsets. That is something you'll have to ask him about. But for now, it's usually a safe bet to choose something like this."

Dante took Mattie's offering, fingering the fabric. "Is this going to fit?"

"They come in different sizes, just like clothes do. With these, there is extra room in the front to accommodate our cocks." Dante coughed, and Mattie smiled. "If I can't say the word, I shouldn't be in the business."

Dante chuckled. "I guess. So how do I know his size?"

Mattie exhaled. "That's a little trickier. As this is your first buy, I would estimate. Is he a similar body shape to you?"

Dante shook his head. "He's a similar height, but he doesn't have as much muscle mass. He's muscular, don't get me wrong, but not what I call military muscular."

Mattie nodded. "I know what you mean. And his cock? Generous or…"

Dante rubbed his cheeks and then sighed. "Fuck it," he mumbled. He held out his hand as if wrapped around a shaft. "Roughly that thick, and this long." He held his hands again.

Mattie loved he did that. "Great. Then I think…" He flicked through the rack. "This one might fit. I do exchanges for size issues, so just come back or send your boyfriend back and I can sort it out if it's wrong."

Dante exhaled. "Thanks. That was less painful than I expected."

Mattie chuckled. "You'll get more relaxed once you know what he likes and what size he is. It's a little easier that way." He glanced over at the counter. "Do you want me to get rid of your friends before you pay?"

Dante's eyes narrowed in the same direction, and he stood a little taller. "No. I'm good."

"Okay."

Mattie led the way to the counter, slowing when he saw three grown military men fawning over his smiling daughter. He excused himself and slid behind the counter.

"Thank you for that," he said to Bray. "I'll just ring him up and then I'll take her back."

"No rush," Bray murmured.

Mattie glanced at him and saw the serene expression on his face. He'd love to get to that stage, and he would eventually, but he still had the social worker visit to get through before he'd relax. He and Jordan had taken Ama to the hospital early that morning to get a swab taken for DNA. They'd have to await the results—though he'd had the results expedited—but the social worker, Anthony, was visiting to find out if Mattie could keep her. He'd only had her a day, but he hated the idea of losing her. From what he'd said when he'd spoken to him, he was also going to be in contact with Rhia, Ama's aunt, to confirm, and there were still laws and legal stuff he had to go through to ensure he got to keep her. Whether Rhia got into trouble for what she did was something Mattie didn't know. He hoped not because, although it wasn't the best idea, she was struggling. He would've preferred her to do that than just neglect Ama.

He rang up the item and put it in a small discreet bag for Dante. "There you go. Like I said, any problems, just come back."

Dante nodded. "Thanks."

Mattie turned to Bray and his daughter. "Thank you again. This is the first time she's not cried since I fed her this morning."

"It could be colic, but even if it is, it's nothing to worry about. She'll grow out of it soon enough. It will mean a few sleepless nights, but…" Bray shrugged.

Mattie chuckled. "Luckily, I'm not a complete newbie. My friend has a son, and I was there for him growing up. I just never expected my own."

Bray seemed reluctant to let Ama go, but he gently passed her over to Mattie. "You didn't want kids?"

"Oh, no. I did. I just didn't think I'd ever get it." He cuddled her tightly to his chest, and she didn't cry.

"Not even with your partner? Your best friend, right?"

Mattie's cheeks heated. "Yeah. That's kinda new, too. As in, really new. Life sure knows how to throw several curveballs at once."

Bray chuckled. "Doesn't it?" He glanced at his friends, who were talking amongst themselves a few steps away. "Like I said, if you need anything, let me know." He reached for a pen and notepad that was on the counter and scribbled something. "I promise it's not a come-on or anything. I just remember how it was for my ex-wife. It's a lot when there's only one of you."

Sadness flowed across his face, and Mattie wished he could hug the guy, but he didn't want to overstep. "Thank you."

Bray nodded and headed towards his friends. "Let's go."

"Yeah! Drinkin' time!" one said.

"For you, maybe," Bray said, their voices getting quieter as they moved away. "For me, I get nothing. I've got to get home to…"

The door shut behind them, and Mattie pressed his cheek to Ama's head. "He was nice, wasn't he?" He settled into his chair, once again thinking he needed to change it to an armchair or something, and Ama nestled her face into his neck and sighed. Mattie sighed right along with her. "We'll figure it all out, okay?"

Two hours later, Jordan made a flying visit to the shop after he finished work. He was taking Cody to his first whittling lesson, and the kid was so excited. Mattie would bet a month's takings that whatever he had learned at school that day would've been forgotten by then.

"I just wish I could get a bead on the guy. He seemed…" Jordan shook his head. "I don't know."

"You're not taking Cody to a weirdo, are you?" Mattie asked, pushing Ama in her pushchair, back and forth. Jordan glared at him, and Mattie chuckled. "Just asking."

"Anyway, I better go. I'll see you later. I'll be back in time for the visit."

Mattie's mouth curved at one side. "You better."

Jordan grinned, kissed him, and ran out of the shop. Mattie glanced down at his sleeping daughter. Daughter. How long would it take for him to get used to that? The social worker was due at his house at five o'clock that evening, and he'd been extremely accommodating when he found out Mattie had a business to run.

But time was running out. He was due to get the DNA test results before the laboratory closed that day, and he hoped Jordan made it back in time to meet with him.

When it came to closing time—three-thirty that day because he'd decided he needed that extra half an hour to walk home instead of taking the bus, and because his life was currently in someone else's hands—he finished what he needed to do, left himself a list for things he didn't get done and headed home with Ama.

The walk was a bad idea because he was a hot, sweaty mess by the time he got home. He wasn't sure he had time for a shower, but he put Ama in the crib they'd bought the previous day and jumped in. He didn't bother doing anything other than cleaning off the sweat and then jumped out and dried off, throwing whatever clothes he could find. If he was a mismatched mess when Anthony turned up, so be it.

He was just jogging down the stairs with Ama in his arms when the doorbell rang. Pausing for a second to swallow the butterflies that wanted to choke him, he wandered to the door and opened it, wishing Jordan was there.

"Hi," he said.

"Good evening, Mr Evans. I'm Anthony Rodrigues."

"Nice to meet you, Anthony. Please call me Mattie. And come in."

The guy who held his future in his hands stepped across the threshold and waited for Mattie to close the door and lead the way. He held tightly to Ama, breathing in her scent and hoping he didn't make a mistake that made Anthony want to take her away.

"Would you like a drink?"

Anthony waved his hand and took a seat. "No, I'm fine, thank you." He rifled through his bag and brought some papers out.

Mattie settled into an armchair and cradled Ama in the crook of his arm, staring down at her. Despite having only had her in his life for around thirty-six hours, he couldn't imagine life without her in it any longer.

"I can see you already care for her," Anthony said. "Have you had the DNA results back?"

Mattie's heart jumped, and he grabbed his phone from his pocket. He had become adept at using his phone one-handed. He clicked on his emails and waited while it reloaded. The email jumped out at him. "Yes," he murmured. He opened the email and read the attachment. Relief—and the weight of being responsible for another person—flooded him, making him slump in the chair. "It's a positive match. Ama is my daughter." He held out his phone, and Anthony took it, reading through the document.

"Okay. That makes things a little easier, but there are still a few hurdles we have to jump through."

Mattie nodded. "Nothing worth fighting for is simple."

Anthony smiled, a kind of half-smile that made Mattie think he truly understood what he meant. "I haven't spoken to Rhia yet. I wanted to speak to you first, to see where we were. I will need to speak to her, though."

Mattie swallowed. "Could she change her mind and take Ama away?"

Anthony linked his fingers. "From what I know of similar situations, it's unlikely to happen. And because she's already given Ama up once, we wouldn't look as kindly upon giving her a second chance. You are her father, though, so you get more options now that you're in the picture and know about Ama, especially as you're named on the birth certificate, too."

Mattie blew out a breath. "Okay, what do we need to do?"

While they went through everything, Mattie changed Ama's diaper and made a bottle for her dinner. His mind was all over the place with possibilities and legal requirements and more home visits and safety concerns and…

"Mattie, you'll be fine. Let's just take it one step at a time," Anthony said.

Mattie settled the now-sleeping Ama into her daytime crib in the living room and sank into the seat beside her.

"I need to find childcare," he said.

Anthony nodded. "I'm sure Corey at Charmers Day Care will have space. Her staff are extremely competent and well versed in children of all ages."

"Okay. I'll call them tomorrow."

Anthony placed the paperwork into his bag. "For now, Mattie, I'm happy Ama's safe and well looked after. I have no reason to remove her from your care unless you feel it's necessary."

Mattie shook his head. "No. I want her. She's mine."

Anthony smiled. "She is, and she's a beauty." He stood.

"One word of caution. Don't let me hear you take her to work with you instead of finding childcare." He raised his eyebrows. "I'll let it slide now, but it's not to become a regular thing."

Mattie's cheeks burned. "I know. I'll call Corey straight away tomorrow."

"Good. Take care and call me if you need anything. I'll be in touch as soon as I have the next hoops to jump through."

"Thanks, Anthony."

He saw Anthony to the door and then settled back beside Ama. He had plenty of things to get done, but he couldn't find the energy for them.

The most important thing at that moment in his life was watching his daughter breathe.

His daughter.

His.

He smiled.

CHAPTER 8

JORDAN

Cody had been beyond excited when Jordan had picked him up from school. He hadn't stopped talking for the entire bus ride to Conway Heights, asking questions Jordan couldn't answer. But when they finally arrived at the address, Cody fell silent, staring at the door as if it was about to bite him. Jordan's feelings weren't much different, though his were about the man behind the door.

The door opened, and Bray's imposing body filled the frame. "Afternoon, come on in." He held the door wider. "You must be the whittler-in-training." He held out his hand to Cody.

Jordan squeezed Cody's shoulder and smiled. "Bray, this is Cody. Cody, this is…" He glanced at Bray. "Do you go by Mr Rushden or Sergeant Rushden?"

"Bray is fine. No need for formalities."

Cody squared his shoulders and gripped Bray's still-outstretched hand. "Nice to meet you, Bray."

"And you." Bray thumbed over his shoulder. "Let's start in the workshop. I'll introduce you to some tools you might already know and some you might not." He peered at Jordan.

"Are you learning, too, or would you prefer a coffee and a seat?"

"I'll eavesdrop a bit and make notes if that's okay with you. I need to know what I need to buy for him."

Bray nodded and headed towards the room he'd shown Jordan a few days ago.

Was it only a few days? It seemed longer. It could be because he was back to being a new parent—well, a new uncle—again with Ama. Mattie, despite his uncertainties, was ready to be a dad, and Jordan was happy for him. He glanced at his watch. He hoped he was back in time to meet with the social worker with him; he didn't want him to have to go this alone.

Regardless of his earlier words, he couldn't help staring at Bray instead of making notes. The man was muscular beyond anything Jordan had seen outside of gym commercials. Even some bodybuilders he knew from the beach weren't as ripped as Bray was. Was it all because of his military training, or was that just the way his body was made? Either way, it suited him, and Jordan couldn't look away. He was the type of man Jordan would've made a play for if they'd met at a club or bar. He shook his head and focused on his phone and the conversation. He was with Mattie now, and he couldn't be having thoughts like that.

"Right. Take these with you and you can practise this week. When you come back, we can move on a little further with the lessons."

Cody jumped up and turned to Jordan, smiling. "Look, Dad!" He held up the wood that he'd carved into what looked like the shape of a bear.

"That's cool, Cody. Well done." He stood. "What do you say?"

"Thank you, Bray. This has been awesome!"

Bray chuckled and ruffled Cody's hair. "You're a natural. It won't take you long to pick this up. Why don't you have a look in the living room at what's on the shelves, and you can see what I'm waiting to take to the hospital for the kids."

"Okay." Cody pushed past Jordan.

"Don't touch anything!" Jordan called after him.

"I won't!"

Jordan sighed. "That probably means he will. I apologise in advance."

Bray waved him off as he tidied his workshop. "It's fine. There's nothing valuable in there."

"They're valuable to the kids, I'm sure."

Bray leaned back against the table and crossed his arms. "Maybe," he conceded. He stared at Jordan, and Jordan stared back, his eyes widening when Bray stepped closer and stopped when they were toe-to-toe.

"What is it about you?" Bray murmured.

"Huh?" Bray was too close. He needed to push him away.

"You're magnetic," Bray continued. "All I want to do is be near you, and I'm never like that. I haven't…" His voice wavered. "I haven't touched a guy since before I joined the Army, but I want to touch you."

Jordan wanted him to, as well. There was a reason they couldn't, but he couldn't remember what. Bray's scent invaded his nostrils as he breathed, and he inhaled deeper to take more in.

Bray's hand lifted, and he skimmed a finger across Jordan's jaw. "In the short time I've known you, you've made me want things I had pushed deep inside, locked in a box. How is that possible?"

His finger caressed Jordan's lips, and Jordan's eyelids fluttered. As they closed, an image of Mattie rose, and Jordan jerked away.

"Mattie," he said.

Bray's forehead creased. "Mattie? The guy from the lingerie shop? What's he…" He trailed off. "You're the best friend." He shoved his fingers through his hair and stepped away.

"Best friend?" Jordan repeated.

Bray exhaled and resumed his lean against the table. "I met Mattie earlier when I was in his shop. I helped a bit with Ama while he dealt with my friends. He mentioned having just started a relationship with his best friend. Which seems to be you. I'm sorry for crossing a boundary."

Jordan blinked. "Small world."

Bray's mouth quirked. "Too small sometimes."

A crash sounded, and Jordan cursed as he headed towards the noise. He entered the living room to find Cody kneeling on the floor, picking up some wooden pieces.

Cody glanced up. "I'm sorry! I caught them with my jacket."

Jordan rubbed a hand over his face and apologised to Bray. But Bray shook his head. "It's fine. They're hardy things, and these are mine. No harm, no foul."

Jordan picked one up. "Chess pieces? You play chess?"

Bray shrugged. "Sometimes."

The guy was definitely an enigma, and despite his new relationship with Mattie, Jordan wanted to find out more. But where did that leave him and Mattie? He couldn't ignore what he felt for his best friend, but he also couldn't forget how it'd felt to be touched, however innocently, by Bray. Jordan closed his eyes and shook his head. Checking the time, he cursed.

"Cody, we have to go."

"You can stay a little—" Bray started.

"We could've, but I promised to be..." The guy already knew about Ama. "Mattie has his social worker visit, and I promised to be there. I'm late."

Bray straightened immediately. "It's okay. Go. Be there for him."

"When's the next bus, Dad? Will we get there in time?" Cody asked.

Jordan pulled out his phone. "I don't know. I'll check. It'll be okay." He clicked on the bus times.

"I'll drive you. Come on." Bray headed for the door, grabbing his keys as he went. "Hop to it," he added when Jordan just stared at him.

Cody followed, but Jordan froze. "Are you sure?"

Bray nodded. "That little girl has me wrapped around her finger already." He winked. "I'll be happy to help."

Jordan chuckled as they strode for Bray's car, Cody climbing in the back. "She is adorable, isn't she?"

Bray started the engine and aimed the car towards the address Jordan gave him. "She truly is. I have twin boys, but they're twenty now."

"And you've just got me, haven't you, Dad?"

Jordan chuckled. "You're more than enough for me, bud." But that wasn't true, was it? And even Bray seemed to be thinking along those lines because he glanced at Jordan with a raised eyebrow. Jordan shook his head, hoping he got across the message that Cody didn't know about him and Mattie yet.

As Cody was staying with Ash that night and they passed his house, despite Cody's argument at wanting to see Ama, Jordan dropped him home as quickly as he could. When they finally pulled up to Mattie's house, there was no car in sight, and Jordan's heart sank.

"I'm too late. Damn it!"

Bray squeezed his shoulder. "You'll still be able to be there. He'll have been given a lot of information. He'll need to digest it all, I'm sure. Go."

Jordan made a split-second decision. "Come with me. You've already met him. I'm sure he won't mind an extra pair of hands and ears."

Bray shook his head. "This is for you two. You don't need me pushing—"

Jordan grabbed Bray's hand. "I think we might."

He couldn't understand it, but something was pushing him to bring Bray into the house. Something wanted him there with him—them.

"Come with me," he said again.

Bray studied him for a moment and then turned the engine off. Jordan took that as an answer and climbed out, racing up the path. He unlocked the door quietly so he wouldn't disturb Ama if she was asleep and glanced over his shoulder to check Bray was with him. He was.

He led the way into the living room, seeing Mattie slumped on the sofa, staring into space, with Ama asleep in her crib. He moved closer, crouching in front of Mattie.

"Mattie? Sweetheart? Is everything okay?"

Mattie blinked and stared at him for a second before he smiled. "Hey, you. Everything go well?"

Jordan smiled. "Yes. I'm so sorry I wasn't here. What did the social worker say?"

Mattie sat upright and glanced behind Jordan with raised eyebrows. "Bray? What are you doing here?"

Bray smiled. "It's a small world."

Jordan chuckled. "Bray is the woodworker I mentioned. He said you two met today, and he helped with Ama."

Mattie brightened. "He did. He was amazing." He stood. "Would you like a drink?"

Bray waved him away. "Sit, rest. We're fine."

Mattie sat again, and Jordan moved to the sofa, still within reach of him, because Mattie seemed to be avoiding the conversation. "Talk to me, Mattie."

"The social worker was really nice. Anthony, that's his name. He said there are some legal hoops we have to go through, but he didn't seem worried about Ama staying with me. He did say I had to find childcare immediately because he didn't want me taking her to work."

Jordan nodded. "Understandable."

"I've heard Charmers Day Care is good," Bray said. "It's been too long for me to recommend somewhere I used, but I've heard good things on the grapevine. There's also Tiny Tots Daycare."

"Charmers is where Anthony suggested, too. I'll call them in the morning."

"So, it all looks good?" Jordan checked.

Mattie nodded, but his expression said otherwise. "They need to find that I'm a fit parent; otherwise, they'll take her away."

"You are, Mattie," Jordan said.

Mattie didn't reply, staring into the crib at Ama. Jordan glanced at Bray, unsure what to do for the first time in a long time. If the subject hadn't been so heavy and important, he would've made a joke, but he couldn't. Not then.

Bray clasped Jordan's nape and squeezed, and then he sank into a crouch in front of Mattie. "Mattie?" He waited until Mattie met his gaze. "Get some sleep. I'll take the night shift. We can sort everything out tomorrow."

Mattie stared at him for a long moment, and Jordan thought he was going to refuse. What he did do shocked him —Mattie leaned forward and kissed Bray on the lips. A mere brushing before he pulled back, eyes wide.

"Oh, god! I'm so sorry!" He glanced at Jordan, his hand covering his mouth. "I didn't... I..."

Jordan took his hand. "Don't be sorry," he whispered, seeing a possible answer to what he'd thought was an impossible situation. If Mattie was attracted to Bray, was Bray attracted to Mattie, too? Could they *all* be together?

Mattie's eyes filled, and Jordan slid his arm around his shoulders, despite the uncomfortable position it put him in. "It's okay. It's all okay." He stared at Bray while he murmured to Mattie. Bray's gaze bounced between the two of them, a slight frown between his eyebrows. "It's okay," he said to Bray that time.

Bray's expression cleared, and he rested one hand on Mattie's knee, the other on Jordan's arm. Jordan's body relaxed, and he smiled at him. Could he have both of them? Would they want that? That night wasn't the time to broach the subject, so he pushed it down. Tomorrow would be soon enough for such a heavy conversation.

Ama started stirring, and Mattie pulled away, but Jordan stayed him. "Will you let me and Bray take over so you can sleep?"

Mattie stared at him. "If you're sure." He glanced at Bray, who nodded.

Bray stood and picked up a fussing Ama, and Jordan led Mattie to the stairs. "I'll be back in a moment," he said to Bray over his shoulder.

"No rush."

When they got to Mattie's room—the room he'd shared with Jordan for the last two nights—Mattie was apologising again.

"I'm so sorry, Jordan. I don't know what happened. I—"

Jordan kissed him. When Mattie was pliant in his arms, Jordan pulled back. "It's okay. We need to talk about it because I have lots of questions for the three of us. Yes, the three of us," he added when Mattie's eyes widened. "But that can wait until tomorrow or another day. Just know that I'm okay with it. It's fine."

"But why?"

Jordan sighed, knowing Mattie wouldn't settle until he relieved him of his worries. "Because I almost kissed him tonight, too."

Mattie froze. "You did?"

Jordan nodded. "I'm with you, Mattie. Truly. But there's something about Bray that pulls me to him as well. I can't really explain it. I would never do anything about it without talking to you, which is what we'll do tomorrow. Please don't worry. I'm not going anywhere."

Mattie sighed and closed his eyes. "It's too much for me to handle tonight."

"Exactly. So let us take the night shift and you go to sleep."

"Yes, sir."

Jordan smiled. "That's more like it."

Once Mattie settled into bed, Jordan sat on the edge and brushed his hair off his forehead. "Sleep. We'll be here when you wake up."

Mattie sighed and closed his eyes. Jordan stayed with him for a little longer, and when he was sure he'd fallen asleep, he closed the door and descended the stairs. He had a feeling he would be having a large conversation with Bray during the night. If they could figure out where they stood, maybe they would have clearer answers for the questions he knew Mattie would have in the morning.

He found Bray and Ama in the kitchen, a bottle in the former's hand. Bray stared down at Ama with a smile as she drank, and she looked equally mesmerised. Jordan leaned against the doorframe and crossed his arms.

"You look good together."

Bray glanced up at him. "Which of us?"

Jordan knew what he was asking. "Both."

Bray shook his head. "I wasn't expecting that."

"I know. Neither was he."

"And you're okay with it?"

Jordan pushed off and sat in the chair beside him, inhaling deeply as he bared his soul. "Surprisingly, yes. I felt nothing but arousal from that kiss you shared, and I'd like more if you're willing to explore it?"

CHAPTER 9

BRAY

AND WASN'T THAT THE QUESTION OF THE NIGHT? WAS BRAY willing to explore a triad relationship—if that was even what Jordan was suggesting? Could he bring himself to step outside of his comfort zone and date not one, but two guys?

He kept quiet as he delved deep inside himself while he fed Ama. Ignoring his attraction to Jordan would be difficult, but it was true that he'd felt a frisson of awareness of Mattie when they'd met that afternoon and also during the kiss. Could it be as easy as just saying yes?

"Yes," he said, taking a risk.

Jordan's smile rivaled Ama's, and he said, "We might have to persuade Mattie tomorrow. Expect lots of questions and planning to go into this."

Bray frowned. "Why?"

"He's an organiser, a planner. He likes to know where things are going, what's going to happen, and where things belong. It's his way."

Bray shrugged. "Fine by me. I'm not so bad, but knowing and planning are all good."

"Are you sure about taking the night shift?"

"Yes, I'm sure. You should get some rest, too. I'm sure you have to work tomorrow."

"I've got to be at the beach by lunchtime tomorrow, so I can stay up a bit longer."

Bray glanced at him. "You're a lifeguard, aren't you?"

Jordan raised his eyebrows. "How did you know?"

"I saw you just before lunch. You were on the tower, laughing. It was just before I met my friends."

Jordan leaned back and crossed his arms, his mouth twitching. "So, you were sneaking looks at me, were you? Why didn't you say hello?"

"You seemed busy."

Jordan watched him as he lifted Ama to his shoulder and patted her back. Bray didn't want her to go back to sleep with wind because she'd wake the household with tummy pain later.

"Do you want a drink?"

Bray grinned. "Coffee would be good, thanks."

Jordan boiled the kettle and moved around the kitchen with ease.

"How long have you wanted Mattie?" he asked.

Jordan blew out a breath and brought over his coffee. "That's a tough question. I think there might've been this... awareness for a while, but I didn't acknowledge anything until Tuesday. I don't know if I just didn't want to rock the foundation of our friendship and that was why it took me so long to understand. I don't know. I separated from Ash five years ago. Was I not ready to admit it?" He shrugged. "I know now, though, that I'm all in. What're your thoughts on it?"

"Now who's asking hard questions?" Bray smiled.

Jordan chuckled. "I think there is going to be nothing but hard questions for the next few days."

Unable to brush away something so important, Bray considered his answer. "I'm unsure. Not about you and

Mattie, but about my part in it. I've only ever been with a man once, and that was before I went into the Army. After that, I pushed it aside for obvious reasons and met Sarah, who gave me two kids. Although I've thought about men since I've never acted on it."

"Are you still wanting to keep quiet about your preferences?"

Their potential future hinged on Bray's answer. "No. It doesn't bother me, although I have to have several conversations with people before I announce it to the world."

Jordan nodded. "There's no rush for anything. I'm just happy you didn't turn my idea down flat. I never expected it, but I'm not against it. I've seen triads on the beach before, but never expected my life to go in that direction. I don't see it as a problem. Just as a hill we need to climb carefully to avoid the rocks."

"Agreed."

"Now to convince Mattie."

Bray frowned. "I don't want to coerce him."

Jordan chuckled. "No, it's not like that. He wouldn't have a problem with this unless he felt it would affect our kids or our families. He would happily sacrifice his happiness if it meant someone else stayed content instead of rocking the boat."

"No one can live like that," Bray said.

"Exactly, but he's a people pleaser. Something I've been trying to drum out of him over the years." Jordan yawned.

"Go to bed, Jordan. I'll look after Ama, and I'll still be here in the morning."

"You better be." Jordan stood but hesitated. Then he leaned down and kissed Bray, just a brief touching of lips similar to what he'd received from Mattie. "Not the kiss I want to give you, but that'll have to wait." He winked and disappeared, leaving Bray with a hurricane of thoughts and emotions.

Bray settled Ama into her crib in the living room and settled onto the armchair, realising it had a footrest that slid up when he pushed back. He'd be able to doze on that while Ama slept and then be awake the moment she cried so she wouldn't disturb Jordan and Mattie.

And dozing was all he did because images of the three of them bombarded him, and not all of them were of a sexual nature. Random flashes of them walking down the street or sitting in a restaurant made him yearn for what he'd never wanted before. For what he'd never had before. It wasn't Sarah's fault he'd never had that. He'd left her with twins to take care of while he went and did his job in Afghanistan, and they'd barely done anything as a couple when he'd been home. They'd drifted apart, and when Sarah asked for a divorce, he'd seen no reason not to give her one. As much as he hated to admit it, he wasn't sure he ever loved her the way he should have. He'd seen her as what his life should look like and gone after it without thinking of the consequences. He didn't regret marrying her or having two wonderful kids, but he hated what he'd put her through. How she didn't hate him, he didn't know.

Ama woke around two in the morning, and he fed and changed her again before she settled down to sleep some more. He dozed for a while longer, and then voices woke him at six-thirty.

"—is fine. Let them sleep."

"But I don't want Ama to wake him. He's been up all night," Mattie said.

"You going in there and quietly lifting Ama is more likely to wake her screaming and then him. If she starts to fuss, we can get in there quickly," Jordan replied.

Bray smiled and carefully rose from the chair with barely a rustle. He slipped out of the living room door, making them both jump.

Jordan shook his head. "I keep forgetting you're sneaky. I

think it's highly unfair that you have training that makes it possible for you to sneak up on us."

Bray grinned, feeling lighter than he had for a while, though he hadn't realized something had been weighing on him until that moment. It was something to consider when he had time.

"I'm sure it won't be long until Ama's awake, so let's grab a coffee to start the morning right," he said.

Mattie snapped to attention and headed for the kitchen, just like Bray thought he might. Giving the guy something to do seemed to be the best way to keep him balanced and not ready to jump at the slightest word. They followed him and settled at the table while Mattie made drinks. When he joined them, Mattie brought up the subject that had obviously plagued his dreams.

"I'm sorry for kissing you yesterday. I… Okay, I'm sorry I did it without asking, and I'm sorry I basically cheated on you, Jordan."

"I was right there, Mattie. You didn't cheat on me. Is it something you want to talk about now, or do you want to think about it some more?"

"Give me the basics of what you see, Jordan. Of how you see this working. I'll ponder over it during the day, and we can discuss it tonight if that's good?"

Bray nodded. "Sounds like a great plan to me."

Jordan scratched his chin. "Well, I don't have a vision of how this works. I thought we could just go with it and see what happens. It's not like I've done this before, either."

That news seemed to make Mattie more tense than ever, so Bray took control. "Okay, so let's look at the different aspects of this. First, are there any objections to us being together as couples when the third isn't there, or do you want us to remain a triad at all times?" When he received frowns, he clarified. "So, if you were at work, Jordan, and I wanted to spend some time with Mattie, what are your thoughts on that?"

Jordan tilted his head. "I don't have a problem with it."

"Mattie?" Bray asked.

"Me either."

"That makes three of us, so we don't need to worry about stepping on toes. Communication is vital for me, though, so while I don't mind you being together, maybe a heads-up to each other to make them aware?" The others nodded.

"How do we even know we're compatible?" Mattie asked.

Jordan chuckled. "I don't think we have to worry about that, but how about we make sure our first time is together, and then we can decide from there?"

Mattie's cheeks flushed, and Bray wanted to see just how far down that flush went. There was a bang on the front door, and Bray shot up, racing towards the hall. He stopped outside the living room door when two women and a man entered. They froze at the same time he did.

"Who are you?" the older woman asked.

Mattie came up behind him. "Mama, what are you doing here?"

The woman, who Bray could now see had Mattie's eyes, sighed. "I hear from my neighbours that my boy has a daughter and not from my son? And then I hear he's been taking her to work with him rather than calling on his mother to help babysit her granddaughter. What am I to think?" She stared and then smiled. "Hello, Jordan, dear. How are you?"

"Very well, thank you."

Mattie exhaled. "Ama is asleep at the minute. Come into the kitchen, and I'll explain it all."

Bray didn't want to get in the way. "I'll head home."

Mattie reached for his hand and shook his head. "Please stay?"

Bray stared at him, wondering if he was ready for the questions that would undoubtedly get thrown their way if he stayed, but nodded when Mattie's expression almost pleaded with him. The relief that cascaded over Mattie's face made Bray wonder what he'd let himself in for.

"Mama, Papa, Lia, this is Bray. Bray, this is my mother, Evie, my father, Paul, and my sister, Lia."

Bray held out his hand to Mattie's father first. "Nice to meet you, Mr Evans, Mrs Evans." He gently shook Evie's hand and then turned to Mattie's sister. "And you, too."

"Are you military?" Paul asked.

"I am. Sergeant First Class, retired."

"Thank you for your service."

Bray nodded but didn't reply. He never knew what to say when people said that to him.

"Go on through to the kitchen. We'll be there in a minute," Mattie said.

When they were alone again, Mattie apologised. "I should never have given her a key."

"It's fine," Bray said. "But are you sure you want me to be here? They'll ask questions."

Mattie nodded. "Yes, they will. But not today. They'll wait until I'm alone and then ask."

"I'll do whatever you prefer."

"Stay. Please." Bray nodded. "Thank you." Mattie rested his forehead on Bray's shoulder for a moment and then stood upright again. "Let's go."

He headed for the kitchen, and Jordan whispered, "They are nice people, except when someone hurts one of their own, and then they're like snakes in a pit."

Bray smiled. "Nice to know."

When they entered the kitchen, it was to hushed whispers from Mattie and his mother. It subsided when they saw them. Evie smiled. "So, Mattie, what happened?"

Mattie squirmed. "I obviously wasn't careful enough, and Dionne ended up pregnant."

"Dionne? You weren't with her for long, were you?"

Mattie wrung his hands. "No, not long at all."

"So where is Dionne now?" Evie asked.

Mattie fell silent, staring down at his hands, and Jordan stepped behind him, resting his hands on his shoulders. "Dionne died in childbirth."

Evie gasped, her hands flying to her mouth. "Oh, my. That poor girl." Tears filled her eyes, and she wiped at them. "Well, little Ama won't want for anything, and we'll make sure she knows her mama."

At that moment, Bray understood how alike Mattie and his mother were. His mother would fight for her child to the ends of the earth, and it didn't matter what she had to do. Legal or not, she would ensure her child was safe and loved. Ama would have that.

"I can't wait to meet her," Lia said. "I always thought you'd be a great dad, Mattie, but I can honestly say I never thought it would happen."

Mattie chuckled, lightening the mood. "Me either." He stood, heading for the kettle.

Evie glanced at Bray. "So, Bray, what do you do now you're retired?"

"I suppose you could say I'm a woodworker. I make toys for the children at the hospital."

She gasped. "I've heard about you! I visit the children when I can, which is less often than I'd like, and they often have little wooden toys on their bedside tables. They're wonderful. You make those?"

Bray nodded, shifting in his seat, a little uncomfortable with the praise. "It's nothing big, but it keeps my hands and mind busy."

"It's a big thing to those children. To be able to have something that is just theirs to keep is a worthy cause."

Bray said nothing, gratefully taking a mug of coffee from Mattie as a distraction. "Thanks."

"How did the camping trip with Cody go, Jordan?" Mattie's dad asked.

As they got into a discussion about camping, and how much Mattie hated it, Bray realized he had yet more in common with Jordan, and no doubt, he'd find something else he and Mattie liked and Jordan didn't.

Ama started crying, and Bray stood. "Let me get her."

He strode down the hall to the living room and smiled down at the beautiful girl, who had woken with a cry but ended with a gummy smile when she saw him.

"Hey, sweet girl," he said, picking her up and cradling her against his chest. "Are you ready to meet some more of your family? You've got lots of people who would love to meet you, but let's start with Daddy's family, yeah?" He pressed his lips to her head and turned for the door, finding Mattie's mother leaning against the door frame. He paused, but all she did was smile and lead the way back to the kitchen. When they entered, she held out her hands.

"Can I?" she asked Bray, and Bray looked to Mattie, who nodded.

He handed her over and immediately missed her warmth. Evie cooed over her granddaughter, and Mattie came over to him, leaning against him.

"I hope she didn't say anything."

"No, just stared at me."

Mattie shook his head with a smile. "She's not stupid."

"Not in the slightest." Bray chuckled. "I am going to go, though. I need to get some sleep. If you need someone to look after her at any point until you find childcare, let me know." He raised his voice. "It was nice to meet you all, but I need to go."

He said his goodbyes, and Mattie and Jordan saw him to the door.

"Will you come back tonight?" Mattie said. "And I don't mean for the night shift. I'd like us to talk some more."

Bray nodded. "Sure. Let me know when you're home and I'll come over."

He leaned down and brushed his lips across Mattie's lips and then Jordan's, something as easy as the way he breathed.

"See you later."

CHAPTER 10

MATTIE

Mattie touched his lips as he watched Bray leave, the need to shout for him to stay almost more than he could bear. Jordan's arm came around his shoulder, and he sighed, resting his head on his chest.

"What's happening, Jordan?"

"Something none of us expected, sweetheart, but I'm certainly not against it."

"Me either, surprisingly."

Jordan cupped his chin, lifting his head. "Are you ready for the inquisition?"

Mattie chuckled. "No."

Jordan kissed him. "Are you ready now?"

"No?"

Jordan grinned and kissed him again. "Any more and they'll call a search party."

Mattie sighed. "I don't know what to tell them."

"Exactly that. We're working things out and need time to figure out what's going on between us."

"Sounds easy enough, but you know it won't be."

Jordan turned them towards the kitchen, keeping his arm

around him. "Let's get the simple stuff out of the way first, yeah? You and me. Together."

Mattie nodded, and they entered the kitchen. His mother smiled at them, a knowing look in her eyes.

"I wondered how long it would take you to find each other," she said, bouncing Ama in her arms. "Took you longer than I thought."

Mattie ducked his head. "I didn't think he wanted me that way."

Evie smiled, pressing her cheek against Ama's head. "You're an idiot."

Jordan chuckled. "Hey! I didn't realise until the other day. How did you know?"

She shook her head, as did his sister, and Lia replied, "It's so obvious."

Mattie groaned and covered his face. "Enough. We're together. That's all you need to know."

"And Bray?" his mother asked. "Where does he fit in?"

Mattie wasn't sure how to answer, but luckily, Jordan spoke for him. "He's someone we've realized we care for, and we're trying to figure out what that means."

Evie didn't seem surprised, offended, or disgusted, which was a good thing. His father, however, looked confused.

"How would that work?" he asked.

Jordan shrugged. "We don't know yet, and we'll let you know as soon as we do."

"Okay, then. So, how old is this beautiful girl?" his mother asked, changing the subject.

Mattie moved closer, resting his hand on Ama's back. "She's two months from what the birth certificate said."

"And you have custody?"

Mattie tilted his head back and forth. "Kind of." He sighed. "I'm on the birth certificate, which helps, but the social worker says there are still a few things that need to happen before it's all set in stone."

"Like what?"

"Home visits to make sure I'm fit to be a parent. A court case to give me full custody, which can take a while. Anthony doesn't think there will be a problem with it all, but it'll still be a while. He insisted I call about childcare, though."

His mother glared at him. "I agree. Taking her to work with you! What were you thinking? Especially when I could've helped."

Mattie sighed. "I know, Mama. I'm sorry. I needed to get my head on straight, and I was still in shock."

She tutted at him. "Anyway, today, she's all mine, got it? And you can rest assured that you have time to look at child-care options. It'll be good for her to be around other children, so daycare is a good idea, but there's no rush, okay?"

"Yes, Mama."

"Good. Go get ready for work, then."

"Yes, Mama," he sassed with a grin.

She glared at him and then smiled. "Despite the shock of having a granddaughter I wasn't prepared for, I'm so happy for you. You'll be a great dad."

Mattie felt tears filling his eyes, and he turned away, exiting the kitchen. He climbed the stairs and sat on the edge of his bed, the weight of being the sole person responsible for Ama lifting. He was her dad, for sure, but he wasn't alone. He had Jordan, Bray, his family, Jordan's family… Did Bray have family around? He couldn't remember if they'd talked about that. But regardless, he had support, and he couldn't be happier about it. He couldn't be happier that he was a dad. The tears won and streamed down his face, but they weren't sad tears, they were happy ones. Everything seemed to be falling into place, and he couldn't wait to see where his future went. Him, Jordan and, hopefully, Bray.

How had that happened?

A triad.

It was something he'd never noticed in Gaynor Beach, and

undoubtedly, it would make them fodder for gossip, especially throwing Ama in the mix, too. But he didn't care. He would shield his daughter and Cody as much as he could, but they would live to their own rules. Not anyone else's.

Wiping his face, he jumped in the shower, dressed and descended the stairs, finding everyone in the living room. Ama was asleep in his dad's arms, Jordan and Lia were talking, and his mother was looking at her phone. She glanced up at him.

"The Vine is busy," she said with a wink.

The Vine was a group of Gaynor Beach residents who had a chat that gossiped about everything. It was open to anyone who lived in Gaynor Beach, and although his mother wasn't a gossip herself, she was part of it to "keep an eye on things." It was how she'd found out about Ama, he was sure.

"I can imagine," he said, rolling his eyes.

He leaned over his father, pressing his lips to Ama's head, and then kissed Jordan chastely, his cheeks burning at the new affection he could show his boyfriend in front of his family. Kissing his mother's cheek, he said goodbye to everyone and left.

By the time he'd caught the bus and stood in front of his shop, his mother had sent him a dozen photos of Ama. Jordan had sent two as well. He couldn't help smiling. Unlocking the shop, he flicked the closed sign over to open and headed for the back to set up the checkout.

Things picked up straight away. Undoubtedly, the people of Gaynor Beach were still interested in Mattie and Ama, as they all asked about her and where she came from. Some were downright rude about it, but he answered their questions with a smile. Nothing would stop him from feeling happy about his situation at that moment. Even before Ama had turned up, he and Jordan had been starting their journey together, and with Ama and Cody, they had a family. Throw Bray into the mix, and Mattie knew he was a lucky guy. He just had to figure out what was happening between the three of them, and he would be golden.

When he had a moment to spare—in other words, when he had no customers—he called Charmers Day Care and asked to speak to Corey.

"Hey, Mattie! It's lovely to hear from you. Anthony mentioned you might call. How are things?"

Mattie couldn't help but smile, even though Corey couldn't see him. "Things are good, thanks. If Anthony mentioned me, you probably already know my situation."

"Oh, god, no. Anthony wouldn't tell me anything more than you might call. It was the rest of the parents that told me about your situation." She chuckled. "Gaynor gossip at its finest."

Mattie rubbed a hand over his face. "I can imagine. They even got to tell my mother before I did."

Corey sucked in a breath. "Ouch."

"Yeah. She wasn't best pleased." He snorted. "Anyway, I wondered if you had any space for Ama, please? I don't want her to be in full-time because I'd like to spend some time with her and get her used to me being around, but do you have something available?"

"Yes, of course. I currently have one full-time space and several other part-time spaces, too. Why don't we talk through what I have available, and you can go from there?"

They spent the next ten minutes talking about his options, which were good, thankfully. He promised to contact him the next day after he'd spoken with his family. He was sure his mother, at the very least, would want to look after Ama for some of Mattie's working hours, but he wasn't sure how many. After he'd seen and discussed the situation with Jordan and Bray, he would see where he ended up.

The afternoon got busy again, and time flew. By the time he shut the store, he was exhausted but energised. Even the packed bus journey home didn't dull his joy, and it gave him time to get his thoughts in order, which he wrote on his phone, ready to throw them into the wild when Jordan and Bray arrived.

When he entered the house, it was to laughter, and Mattie immediately grinned. He could get used to coming home to that sound.

"I'm home!" he called, removing his shoes and dropping his bag to the floor. He'd clean it up later.

"Living room!" his mom called back.

He leaned against the doorframe and watched Evie feeding Ama while Paul and Bray fought with building something.

"What are you doing?" he asked.

His father glanced at him, wiping the sweat from his fore-head. "Bray brought over a playpen for you to use. We thought we'd get it up now."

Mattie frowned. "Isn't she a little young for a playpen?"

Bray met his gaze, and Mattie's stomach swirled with butterflies. "She is for actually playing in it, but you can use it as a sleeping place, too. It's what we had for the twins. I wasn't sure if I still had it, so I went looking, and…" He waved his hands towards the wooden pieces of wood. "I'd forgotten how complicated it was to build, though.

Mattie pushed off the doorframe and moved closer, crouching beside him. "It'll be great. Thank you."

He wanted to kiss him, but he didn't want to presume, so he just smiled and refocused on his daughter before he made a mess of things. He strode across the room, and Ama's gaze found him immediately. Her arms pumped, and the bottle fell from her mouth as she gave a gummy smile. He grinned back, grasping her hand and rubbing his thumb over the back.

"Hey, sweetpea. Have you had a good day?"

"She's just woken from a nap, haven't you, sweetie?" Evie said. "She seems to have her routine a little backward. She'll fall asleep before a bottle rather than after it, like some babies do, but it's not a problem. Whatever works for you, isn't it?" Her last words were spoken in a baby tone and directed at Ama, which Ama loved. Ama's arms rose and fell several times, and her legs kicked.

Mattie's heart skipped a beat, and he chuckled. "I called Charmers Day Care today. They have space for her. I just need to figure out what days and hours I need."

Evie nodded. "Well, you know I don't mind doing some. I just need to work it around my current schedule."

Mattie smiled. "Thanks, Mom. Let me know what you want to do."

"Paul, honey, could you take Ama while I get my diary, please?"

His father rose, clapping Bray on the shoulder. "I'll leave this in your capable hands." He took Ama from Evie's arms and pressed a kiss to Ama's cheek before settling her against him and reaching for the bottle.

As much as Mattie wanted to hold his daughter, he would do so after he'd spoken with his mother. She obviously had something she wanted to say to him.

"Would you like a drink, Bray?" he asked.

"Yes, please."

"Coffee, black, no sugar, right?"

Bray nodded and winked. "Good memory."

Mattie smiled back and followed his mother, who had disappeared into the kitchen. He filled the kettle, not even asking his father if he wanted a drink because he would, and set it boiling, fetching everything he needed before broaching the subject with Evie.

"So, what's up?"

Evie chuckled and rested her hands on her diary. "Nothing per se." She sighed. "I'm going to say something you don't want to hear but need to, okay?" Mattie braced himself and nodded. "Are you sure you want to become a…

triad, is it?" Mattie nodded again. "Are you sure? I'm going to be the devil's advocate here. I want you to think about what this could do for Ama's future. I have conflicting thoughts about it, and I can't figure out what's best."

Mattie knew better than to answer his mother's questions without thinking things through, so he made the drinks while he considered her words. She wasn't being mean at all. He knew that. And her concerns were valid. His relationship with two men could cause an issue in Ama's future, but was he willing to stop it before it started on the off chance it did?

No, he wasn't.

He took the drinks into Bray and his dad, sharing a smile with Bray, and then settled opposite his mother at the kitchen table. He placed her drink in front of her and slid his closer.

"You're right. It might cause problems for Ama, but I don't think... No, I know I can't be without them now I've found them. I've already thought about the consequences, and we can bring Ama—and Cody—up with the skills they need to be able to push the opinions of others aside. It won't be easy. I know that. But why would I push aside my chance at happiness for something that might not happen in the future?"

Evie smiled at him. "Good boy."

Mattie frowned. "What?"

"I was being horrible about your situation, and you told me how it would be. That's the kind of strength you'll need to power through the years to come." She reached forward and covered his hand. "I want this for you, Mattie. I truly do. I can't remember a time when I've seen you so happy, and I believe it'll only increase as time goes on." She squeezed his hand and let go, returning to her diary. "Okay, so I have my meeting on Tuesdays, knitting club on Thursdays..."

As they went through her diary to find out when she wanted to look after Ama, Mattie thought through her words. He would fight for them because he wanted this for himself.

He wanted Jordan and Bray, and he would do anything to make it work. But he now needed to consider Ama; his mother was right about that. His decisions now needed to be filtered through the "parent perspective." And wasn't that a turn up for the books?

CHAPTER 11

JORDAN

Jordan dropped by Ash's house on his way to Mattie's, knowing Cody was at his after-school club. He hadn't been to his own apartment for the past few days, but he would need to grab some things eventually. He couldn't rely on having three changes of clothes indefinitely, even with the use of Mattie's washer and dryer.

"Hey, come on in," Ash said.

"Thanks." Jordan closed the door behind him and followed him to the kitchen. "I'm returning the favour from the other week."

Ash raised his eyebrows and waited, something that used to annoy Jordan in the beginning, but then he'd realized Ash was giving him the chance to start wherever he needed to, rather than pushing him. It was something he'd grown to like and wished more people did.

"I've started seeing Mattie."

Ash's smile was instantaneous, and he pulled Jordan in for a hug. "I'm so pleased for you both." He held up his hands once he'd set Jordan free. "I'd never wondered during our relationship if that was something you thought I would be worried about. But after, I did see something brewing. I never said anything though because it wasn't my place."

Jordan chuckled. "Yeah. I was completely blind to it until the other day." He inhaled. "But that's not the only thing I have to say." He leaned against the counter and crossed his arms, preparing for something, though he didn't know what. "We might be adding a third into our relationship as well."

Ash stared at him, and Jordan fought the urge to fidget. Ash kept blinking at him and then nodded once. "Okay."

"Okay?" Jordan repeated.

"Yeah, okay."

Jordan blew out a breath. "I thought I'd get more than an 'okay'."

Ash shrugged. "What do you want me to say? No, you can't do it? No, that's not right? No, think about Cody? There's no point because I know you wouldn't go into anything without thinking about your son and any repercussions." He shrugged again. "I trust you."

Jordan exhaled. "Thank you. We're going to discuss it tonight, so I'll be able to tell you what the plan is after that."

"Whatever you decide is fine by me. I'll support you however I can. If there's any kind of fallout, we'll all support Cody, I'm sure. And little Ama, too."

Jordan grinned. "Little Ama is right. Though she won't be for long."

"Definitely not. You've got your hands full starting from the beginning again."

Jordan's chest squeezed. "I'm looking forward to it."

"I'm happy for you, Jordan. About all of it."

"How are things with your new guy?"

Ash scrunched his face. "Okay. Our schedules are not easy, but we make it work. I'm hoping to talk to Cody about it soon."

"Should we do it together and get it all done at once, or would that be too much upheaval for him at once?"

"I don't know. Maybe getting it all out there at once will give him time to process all his feelings and thoughts and questions in one go. We won't know until we do it, unfortunately."

"Okay. Well, let me know when you want to do it, and I'll make sure we're all on board with it."

The front door clicked. "Papa, I'm home!"

"Speak of the devil," Ash muttered. "Hey, I'm in the kitchen."

"Dad!" Cody shouted when he saw Jordan and rushed in for a hug. "I wasn't expecting to see you until tomorrow."

Jordan hugged him. "It's just a flying visit today. I have to get back to Mattie's to help him with Ama." He didn't have to help with Ama at all, but what else could he say?

"Can I come and help? Please? I've not seen her yet."

"Not today, bud. I'll arrange it for tomorrow. How about that?"

Cody's face fell, but he nodded. "Okay."

"Did you have a good day at school?" Ash asked.

"Yeah, it was good. Math sucks."

Jordan and Ash chuckled. "Yeah, it does. But you'll get there," Ash said. "I'll help you tonight."

"Thanks, Papa."

Jordan pushed off from the counter. "Right, I'm going to go now I've had my hug for the day. I'll see you tomorrow, all right?"

"Okay."

He hugged Cody again, waved at Ash and left, bundling himself onto the bus again to take him the rest of the way to Mattie's house. His stomach swirled and churned, a hurricane of butterflies and worry. He had no idea what the evening would bring, but he hoped it would be favourable.

He knocked on the door and let himself in as he usually did, almost bumping into Mattie's parents.

"Oh, hey!" he said as Evie hugged him. It was a day for hugs, apparently.

"Hey, yourself. We're just heading off, but we'll see you soon, sweetie," Evie said, ushering Paul out of the door.

Jordan stared after them. "Okay, bye," he muttered, wondering what the heck that had been about. He glanced in the living room, but no one was there, though something new was, so he went to the hub of the house—the kitchen—where he found Mattie, Ama and Bray.

"Hey!" Mattie said, rising from the table to greet him with a kiss and a bundle of joy between them.

Jordan returned the kiss and glanced down at Ama. "Hey, sweetheart. Have you been causing trouble today?"

Mattie chuckled. "If she did, Mom didn't tell me."

"Grandparents wouldn't. They keep all the troubles to themselves," Bray said. "How was work?"

Jordan shook his head. "Busy. I know it's the height of summer, but some people have more swimming costumes than brain cells."

"I can imagine," Bray said.

They dropped into silence, and then Jordan chuckled. "Let's clear the air, shall we? All I can feel is static at the minute, and as much as I like my hair standing up, I'd prefer it to be after I've been in bed." He purposefully made it an innuendo to see what they'd do, and Mattie rewarded him with flushed cheeks and ducked head, and Bray's darkening eyes.

"Let me have this little one for a few minutes," Jordan said, lifting Ama from Mattie's arms.

Mattie pouted. "I've only just had her."

Jordan chuckled. "Bray, do you agree that he'll find most visitors won't care that he's not held his daughter and will steal her away at every possible moment?"

"I agree wholeheartedly."

Mattie sighed. "Would you like something to eat?"

"Let's order takeaway, then we'll have more time to talk." He paused. "Although that just reminded me. I've missed something." He stepped closer to Bray and leaned down, waiting for Bray to meet him halfway. Their lips brushed, and Jordan closed his eyes before standing straight again. "Can't meet one and not the other."

He settled into a chair, and then rose again, heading for the living room. "Comfy chairs, I think."

His "got it together" attitude would only last so long, but if he didn't pretend he wasn't in knots, he wouldn't be able to say anything. So pretend he did. Settling on the sofa with the bundle of joy against his chest relaxed him somewhat, but it wouldn't last. Mattie and Bray entered, closing the door despite no one else being in the house. It was a good idea in case someone let themselves in, though.

Mattie sat beside him, and Bray chose the armchair next to them.

"So…" Mattie said. "I don't really know where to start. I wrote a list, but it only helped to clear my mind, not to tell me what I was worried about. I'm not sure."

Jordan wasn't sure either.

"How about I start then?" Bray said, leaning forward and resting his elbows on his knees. "When I first met Jordan, I was attracted to him straight away. But the moment I knew he was with you, I ignored my attraction. I'd never have done anything to make someone cheat on someone else."

"I know you wouldn't," Jordan said. "I wouldn't have either, but it was close." He glanced at Mattie. "I'm sorry for that."

Mattie shook his head. "You didn't actually kiss him, whereas I did." He chuckled. "There's definitely a three-way attraction here. Do you agree?" Jordan and Bray nodded. "So, where do we go from here?"

"Let's cross off any issues we see first. If any of them are insurmountable, we need to know before we agree to go any further," Bray said.

"Okay. Well, the only issue I see is gossip," Jordan said. "We'll be the talk of the town, and therefore, so will our kids and our families."

"I think we need to grow thick skin for that," Mattie said. "Mom brought this up earlier, and I'll tell you what I told her. I won't let what *might* happen dictate what I do now."

Jordan could've kissed him. "I agree, although I think we need to figure out the best way to explain *us* to people—and Cody."

Bray nodded. "Yes, we need something we all agree on."

"A triad?" Mattie said.

"I think that's the best word to describe us, but what do we tell people?" Jordan said.

"Do we have to tell them anything?" Bray asked.

Jordan and Mattie shared a look. "The Vine will give us the third degree unless we satisfy them with more than that."

Bray shrugged. "I've only ever had to explain myself to my family, friends and my superiors. No one else has mattered."

Jordan laughed, startling Ama. He soothed her for a second and then explained his humor. "You'll have to deal with that. Especially with you living on the outskirts of Gaynor Beach. People will want to know everything about you. They will delve into your psyche, your life, your past, and they will uncover everything they can. They'd be great in the military for getting people to talk."

Mattie and Bray chuckled.

"So, I think we can safely say that it doesn't matter what we say to people, they will make their own assumptions," Mattie said.

"Agreed."

"But what do we tell Cody?"

Jordan sighed. "I think the easiest solution is the easiest

explanation. We are together just like a couple would be, but we have three times the love."

Bray smiled. "I like that."

Mattie leaned closer and stroked Ama's hair as she dozed. "There's more than enough love to go around," he whispered.

"True enough." Jordan kissed his head.

"What other issues?" Bray asked.

"Boycotting?" Mattie said. "I have a business to run. It's my livelihood. If people get up in arms about us, it could affect that."

"Money is of no concern," Bray said. "I know no one likes to talk money, but I have plenty to support us should the need arise. But yes, there is the chance people will stop buying from you, but if we can weather that, they'll soon come back again."

"Unless they get me shut down."

Bray shook his head. "I won't allow that. We have the law behind us."

"Yeah, but would the residents support that or make to change the law?" Mattie said.

"I don't know if they could, but they could always try. Don't borrow trouble, Mattie," Jordan said.

Mattie sighed. "It's hard not to."

"I know. Let's get through the issues we can deal with for now, and then it'll only leave those we need to work on," Bray said. He shifted forward in his seat. "The only concern I have is regarding the bedroom."

Heat flooded Jordan as memories of his dreams invaded his mind. He had no idea if any of them were possible, but he'd die trying. The thought of the three of them in a tangle of limbs was almost more than he could bear, and he focused on Ama to dispel them.

"What's that then?" Mattie said, his voice cracking.

"If we're compatible. We might be as twos, but are we as a triad?"

"I don't think we'll have any problems in that area, but we won't know until we try, will we?" Jordan said.

Mattie cleared his throat. "Look, I know we probably have more issues to go through, but can we just try being together tonight? Watching TV, talking, laughing, looking after Ama—together."

"I think that's a great idea," Bray said, sliding off the chair to kneel in front of them. He leaned over the sleeping Ama, brushing his fingertip against her cheek. "Let's get her into the playpen, and we can choose a movie."

Bray rose, reaching for Ama, and Jordan handed her over. He was so careful with her as he wandered over to the new addition—a wooden frame surrounding a comfortable-looking pad. He knelt and laid Ama gently on the fabric. Then he stood and backed away. Jordan's heart melted just a little more over his actions, and he slid his arm around Mattie, who seemed just as overwhelmed. He didn't think they'd have any problems at all. In any area of their relationship.

"What are we watching?" Bray asked, slipping onto the sofa beside Jordan and squashing him between him and Mattie.

"Well, the first thing we need to look into is getting a bigger sofa," Jordan said, pulling his arm free from where it'd been stuck.

Mattie laughed. "We can do that. Especially as when the kids get older, they'll be climbing on us, too."

As Mattie grabbed the remote and set about finding something to watch, Jordan lost himself in his thoughts again. This time it was about Mattie already thinking of them years in the future. Jordan had never really considered the future to be different than what he was living now, but now he was with them, he could see things changing and moving and rearranging. He couldn't wait until they were out in the open about their relationship, and they could tell anyone and everyone about them. He didn't want to have to hide, but he would if he needed to. They had so much love to give, it would be awful if they couldn't share it.

He sighed as Mattie snuggled back into his side, and Bray slid his arm around them both. Jordan rested his head on Bray's chest, and they fell into a comfortable silence as the movie played. It wouldn't be long before Ama woke, and then they would have a different dynamic to work out. Every day would be a learning curve, and he couldn't wait to explore it all.

CHAPTER 12

BRAY

Bray had missed having someone in his arms, but he hadn't realized how much. As he sat with Jordan and Mattie, he couldn't say what they were watching because he was concentrating on remembering the feel of them, the sounds they made, the noises of the house. He didn't want to forget this moment of peace. He doubted it would stay that way for long. Not only because Ama would wake soon, but because the people outside of the house were unlikely to be as easy-going as Bray wished they would be. As much as they spoke of standing their ground and sticking up for themselves, when it came down to it, would they be able to do it, or would the peer pressure push them in another direction?

Their takeaway was delivered, and they ate it while Ama still slept and the movie played. Their banter was something Bray loved. It reminded him of his friends, which came with the realisation he needed to tell them what was happening—when he knew.

When Ama's sleepy snuffles turned into babbling, he wanted to pick her up and settle her against his chest, but Mattie beat him to it. Only fair, as he had hardly held his daughter since he'd been home.

"Hey, sweetpea." Ama stared at Mattie and waved her hands. Mattie smiled down at her. "Let's get you changed, shall we?" He moved to the floor where the changing bag was and laid her down on the mat already covering the carpet.

Jordan tilted his head to look at Bray. "He's a natural," he said, not keeping his voice down.

"I can see that."

Mattie's cheeks tinged red, and he glanced across at them. "I've had practice with Cody, remember?"

Jordan shook his head. "You did, but you were a natural then, too. It's built in with you. You've always wanted kids."

Mattie chuckled at Ama. "And now I have one, don't I, sweetpea?"

"If you think about it," Jordan continued, "if we're going ahead with our relationship, you actually have four."

Mattie's hands froze for a second, and Bray opened his mouth to take Jordan's words back, saying Mattie didn't need to worry about his kids, but then Mattie lifted a beaming smile at them. "I have four kids. I've gone from none to four in days." He looked at Ama and smiled again. "Aren't I the luckiest man alive?"

Bray shook his head. "For someone who likes things to be planned and organized, you're sure going with the flow."

Mattie said nothing as he finished changing Ama's diaper, and when he picked her up and settled her back against his chest so she could see them, he sighed. "I know. I don't understand it, either. I honestly thought I'd be a mess right now, but everything just seems to be slotting together. Don't get me wrong, I have a list as long as my arm of things I need to do or buy, but it's not weighing on me."

Jordan leaned forward, and Bray immediately missed his warmth. "A problem shared is a problem halved…or thirded, or whatever." He hissed and waved his hands. "Not that Ama is a problem."

Mattie chuckled. "I know what you mean." He shrugged. "I don't know. But I'm not complaining about being relaxed. It won't last. Anthony will be doing some spot check visits, both here and at work, to make sure I don't have her hidden in the back room." He snorted. "Thinking about childcare, though. I need to finish figuring out what hours I need."

Jordan pulled out his phone. "What did your mom choose?"

"She said she can do Monday and Thursday afternoons."

Jordan studied his screen. "Well, I can ask for permanent afternoons at work and then I can do mornings?"

Mattie shook his head. "No. Keep your work as it is. I know you like to be available for Cody when Ash is working. Corey was great in saying that I could put her in for different hours each week if I needed to."

Bray inhaled. "And don't forget, I can do some, too."

Mattie leaned his cheek against Ama's head, and Bray could see he was emotional. "Thank you. Both of you."

"Let's get a quick plan down for the next two weeks because that's how far my shifts go," Jordan said. "Then you can call Corey in the morning and let him know what you need."

They relocated to the kitchen table, and Mattie made a bottle for Ama. When he came to sit, he asked, "Who wants to feed her?"

Bray did, but he let Jordan answer first, not wanting to push in on his chance.

"Let Bray," Jordan said. "I'll help you figure this out."

Bray's heart skipped a beat as Mattie put Ama into his arms. "Here you go."

Adjusting her position, Bray picked up the bottle and teased her lips with it. She latched on straight away, and Bray stared down at her angelic features, so reminiscent of Mattie apart from her eyes, which he assumed she got from her mother. It was such a terrible thing to have happened to her, but they'd make sure Ama remembered her mother. Had Mattie got any photos of her? He'd have to ask because if not, they'd have to get in touch with the sister to ask. No way was Ama growing up with no idea what her mother looked like. Not on his watch.

It didn't take them long to figure it out, and with Mattie's mom's advice of giving Ama the chance to interact with other children her age and older, Mattie decided on giving her four half days at daycare, to begin with. Bray agreed with his choice because it was the best of both worlds. His mother could have her for two half days, Jordan for another two half days, and Bray would take up whatever slack was needed after that. The only times he couldn't do was when he visited the children's hospital, but that could be moved around as needed.

A couple of hours later, Ama was safely asleep in her cot, with the monitor clipped to Mattie's pocket so he could hear her if she cried.

"I better go," Bray said. He wasn't sure whether he said it because he needed space to think or if it was because it was what he would normally say.

Jordan shared a glance with Mattie and stepped closer to him in the hallway. His hands rested on his chest and smoothed upwards. "Before you go…" Jordan's lips claimed his, and Bray's eyes closed as the scent of him invaded his nostrils. He slipped his hands around Jordan's back and head, holding him in place as he licked across his lips, requesting entry.

This kiss was harder and deeper than any they'd shared so far, and Bray didn't want it to end. He turned them and pressed Jordan against the wall, giving him leverage to grind against him. Jordan whimpered into his mouth, and a second later, another body pressed against his side. Bray pulled his mouth free and glanced at Mattie, cheeks flushed, eyes dilated. Jordan's hand was wrapped around Mattie's T-shirt, having obviously pulled him closer.

Bray didn't hesitate. He slid an arm around him and took Mattie's mouth the same way he'd taken Jordan's, nipping his lips, taking his air, exploring his taste.

"Fuck. That's so hot," Jordan muttered.

Bray pulled back, panting, and stared at Mattie's bruised lips for a second before focusing on Jordan. "Your turn."

Jordan frowned, but when Bray tilted his head towards Mattie, he grinned. "My pleasure." He yanked him closer, fusing their mouths in a kiss that set Bray's blood on fire. Jordan was right. It was fucking hot. He watched as their tongues duelled, their teeth nipped, their lips sipped, his arousal heightening with each passing second.

Keeping his hands on them, he leaned down and took Mattie's earlobe gently between his teeth, tugging and then sucking on it. Mattie's head fell further back, giving him access to his neck. Letting go of his ear, he lowered to the exposed column, licking a stripe down and latching onto the skin at the base. He sucked hard, and Mattie groaned, gripping Bray's head. Bray let go of his skin, his heart racing at the mark he'd purposefully left behind. He licked over it, then turned to Jordan. He grasped Jordan's hair, tilting his head away from him and exposing his neck, and then he repeated the actions on him, marking him, too.

When he came up for air, Mattie was helping to hold Jordan against the wall as he panted and dropped his head back with a thud.

"Holy…fucking…hell…" Jordan muttered.

"I agree," Mattie said, staring at Bray.

"Hoo-yah," Bray whispered, earning a chuckle from them both.

"You can stay," Mattie said.

Bray wanted to, and that, more than anything, told him he

shouldn't…yet. "Soon. Let's get used to us before we have sleepovers."

Jordan pouted. "We can keep playing, though, can't we? I can't go a day without one of those kisses ever again."

Bray chuckled. "We can play. And we can see what we all like. I, for one, have some ideas about what I'd like to do to the two of you." His voice was rough and deep, vibrating in his chest at the images bombarding him. But he swallowed them down and stepped back, both Jordan's and Mattie's hands falling from him. He wanted to step right back into them again, but they all needed to think things through and make sure they were okay with where they were headed.

Because once they decided, Bray wouldn't be changing his mind without a big reason.

He'd thought about being with a man—but never believed he'd find one who *fit* him—but a triad had never crossed his mind. He wanted them to make sure this was what they wanted before they went any further and hurt each other, and he told them as much.

Both appeared to want to argue, but he held up his hand. "Just a few days. Okay?"

"Kisses are still okay, aren't they?" Jordan asked.

Bray chuckled. "Yes. As I said, we can play, but we need to go slow. I'd hate for either one of you to get hurt."

"What about you?" Mattie asked.

"What about me what?"

"What about you getting hurt?"

Bray smiled. "All three of us getting hurt. Is that better?"

Mattie nodded and leaned his head against his chest. "Much. You're as important as we are."

Bray didn't think so, but he'd be happy to make them think he did. "Get some rest. She'll be awake again soon. Ring me if she doesn't settle, and I'll do the night shift again."

Mattie lifted to his toes and kissed him, more gently this time, and then moved back. "I will."

Jordan leaned in, brushing his lips across Bray's, and sighed. "I don't know where you both came from, but I'm glad you're here."

Bray's heart melted. The once strong-willed sergeant was melting. At words. He inhaled, cupped Jordan's cheek in one hand and Mattie's in the other and left.

He needed to speak to his mother.

Though if she was as much of a witch as he believed her to be, he guaranteed she would call him the moment he set foot in his house.

She didn't, but it wasn't much later than he'd expected.

"You would be priceless to the Army, you know?" he said. "I swear you have cameras in my house and know when I'm here."

"My secrets die with me," his mother said with a croaky laugh.

"Don't even joke about it. Remember, you and Roscoe are stubborn." He hated the idea of her joining his father, though it was inevitable. He pushed the thought away.

"So, Bray, what's got your panties in a twist?"

Bray chuckled. "How do you… Do you know what? I give up." He sighed. "I have…a situation."

"Mmhmm. What kind of situation? Is this to do with that guy you met?"

"Yes. And no." Bray settled on the sofa and kicked his feet up on the coffee table. "I'm in the middle of figuring out a triad relationship." He threw it out there and waited for her answer.

She was silent for a few seconds and then burst out laughing. Bray raised his eyebrows and waited her out, shaking his head. Her laughter turned to coughing, and he winced at the rattle.

"Oh god. I needed that." She coughed again and slurped a drink. "Ahh. Right, I'm back. So, you have two men?"

"Yes." Short and simple.

"And what are you trying to figure out?"

Bray exhaled. "Not figure out as much as I don't want to hurt them. There are kids involved. Not least of which is my two."

"What makes you think you'll hurt them? Actually, don't answer that." She inhaled, and Bray imagined her sucking on her cigarette. "They're not Sarah, you know. Things are different now."

Bray closed his eyes, rubbing his eyelids. "It wasn't her fault, Mom."

"Wasn't it? Yes, you were gone a lot, but she knew you would be. She agreed to marry you. She understood the lifestyle."

Bray sighed. His mother had never been a fan of Sarah, but she had never been unkind until Sarah filed for divorce. After that, his mother had ranted about her leaving him alone. Bray had eventually told her to cool it, and she had. Sarah had never given him any grief about his absences and made sure he always had access to his kids. He couldn't fault her for not wanting to stay in a loveless marriage.

"Look, Bray. You're no longer in the military. You have time to spend with them and with the kids. You won't be leaving them for extended periods. There is time to see where this is going. Take it. The only way you'll hurt them is by not talking to them. Communication is key. You learned that in the Army."

"*'Send three and fourpence. We're going to a dance,'*" he said, repeating the start of one of his father's favorite phrases.

"*'Send reinforcements. We're going to advance,'*" his mother finished. "Exactly my point."

Bray stared at the ceiling. "Are you not going to ask about them?"

"Do you want to tell me?"

Bray smiled. "Yeah. Actually, I do."

Bray settled further into the cushions of the sofa and

began to talk. He didn't realise how much he'd picked up about Jordan and Mattie until he relayed it all to his mother. Her questions, though nosey, gave him an insight he hadn't known he had. And by the time he said goodnight, he couldn't wait to see his guys in the morning.

CHAPTER 13

MATTIE

MATTIE SLEPT FITFULLY. AMA WOKE ONCE FOR HER BOTTLE, AND then at around six o'clock the following morning, Mattie didn't see the point in going back to bed after she'd woken for the day. Jordan had woken when Ama had, but Mattie had told him to sleep. He'd need his rest for the day. As would he, but Ama was his daughter. He would have to deal with it for many years to come.

He held Ama as he fed her the morning bottle and looked longingly at his cooling coffee. That would be something else he needed to learn—either making a coffee after he'd fed her or getting up slightly earlier than her and drinking it beforehand.

He heard Jordan's yawn before he saw him, and he grinned. "You should sleep some more."

Jordan settled beside him, leaning his head on Mattie's shoulder. "It's not the same without you."

Mattie's heart skipped, and he turned to kiss Jordan's head. "I know I've asked before, but you're welcome to move in. Not because we're more than friends now, but because I have a spare room and you would save rent money."

Jordan chuckled. "I know. Let's give it a little while longer. It's been less than a week since we got together."

Mattie sighed as Ama finished her bottle and repositioned her against his chest. "I know. I just don't like you being there when there's a space here. You don't even have to sleep in my room, you can have the spare room."

Jordan lifted his head as well as his eyebrows. "And where will little miss sleep?"

Mattie opened his mouth, but Jordan had a point. "Crap."

"It's fine. We have time, and I have a separate place to lay my head if I need to, but I love being in your bed." He glanced at the window. "It would be nice for Bray to be here, too, but I understand his hesitance."

"The same as yours."

"Not rushing is a valid reason."

Ama gave a burp. "I didn't say it wasn't. I'm just eager for things to progress before you both change your mind," he muttered.

"Change our minds about what?"

"Me."

Jordan shifted around to face him fully. "I'm not planning on changing my mind about you. You're perfect for me. I'm so stupid that I didn't see it sooner."

"You don't *think* you'll change your mind."

Jordan sighed, reaching for Ama and holding her close. "I won't change my mind, Mattie. I can see us together. It's not a difficult thing for me to imagine. I won't leave you."

Mattie stood and headed for the door, not wanting to think about the possibilities. "Don't promise things you can't control."

"Mattie..."

"I know. I know. I'm fatalistic, or whatever you call it. I just hate the idea of this ending before it begins."

Jordan stepped towards him, bouncing Ama against his

shoulder. "It won't. If we take our time, like Bray said, we will be fine."

Mattie kept swaying from one side of the coin to the other when it came to their triad. One minute, he believed they were powerful enough to stay together and weather all storms. The next minute, he couldn't see a future for them. It was driving him crazy.

"I know. I'm sorry." He rubbed his face. "Ignore me. Do you want coffee?" He entered the kitchen with Jordan following him, Ama's gurgling music to his ears.

"Sure. And no, I won't ignore you. Your worries are as valid as any other. You need to tell us what's going on in that brain of yours, Mattie, or we won't be able to help."

Mattie focused on making drinks, but when they were done, he settled at the table beside Jordan. "I'm scared this is all a dream." Jordan reached for him, but instead of resting his hand on him like Mattie expected him to, he pinched him. "Hey! What was that for?"

"Do you believe you're dreaming?" Jordan smirked at him.

Mattie tilted his head and grinned at him. "No. I definitely have an annoying lifeguard busting my balls."

"I'll do other things to your balls if you like," Jordan murmured, leaning closer for a kiss.

But before their lips touched, Ama squealed and kicked her legs, putting her foot right in Mattie's chest.

"Oof," he said, rubbing the area. "Are you going to be a footballer when you're older, sweetpea? You've got one hell of a kick on you."

Jordan laughed. "I bet she has. So do you. You kick out in your sleep."

Mattie's cheeks heated. "Do I? God, I'm sorry. I never realized. I've never..." He trailed off, not needing to explain that he'd never had anyone who could tell him about his nocturnal activities.

"It's fine. I've found that if I run my hand across your stomach, you curl back in on yourself and stop being a starfish."

Mattie covered his face with his hands and snorted. "Oh, god."

"Anyway, we need to start getting ready for the day. It's Saturday, so who have you got looking after her today?"

"Bray said he could look after her this morning, and then Lia is taking over this afternoon for a couple of hours until Mom turns up." He shook his head. "I hate that I have to rely on so many others so that I can go to work."

"If necessary, I can change my shifts so I don't work Saturdays. It's not a big deal, Mattie. We'll work it out. And don't worry about others looking after her. She'll get experiences with each of them she probably wouldn't with just you or us. It'll be good for her."

"It feels a bit like pass the parcel, though."

Jordan chuckled, lifting Ama into the air towards Mattie. "Daddy's turn." Mattie took her. "It is, but she's a beautiful, bouncing baby. No one minds."

"I wonder when Anthony will turn up."

"Probably tomorrow. He knows you're at home, so he'll probably drop by then to see how you're coping."

Mattie kissed Ama's cheek. "I feel like I'm coping well. As long as I have someone to look after her while I work." He frowned. "I think I'm going to employ someone else to work with me. I'll be able to spend more time with her that way."

"You don't have to, but it might be a good idea. You do spend an awful lot of time at the store." He held up his hands. "Not that I mind, but you need a breather. You always have, but you're stubborn."

Mattie nodded. "I know. I'll look into it today and see what I can work out. Then I'll put an advert out for a helper."

Jordan kissed his cheek, grabbed his chin, and kissed his mouth. "Perfect. Let me know what I can do to help. But in the meantime, I think it's time to get some breakfast before we get ready for our day. What do you think, little miss?" He tapped Ama's nose, and her arms went wild.

They laughed, and despite Mattie's earlier hesitations, he felt a lot better now he'd spoken to Jordan about it. They ate, had another coffee, and headed up to get ready. They took it in turns to shower, each one entertaining Ama while the other got dressed, and when the doorbell rang, Mattie jogged down the stairs with Ama in his arms and opened it.

"Good morning," Bray said as he stepped inside, closing the door behind him. "How are my favorite people this morning?" He dropped a kiss on Mattie's lips and Ama's head before looking behind them.

"Jordan's finishing getting ready. And we're good. How are you? Did you sleep well?"

"I did, thank you."

Look at them being all posh and well-mannered. Mattie pushed the thought aside. "Would you like a drink?"

"Nah, I'm good." Bray slid his arm around Mattie's shoulder. "The better question is, how did you sleep?"

"She woke once for a bottle, but that was it. We were up at around six, but I think she's settled really quickly compared to what I was expecting."

Bray nodded and steered them towards the stairs, where Jordan now waited. Bray and Jordan kissed, and then Bray said, "She's done extremely well. I'd love to know what the social worker thinks about it."

Mattie blew out a breath, his stomach churning at the thought of the visits. "I hate being unprepared."

Jordan chuckled. "It's not a test, Mattie. You don't need to study for it."

Mattie rolled his eyes. "Well, it kind of is a test, but one I can't study for. That's what's bothering me."

Bray tightened his hold on him. "You have nothing to worry about. You have everything she could ever need already. We can work on fixing up the nursery. Stop worrying."

"That's like telling him to stop breathing," Jordan joked. He glanced at his watch. "I have to get going. And so do you, Mr Worrier."

Mattie exhaled and peered down at Ama. "You have a good day, sweetpea. Okay? Don't give anyone grief." He pressed his lips to her head and closed his eyes, inhaling her scent.

"She'll be here when you get home."

Mattie chuckled. "Not if my mother has anything to do with it. She'll probably parade her around Gaynor Beach if she has her way. And with me not being here, I have no say in the matter."

Bray frowned. "I can tell her not to do it if you prefer?"

Mattie shook his head. "I'm only joking. I don't mind at all. Ama's already the talk of the town. She might as well make an appearance. Knowing Mom, she'll bring her to the store to see me, anyway."

Jordan touched his back. "Come on, or we'll both be late."

Bray reached for Ama, and Mattie reluctantly let her go. Not because he didn't think Bray could look after her, but because he wanted to spend time with her. He reminded himself that he could spend all the hours with her the next day when he had his day off.

And probably the visit from Anthony.

The three of them shared another kiss, and Mattie and Jordan left, catching the same bus for some of the distance.

"Don't worry about her," Jordan said.

"I'm not, actually. I'm thinking if I know anyone who might be interested in a job, instead of having to go through the recruitment process."

Jordan stared out of the window. "I can't think of anyone. Everyone I know either already has a job or is too young for it." He chuckled. "I'm sure Cody would love to do it, but I don't think he's quite the right age yet."

Mattie laughed. "Yeah. Not yet." He shrugged. "Never mind. Recruitment process it is, then."

He kissed Jordan when his stop came up and waved as he climbed off. The walk was only five minutes from the bus stop, and he unlocked the store, keeping the sign on closed for the moment. Readying the store for the day took him ten minutes at most, and after taking a second to breathe, he flipped the sign to open and unlocked the door again.

The hours went by both slowly and quickly. It was still a lot busier than usual, which he put down for two reasons. One was the new stock that had come in the day before, and the second was he was still news to people, and they wanted to see what gossip they could get from him. He was ready to put Ama's photo next to the till so everyone could see her instead of asking to see a picture of her. His phone had been used more than ever that morning.

He'd just started on his lunch when the bell tinkled to say someone else had entered. He withheld his groan and stood, pausing when he saw Anthony.

"Oh, hey." He swallowed. "Everything okay?"

Anthony smiled. "Yes, everything's fine. I just wanted to check up on you before I started my weekend properly. I'm glad to see you haven't brought Ama with you. How is she doing?"

Mattie's heart pounded so hard, he thought Anthony would be able to hear it, but he breathed deeply. "She's doing really well, I think. She only woke once last night, which is a record since she's been with me."

"That's great news. Who is looking after her today?"

Mattie rubbed a hand over his face. "Several people. Bray has her this morning, but Lia should be taking over at one o'clock. Then my mother will be having her from three o'clock until I finish."

"Sounds like you have it all worked out. That's great, Mattie."

He blew out a relieved breath. "Thanks. I spoke to Corey as well, and I'm going to discuss hours with him on Monday. I've worked out the schedule for who can have Ama while I'm working, but I'm also… I'm going to start looking for someone to work here so I can take more time off. I hate the idea of Ama never seeing me apart from dinner and bedtime."

Anthony nodded. "I know what you mean. No matter what, though. As long as she's looked after by capable people, you're doing a brilliant job. You'll figure the rest out as you go along."

"Thanks." Mattie relaxed a little. "Do you have any news from your side of things?"

"Everything is going as expected. I'm waiting for a few things to come back to me, but I fully expect you to have full custody of Ama. We need to wait for the courts to confirm it, which can take a little time, but everything is looking great from our end."

"Did you hear from Rhia?"

Anthony nodded. "She's rescinded all custody of Ama and signed and returned the documents we needed her to. As far as I'm concerned, there shouldn't be any problems with the courts in that respect."

Mattie clutched at the counter as a wave of relief flooded him. "I'm glad. I'd hate the idea of having to give Ama back when she's already become such a big part of our family."

Anthony smiled and held out his hand. Mattie shook it. "You're doing great, Mattie. Don't forget that. I'll see you again soon." He turned to leave, but then said, "Oh, I forgot." He rummaged in his pocket and pulled a piece of paper out. "There's a kids' get-together thing happening in a few weeks. It's on a Sunday. I thought you might be interested. You could meet some of the other parents around here. Parents of younger children, I mean."

Mattie took the paper. "Thank you. Yeah, I don't know anyone with younger kids. Jordan has Cody, who's eight, and Bray has twenty-year-old twins. Not quite close enough in age."

Anthony tilted his head. "Bray?"

Mattie's cheeks coloured. Maybe he should've kept that tidbit to himself. "He's…a friend?" Anthony's eyebrows rose at the questioning tone, and Mattie sighed. "I hope to god this doesn't go against me, but Jordan and I got together, and then Bray, kind of, became, uh, close to us as well." He swallowed. "We're working out if we go together as a triad."

Anthony stared at him for a second and then smiled. "I'm happy for you, Mattie. I'll need to add that information to your records, but I don't see there being a problem with that."

Mattie exhaled. "I'm glad. I'd hate for it to be something that would make my custody chances fall."

"You should be fine. I'll look into it, though." He turned away again. "Have a good weekend, Mattie," he called over his shoulder.

Mattie slumped against the counter and closed his eyes. One visit down. However many more to go.

CHAPTER 14

JORDAN

It was as difficult leaving Ama as it had been leaving Cody when he was a baby. Jordan loved kids and had always hoped for more. When Mattie had claimed not only Ama but Cody and Bray's kids, too, it had lit a fire in Jordan. He wanted that, and he hoped it would happen. As much as Bray said they needed to take things slowly, Jordan wondered if he could entice him to play a little with phone sex. It was something they could do while Bray was at his house, and they wouldn't have to worry about going too far when they were all together until they wanted to, that was.

Thoughts and ideas ran rampant around in his mind all during his shift, and though it didn't affect his work, his colleagues noted his distraction. It had been a rather boring shift, but he'd never wish to be busy. Not when someone's life was in the balance.

As he took the bus back to his apartment, he realized he'd already decided about Mattie's offer of moving in. Without actively acknowledging it, he didn't even think of his apartment as home any longer. It would truly make sense, and he had never fully understood his hesitance for Mattie's past offers. Why had he taken so long to see the best course of action? Had he somehow already known that he was attracted to Mattie and hadn't wanted to rock the boat? He might never know, but he was going back to the apartment now to give his roommates his notice period and start the quick task of getting his stuff together ready to move over. He didn't have a huge amount of stuff. Most of the items he had owned when he was with Ash, he'd left with the father of his child. If he asked for anything that had been his, he guaranteed Ash would give it to him, but at the moment, there was no need.

It would be yet another fresh start for him. Or not even a fresh start, more a joining of lives. He much preferred that to a fresh start. He couldn't wait to see where they were headed.

When his stop arrived, he climbed off and strode the few feet to the apartment building and let himself in. And when he entered the apartment, it was to shouts of, "Where the hell have you been?" and "I thought you were dead."

He laughed and dropped his bag to the floor before joining in the joking. "Yeah, I'm dead. Definitely. How have you all been?"

He shared the apartment with two guys who were students, and they all got on well, even though they had nothing in common. They chatted for a bit before Jordan brought up the subject he needed to.

"I actually need to let you know that I'm moving out."

Luke held out his hand to Trey, who groaned and reached into his back pocket for his wallet. "I told him you'd found someone."

Jordan chuckled. "How did you know I have? I could just be moving to a new place."

Luke rolled his eyes. "News of you and Mattie, plus a little cute baby, is making the rounds, if you didn't know."

Jordan sighed. "Yeah, I should've realized. Yeah, so I'm moving in with Mattie and little Ama."

Trey leaned forward. "I'm happy for you, man. I'm sure

we'll have no problem finding someone to take your place. No offence."

Jordan laughed and stood. "None taken. I'll still pay the rent for the notice period."

Luke waved his hand. "If we find someone quick enough, we'll let you off that."

Jordan nodded. "Thanks. Well, I better grab a few more things to take with me. I'll get the rest of it this week sometime if that's okay? Although if you find someone who wants to move in straight away, let me know, and I'll collect it sooner."

They spoke for a few more minutes before Jordan disappeared into his room to collect a bag full of clothes. When he truly took stock of what he had, he reckoned it would take him two trips on the bus maximum to get it to Mattie's house. Although Bray had a car. Maybe he could help him do it in one trip. With that in mind, he hurried to finish and get back home.

Bray wouldn't be there now, but he'd speak to him later when he put his phone sex idea into operation. He just needed to make sure he was at home alone before he started it. He wouldn't tell Mattie because he would just worry about it until it happened, whereas if it was on the fly, it would be easier for him not to become anxious about it being perfect.

He said goodbye to his roommates and headed back for the bus with a backpack and a holdall bag. When he finally walked into Mattie's house, it was empty, and for a second, he panicked. Then he remembered Evie was looking after Ama and had undoubtedly taken her for a visit with all the gossipers of Gaynor Beach.

It was strange being alone in Mattie's house. He'd done it before, but this time seemed different. Instead of dwelling on it, he put his bags in Mattie's room and pulled out his phone. He called Cody on the tablet that they had bought him to play games. It worked as a phone as well, but he didn't use it as one except for when he wanted to talk to his parents and a select few friends.

"Hey, bud. How're things?"

"Good. Papa is just cooking an early dinner because I'm starving." The video picture wobbled as he settled it down.

Jordan laughed. "Aren't you always? If Papa agrees, would you like to come over tonight for an hour to see Ama?"

Cody's face disappeared from the screen, but Jordan could hear him shouting for Ash. Jordan waited patiently for him to return, knowing what the answer would be.

"He says yes!"

"Imagine that," Jordan murmured. "Good. I'll pick you up around six o'clock, okay?"

"I'll be ready."

They spoke for a few minutes until Ash called him for dinner. They'd have more time to talk when he came over. He wouldn't keep him for long because it was Ash's time with him. Just as he went to message his dad to ask if he could borrow his car, he received a message from Ash.

ASH: I'll bring him over if you're okay with that? I'd love to meet the little one if I'm allowed.

JORDAN: Of course you can. And thanks. That makes things a little easier.

ASH: See you around six.

Jordan sent a confirmation and messaged Mattie to tell him what the plan was, just so he knew who was going to be filling his house when he got home.

Evie and Ama still weren't home when Mattie entered at five-thirty, and Mattie gaped at him.

"What are they doing?" he murmured. "It's not that big of a town."

Jordan pulled him into his arms while he called his mother. "Hey, Mama. Where are you?" He listened for a moment. "Okay, well can you bring her home because we've got people who want to meet her." He listened again. "Thanks. See you soon." He shook his head as he ended the call. "They were still at the café being mooned over."

Jordan chuckled. "Sounds like Evie." He dropped a kiss on Mattie's head. "Would you like something to eat?"

"I'll just grab a sandwich or something."

"No, let me at least make you some pasta."

Mattie sighed and leaned against him. "That sounds wonderful, thank you."

Jordan cupped his jaw and frowned. "You're not normally so exhausted after a day at work. What's up?"

Mattie sighed again and burrowed into Jordan's chest. "Anthony came to the shop today to check I hadn't brought Ama with me."

Jordan's heart jumped. "Was he okay?"

Mattie nodded. "Yes, he was fine. Everything's fine. Obviously there'll be more visits, but it's nice to know I'm on the right track with him. I think it's just a release of stress. I just feel so tired."

"Well, I have something that will wake you up again. Food in your stomach, a little girl in your arms, and a quiet night in." He paused. "Once everyone's gone home, that is."

Mattie chuckled and lifted his head. "Sounds perfect to me."

Jordan kissed him. He couldn't help it. Now he had the freedom to touch him, he found he wanted to do it all the time. The kiss deepened, and Mattie moaned into his mouth. His arms found their way into Jordan's hair, gripping tightly. Eventually, he pulled back, his chest aching with the need to breathe, and he pressed their foreheads together.

"I'll make you something to eat. Rest up before everyone

gets here." He dropped a kiss on his lips once more and headed for the kitchen.

The pasta was almost ready when Mattie's mother and Ama arrived. The conversation and laughter floated down the hallway towards him. He finished off the food, plated it and carried it to the living room, where Mattie sat holding Ama and smiling down at her. Evie glanced up when he entered.

Jordan pretended to sigh. "Now how am I going to persuade him to let you go while he eats his dinner?" he said to Ama as he placed the plate on the coffee table. "Daddy needs to eat, little one."

"Do you want me to hang around for a little longer?" Evie asked.

Mattie shook his head, brushing his finger along Ama's cheek. "Ash and Cody will be here in a few minutes. They can have their cuddles while I eat."

"All right. Have a good night, you guys." Evie stood and picked up her bag.

"Thanks, Mom."

"You're welcome, sweetie." She leaned down and kissed Ama's head, and then Mattie's head before facing Jordan. She cupped his cheek. "I'm glad you're here," she whispered, kissing his cheek.

Jordan preened at the words, hugging her. "Thanks. I'm glad I'm here, too."

Evie left, but laughter sounded, and Cody came barging into the room. "I'm here!"

He barrelled towards Mattie, but Jordan caught him around the waist before he became a whirlwind aimed at Ama. "Slow your roll, bud. She's only little, remember?" He slid his arm to his shoulders instead, rolling his eyes as Ash entered.

"Can I hold her?" Cody asked.

"Sure thing," Mattie said. "Sit down, and I'll hand her to you."

Cody did, and Mattie helped him to position his arms around the little girl. Cody was obsessed with her from the moment he held her. Ash stopped beside Jordan.

"He's talked about nothing else since your phone call."

"I'd say I'm sorry, but I'm glad he's showing an interest. I can't think most boys would be interested in babies," Jordan murmured.

"True, but it helps that this is his sister," Ash said.

Mattie must've heard Ash's response because his head whipped around from where he'd been eating his food while watching Cody and Ama. He barely kept the food in his mouth as his jaw dropped. Jordan and Ash chuckled.

"How's your sister doing, Cody?" Ash said.

"She's good. Do I have any more siblings?" he asked.

Jordan and Ash shared a glance, and Ash must've realised what he wanted to do and nodded at him. "Well, actually…" Jordan started. "We've added someone else to our relationship. His name is Bray, and he has two sons of his own. They're older, though. They're twenty. So yes, you kind of have two brothers, too."

"We'll have to meet them soon," Ash said.

Cody grinned. "I have more family!"

This time, Ash and Jordan shared a smile. The slight sting of not having more children together was no longer as painful as it used to be.

"How are things with…" Jordan trailed off, not wanting to say too much in case Cody overheard.

Ash brightened more. "Great. I've decided to mention it next weekend. He's coming over to meet…" He nodded at Cody.

"That's great! I'm happy for you. I'm sorry I didn't wait to mention it." Jordan watched Mattie eating from the corner of his eye, so he saw when he finished his food. Jordan grabbed the plate and took it from him. "Sit down and rest."

"I—"

"Sit down and *rest*," he repeated.

Mattie sighed and gave a small smile before settling beside Cody and brushing the top of Ama's head. He spoke softly to Cody, and Jordan loved the domesticity of it. He glanced at Ash.

"You should sit, too. You'll never get a look in at her otherwise."

Ash chuckled and settled on Cody's other side. Jordan distantly made a note that the sofa comfortably held three smaller people and headed to the kitchen. Despite the food being cold, he devoured a bowl full of pasta while standing, having not wanted to let Mattie wait while he ate his own. When he finished, he tidied up and set the dishwasher before going back to their visitors.

Ash looked very comfortable holding Ama, and Cody was glued to his side, looking over at her again. Jordan had a feeling Cody would become the overprotective brother Ama might not want as they grew, but it would be nice for them. Eight years was a fairly big gap compared to some, and their relationship could go either way as they aged. But no matter what, Cody would be there for her. Jordan knew he would.

They stayed for an hour before Ash told Cody they needed to get back.

"But—"

"No," Ash said, staring at him. "We talked about this on the journey over."

Cody's shoulders lowered. "Okay." He looked at Mattie. "Thank you for letting me hold her."

Mattie smiled at him. "You're always welcome."

Cody brightened. "Could I have a sleepover one day?"

Jordan jumped on the question. "Actually, you'll be sleeping over here whenever you're with me now. I'm moving in." He caught Mattie's shocked but delighted expression and grinned.

Cody pumped his fist, making Ama jump and cry. "Oh,

sorry, Ama." He brushed his hand over her head. "Shh, I'm sorry," he whispered.

Jordan squeezed Cody's shoulder. "She'll be fine, don't worry."

"See you soon, little sister," Cody said.

Jordan's heart expanded a little more. His family was amazing. He saw Ash and Cody to the door, hugging them both before waving them off. When they disappeared, he locked the door behind him, ready to set his plan into motion.

"Okay, then. Time to get little miss her three B's—bottle, bath and bed."

Mattie tilted his head. "Wasn't there something else you wanted to tell me?"

Jordan rubbed his chin, pretending he didn't know what Mattie was referring to. "Was there?"

Mattie stepped closer, lifting Ama to his shoulder and bouncing her. "You know it."

Jordan slid his arm around Mattie's shoulders, bringing them both closer to him. "You asked, and I decided to say yes. If it's still okay with you, I'd love to move in."

Mattie lifted his chin, asking for the kiss Jordan so readily gave him. "I can't wait."

"Well, I already brought two bags with me today. I'm going to ask Bray to help me grab the rest of the stuff as soon as he can. I don't have much."

"Sounds perfect to me."

They shared another kiss before aiming for the kitchen to make Ama's bottle. Her routine was getting easier for them, and Jordan basked in the ability to join in. By the time they had her fed, bathed and dressed for bed, Jordan was secretly planning how to go about bringing out the next step of their evening.

They settled Ama down and closed the door, and Jordan tugged Mattie towards the bedroom.

"What about—"

"Dishwasher is on, kitchen is clean. Nothing else needs doing tonight. We're going to rest."

Mattie sighed. "Okay."

Jordan closed them in the bedroom, putting the monitor on the bedside table, and pushed Mattie back onto the bed. He crawled over him, kissing his neck when he reached the exposed skin.

"I thought we were resting?" Mattie murmured, ending the sentence with a soft moan.

"We are. We're resting our minds," he whispered. He nibbled at Mattie's earlobe and pulled his phone from his pocket. He sat upright, straddling Mattie's legs.

*JORDAN: A*RE YOU AT HOME, ALONE AND FREE*? X*

HE WATCHED CONFUSION PASS OVER MATTIE'S FACE AS HE pushed himself to his elbows. "What are you doing?"

"Waiting."

Mattie paused, and when Jordan said nothing further, he said, "Waiting for what?"

"Confirmation."

Mattie hesitated again and chuckled. "Confirmation of what?"

Jordan just grinned and focused on his phone when it chimed.

BRAY: I AM. WHY*? W*HAT ARE WE DOING*? X*
JORDAN: I'm calling you in five minutes. Be naked. x

HE PUT THE PHONE ON THE BED AND REFOCUSED ON MATTIE, who was still staring at him with a slight curl to his mouth.

Jordan wanted to kiss it off, and so he did. The ferocity with which he attacked Mattie was enough to send them back into the bed, and Jordan took everything Mattie gave him and sent everything right back again. Their tongues danced. Their breaths mixed. Their arms and legs tangled. He couldn't get enough. Slipping his fingers down to the hem of Mattie's T-shirt, he tugged it until he could yank it over his head and throw it aside. His mouth descended onto his warm skin, his slightly furry chest abrading his cheek as he brushed it down to his nipples, where he sucked it into his mouth.

"Oh, fuck," Mattie breathed, clutching at Jordan's head.

His moans fucked with Jordan's head, wanting him to speed things up and get them both where they wanted to be, but he had a plan—one he struggled to remember. He listened to the noises Mattie made while tasting his slightly salty, sweaty skin, and then he remembered. Bray.

He grabbed his phone, though he still fed on Mattie's nubs alternately. He discreetly called Bray and put it on speaker while he nuzzled him. Fate must've intervened, because when Bray answered, Mattie let out the most delightful moan.

"I like the sound of that greeting." Bray's deep voice sent shivers through both of them, even as Mattie's eyes sprung open and his cheeks darkened.

"Glad to hear it. I hope you did as I asked," Jordan said.

"I always follow orders—except when I'm the one making them."

Jordan shivered again, putting that aside to think about later. "Glad to hear it." He spoke to Mattie. "Mattie, we're going to play tonight so we can all get some rest."

"Is that resting, though?" he asked, his voice cracking at the end.

"It will be once you're wrung out from orgasms."

Bray chuckled, and goosebumps pebbled across Mattie's chest. Jordan smiled, following the path with his tongue. Mattie moaned again.

"What's he doing to you, Mattie?" Bray asked.

"He's… He's licking…my chest."

It would take Mattie a little while to relax about their play session, and it was Jordan's job to make it happen. Make him so out of his mind with lust that he didn't second-guess his reactions. He needed him to relax fully. To let go.

"Do it again, Jordan. Pull those sounds from him so I can jerk myself off to them."

"Yes, sir," Jordan said.

He latched onto Mattie's nipples again, and almost immediately, Mattie's moans filled the air. His cock tented his trousers, and he shamelessly rubbed it against Mattie's covered groin. More groans shot to the ceiling, and Bray cursed.

"You sound fucking amazing, Mattie. Next time, I'm going to be there, right next to Jordan, pulling those noises from you myself. But for the moment… Jordan, is he naked?"

"Not yet."

"Do it."

"Yes, sir."

CHAPTER 15

BRAY

The words shot to Bray's groin, sending tingles down his spine. He'd had no sexual connotations for the phrase "Yes, sir" until Jordan had said it when they'd first met. Now, he couldn't imagine hearing it from him or Mattie without that sexual hint to it. Luckily, that didn't seem to bleed into his social life. He'd spent a couple of hours with Dante, Freer and Radar that afternoon, and they often called him sir, but it didn't have the same reaction, thankfully. It would've been rather uncomfortable if it had.

He listened to the rustling on the other end of the phone and closed his eyes, imagining Jordan stripping Mattie of his outer layers and leaving him with glistening skin.

"Holy hell," Mattie breathed, and Bray's cock kicked up, leaving a wet patch on his bare stomach. He didn't want to touch himself yet. He was close already, just with the images his mind conjured up.

"Talk to me, Mattie. What's he doing to you?"

"He's… Fuck… Um, he's licking me."

"Where?"

"My… My…"

Bray's mouth curled. "Is he licking your cock, Mattie?"

"Uh-huh. Oh, god!"

"Jordan, lick the tip. Get your tongue right into the slit and drag that precome from him. I want it streaming from him." Bray gave up the pretence of making this last and wrapped his hand around his shaft. The heat of his swollen cock warmed his skin, and he circled his palm over the head, collecting and redistributing the leaking precome to ease his stroking path.

"Fuck, oh fuck, oh fuck."

Bray hissed as Mattie's curses sent a bolt of fire down his spine, the extra blood pooling in his cock making it ache for a release he wanted to hold back.

"That's it, Mattie. Let me hear you. Jordan, roll his balls in your hand and stroke the base of his cock with your other one. Suck the head of it. Keep him as high as you can without taking him over."

Unintelligible words fell from Mattie's mouth. His moans, groans and curses joined with Jordan's sucking sounds to light up Bray's veins with a rolling wave of fire. He wished he could see them, but it would be certain to send him flying over the edge immediately. The images his mind conjured were enough to keep him on a tightrope right then.

"I'm… I'm…"

"Pull back, Jordan. Don't let him fly yet." Bray stopped stroking, taking his own advice. "Mattie, wrap your hand around Jordan's cock. Let him understand how you feel. Make him ride the edge."

Jordan's whimper of need shot through Bray, and he breathed through it. He wanted them all on the precipice so they could ride the wave together. In theory. He might jump the gun if he wasn't careful.

As Jordan's moans grew, Bray said, "Jordan, do the same for Mattie. Both of you take the other to the edge. I'm right there with you." His breathing increased as he alternated between stroking and rolling his balls in his hand. A good pull on them, and he'd go over.

"Oh fucking hell," Jordan cried. "I'm coming!"

Mattie's whimper joined him, and Bray tugged on his balls and stroked himself through the orgasm that swept through him. He kept the phone pressed against his ear, attuned to every sound coming from his partners.

"Holy shit," Mattie breathed, and Bray chuckled, agreeing wholeheartedly. "That was…"

"One for the books," Jordan finished with a heavy breath.

"Truly," Bray said. He stared at the cooling release on his stomach and chest. "Well, I need a shower."

Jordan and Mattie laughed, just like he wanted them to, and he smiled into the phone.

"Next time, we're doing that together. In one room. Okay?" Jordan said.

"Yes, sir," Bray said softly. "Get washed up and get to bed. You'll be up in a few hours with Ama."

Mattie sighed. "I wish we could kiss you goodnight."

"Close your eyes. Both of you," Bray said. "I'm dropping a kiss on your lips, brushing my lips across yours, nibbling them and making them bruised and aching. I lick across them, requesting entry and sliding deep inside, tasting you, inhaling you. I cradle your head as I deepen it, inhaling through our noses so we don't have to part. Then I soften our kiss, tugging on your lip as I retreat. One more soft kiss before I leave you." He stopped talking, his mind ending the imagery he described to them.

"Oh my," Mattie said.

"Exactly," Jordan added.

"Goodnight, sweethearts."

"Night, Bray," they said in unison.

As much as he didn't want to, he ended the call. He really did need a shower.

———

"So, tell me about them."

Bray shook his head as he sipped his coffee. "I've already told you about them."

His mother cackled. "Tell me again."

Bray knew he wouldn't get anything else out of her until he bared his soul, so he did just that—leaving out the experience from the previous evening.

"Show me a photo."

Bray froze with his cup halfway to his mouth, his lips twisting. "I don't have one."

"Then get one!"

"I'll do it when I next see them."

Paula shook her head and stubbed out her cigarette. "No, message them and get them to send one."

Bray huffed a laugh but did as she asked. There was no denying her when she got an idea for something.

BRAY: SORRY TO DISTURB YOU. MY MOTHER WOULD LIKE A PHOTO of you both if you don't mind sending me one. x

HE PUT THE PHONE ON THE ARM OF THE CHAIR AND REFOCUSED on his mother, who hacked up a lung. He sighed. "Have you spoken to the doctor about your chest?"

She waved him away. "It's just a chest infection that'll clear up by itself."

Bray withheld his sigh that time. "You didn't see one then."

"What's the point, sweetheart? They'll just tell me to quit smoking. As if that'll be the magic cure-all pill."

"It won't hurt, you know."

"It'll hurt me." She huffed, which turned into another

hacking cough. "I'm too set in my ways, Bray. You know that. I don't have many years left on this planet, anyway. Why not spend them how I want to?"

Bray's heart clenched at the thought of being without her, but she spoke the truth. Not how many years she had left, but that she should spend them however she wanted to. That should be the rule for everyone.

His phone chimed, changing the topic again. Picking it up, he opened the message from the group chat he, Jordan, and Mattie had started. He automatically smiled when their beaming faces lit up the screen. Jordan had his arm around Mattie, Ama was in Mattie's arms, facing the camera, and Cody was behind them putting bunny ear fingers up behind each of his men.

He handed his phone to his mother without a word.

"Mmhmm. Nice. I'm assuming the baby is little Ama. Who's the froglet?"

Bray snickered at the use of the name he'd not heard since he'd been of a similar age to Cody. It was what she called anyone who couldn't be called a teen.

"Cody. That's Jordan's son."

"So, Ama is Mattie's daughter, and Cody is Jordan's son. Then you have Kit and Noah. It's going to be a full house at Thanksgiving."

She handed the phone back, and Bray saved the photo as his phone wallpaper.

"I need to tell Kit and Noah about them. I've not spoken to them this week yet."

"I'm sure they'll come racing back for a visit the minute you do."

"I'm sure they will." He watched her as she coughed again. "Look, Mom—"

"Bray, I'm fine." She locked gazes with him, the steel in her eyes so similar to his own. "I'll come and visit you all once this cough has eased. I don't want to pass anything on to the little ones."

The front door opened before Bray could reply.

"Paula! It's Sunday!" Loretta yelled as she entered, Maggie right behind her.

His mother rolled her eyes as if she was a teenager. "Wow, you can understand the days, Lori. Well done."

Maggie gasped and held out her arms as she stalked towards him. "Bray! I wasn't expecting to see you today."

Bray stood, enveloping his aunt, and smiled. "Surprise visit."

"He's got new beaus," Paula said with a chuckle, knowing she was throwing him to the wolves. He glared at her.

"Beaus with a S?" Loretta said, raising her eyebrows. "One not enough for ya?"

Bray shook his head with a smile. "Apparently not, Aunt Loretta. I'm sure you'll get to meet them soon enough." He hugged her and then turned to his mother. "I'm heading out. Have a good Sunday, all of you."

"Can't we persuade you to stay?" Maggie said. "I feel like we don't see you enough."

Inwardly, Bray chuckled. They didn't see each other enough, and Bray could only handle them in small doses. "No, I've got things to do."

"Babies to rear, dicks to suck. Yeah, we get the picture," Loretta said.

Bray cringed, hoping she would tone it down when she met Jordan and Mattie but knowing she wouldn't.

"Send me that photo, Bray," his mother said. "I'll show it to them."

He could hardly begrudge her, so he nodded and did so before he left. The traffic from Oceanside wasn't bad; therefore, it didn't take him long to get home. As much as he'd told the truth about needing to get things done, it wasn't as urgent as he'd implied. He had some more wooden toys to finish and a visit to the hospital to drop a couple of new things around, but it didn't need doing that day. He'd see how things went. How distracted his mind was. Which was a lot because he couldn't stop thinking about what they'd done the previous evening.

They seemed compatible, which was a bonus, and both Jordan and Mattie liked taking orders, which was something Bray needed. He liked being able to take care of his men, whether that was in or out of the bedroom.

He hesitated when he parked in his driveway, staring at the car waiting at the curb. Then he sighed. He might as well get it all out in the open on the same day. Climbing out of his car, he whistled at the occupants of the other car. Two doors opened immediately, one a little slower, but they all came at his call.

"Wasn't expecting you three here. Social visit or something else?"

Dante raised his eyebrows. "Does it matter?"

"Well, your answer depends on whether we have to send Freer to fetch beer."

Dante said nothing and held out his keys to Freer. "Fuck, man. Why couldn't you have said that before? We just got here."

"And you'll be back before you know it," Bray answered, heading for his front door. "Take Radar with you."

He heard but ignored the grumbles and entered his home, leaving the door open for Dante. Dante's car started and the sound slowly disappeared, both because Freer drove off and because Dante closed the door.

"So, what's up?" Bray asked, aiming for the kitchen and flicking on the kettle. "Coffee?"

"Always." Dante dropped into a seat. "And nothing's up."

Bray stared at him for five long seconds and then looked away, making their drinks.

Dante sighed. "Why didn't you tell us?"

Bray didn't answer straight away. He doctored the drinks and handed Dante's to him, and then he leaned back against the counter and cupped his drink, staring at the floor. He remained silent until Freer and Radar returned, barging into his home with ladened hands.

"Jesus, how much did you buy?" Dante said as Bray made another cup of coffee for himself.

Freer grinned. "I assumed things were going to get heavy. Thought we'd need an excuse for flapping lips." He winked, and Bray's mouth twitched despite knowing he was right. It would be easier with alcohol, but he'd never used it as a crutch before, and he wasn't going to now.

"Grab what you want and join me in the living room."

He wandered through and removed his jacket before dropping into an armchair and reclaiming his coffee. His team trickled in with hands full of bottles and settled around the room. Dante placed a bottle on the small table beside Bray and retreated, sitting in another armchair and crossing his ankle over his knee before resting his bottle on it.

Bray wasn't sure exactly where to start, so he started at the beginning. "I've always been into men and women." He frowned. "With how the military was and because I met Sarah, I never made it known that I was interested in men. Didn't need to. When I retired, I wasn't bothered about relationships. The odd night here and there, but nothing to write home about. I didn't feel the need to confess."

Dante took a drink, and Bray could see his hands shaking. "We wouldn't have minded."

Bray's mouth curved. "I know. I wasn't lying to you. Maybe of omission, but I would never do that. I didn't think it would be important." He shook his head, trying to explain. "I didn't think it would matter." He shook his head again, staring at the half-finished chess game. "I'm not saying it right. It matters, but it wasn't something I thought I needed to announce."

"Even when I told you about Milo?"

Bray winced. "I maybe should have mentioned it then, but again, I wasn't interested in anyone at that point. I didn't feel the need. It's only since I met Jordan and Mattie that I knew I needed to tell you. And I planned to do that this week. We have a 'date' on Wednesday night, remember?"

"I'm not mad, Pack. Not really," Dante said. "I just wish…" He sighed. "I wish you'd told me. It might've made things easier."

Bray leaned forward, putting his cup on the coffee table and then linked his fingers and stared at them. "No matter what you told me, Dante, I would've accepted it. And I know you would do the same. I guess… I don't know."

Freer clapped his hands, making Bray tense. "Look, guys, all this emotion and feeling stuff is great and all, but can we get drunk now? I want to hear everything about these new boyfriends of Pack's. There has to be some dirt we can use on them when we meet them." He snorted.

Bray raised his eyebrow and waved his hand towards him. "Be my guest."

"Have you told anyone about your relationship?" Radar asked, starting on his second beer.

Bray chuckled. "Do we ever need to tell anyone in this town?"

Radar froze and then nodded. "True."

"Where did you guys hear it, anyway?"

It was Dante's turn to chuckle this time. "The Vine," the three of them said in unison.

Bray should've known. "That's where Mattie's mother found out about Ama. She wasn't pleased she hadn't heard it from him."

Dante winced. "I can imagine." He downed his beer. "When can we meet them?"

Bray hesitated. He wasn't sure if he wanted to drag it out and have Jordan and Mattie meet them in a bigger space than one of their homes. But then, it didn't matter where they were, did it?

"If you stop drinking, I'll see if we can go now."

Radar and Dante immediately put their bottles down, but Freer stared at him, mouth gaping. "I just fetched these!"

"And you can finish them after you've met them if you want to. But you're not going if you're drunk."

Freer sighed, put down his beer and pointed at the bottle. "I'm coming back for you."

Bray dialled Jordan, smiling when he answered. "Hey, gorgeous. Are you calling for another—"

"Hey," he interrupted, not wanting Jordan to voice his thoughts where his friends could hear him. "Are you up for a visit with some friends of mine? We won't stay long."

"Of course! Any friend of yours is welcome to visit. When?"

"Now?"

"Sure. I'll let Mattie know. We have no plans tonight at all."

Bray smiled at the obvious lie but didn't say anything. "See you soon." He hung up and stood. "Come on then."

They all climbed into Bray's car—they would be finishing the beer off later, anyway—and he drove to Mattie's house, his stomach clenching at how his friends would behave while they were there. He didn't think they'd misbehave as such, but they were his friends, after all. Some ribbing and teasing were to be expected. He just hoped they didn't take it too far.

When he parked up, he gave them a look, and all three nodded. That would usually be enough for them to know his thoughts, but this was a completely different experience to them being in the middle of a gunfight.

CHAPTER 16

MATTIE

There was a knock at Mattie's door, and Jordan opened it almost immediately. Mattie could hear their conversation from where he sat with Ama.

"You don't have to knock, remember? Just come in."

"And I've told you before, you should lock the door to stop people walking in." There was a pause. "Can we come in and I'll do introductions all at once?" Bray asked.

"Of course! Go on through to the living room. Mattie's just feeding Ama."

Bray entered first, and the moment his gaze fell on Mattie and Ama, Mattie's heart skipped a beat. He was gone for these people. He truly was, but would Bray want to hide it from his friends? Bray crouched before Mattie, kissed Ama on the head, and then kissed Mattie softly, answering Mattie's worries without ever having to voice he'd had them. "Hey."

Mattie smiled. "Hey, yourself."

"How is she?"

"Doing good. Slept six hours in a row last night."

Bray smiled and brushed a finger down Ama's cheek. "Well done, little one." Mattie looked behind him, seeing his friends, who looked just as wide and tall as Bray was. Bray stood. "Mattie, Jordan, these are my friends—family, really—Dante, Freer and Radar. Also known as Jamie, Reece and Cole, if you don't do nicknames." Each of them lifted a hand when he said their name.

Dante was the first to step forward and hold his hand out to Jordan. "Nice to meet you."

"Nice to meet you both," Radar said. He stepped closer to Mattie, craning his neck to see Ama.

Bray beckoned him closer. "This is Ama."

Radar leaned down, smiling. "Nice to meet you, Ama," he whispered.

"Would you like to finish feeding her?" Mattie asked Radar.

Radar's eyes widened. "Can I?"

Mattie nodded and gestured beside him. "Sit down, and I'll pass her over."

Radar wasted no time, and before any of them could blink, he held Mattie's daughter in his arms and was feeding her, with a small smile gracing his lips.

Dante's conversation with Jordan appeared to catch Bray's attention, and he crossed the room and slid his arm around Jordan's shoulders, leaving Mattie with Radar.

"Do you have any children of your own?" Mattie asked, wanting to break the ice.

Radar shook his head, his eyes on Ama, his hand steadily holding the bottle for her. "I'd like to. One day."

"Don't wait," Mattie said, startling them both. "Sorry. What I meant is that if you want a family, don't wait for the right time because there never will be one. You need to make it happen yourself."

Radar chuckled softly. "Easier said than done."

"True, but if you're not bothered about the children being biologically yours, there is always fostering or adoption. There are so many kids out there in need of a good parent."

"But how many will agree to giving a child to a single man?"

"More than you can imagine." He changed the subject. "Would you like a drink?"

"Coffee, please."

He left Ama in Radar's capable hands and headed for the group by the door.

"He's good. You should see him," Jordan said.

"Maybe I will one day," Bray said.

Mattie wasn't sure what they were talking about, but it didn't matter. "Who would like a drink?" Mattie asked.

"Coffee all around for us, please." Bray glanced over at Radar, but Mattie wasn't at all concerned.

"Sit down, everyone. As Mom always says, 'You're making the room look untidy.'" Mattie gestured to the chairs before leaving the room.

He didn't mind meeting new people, but it wasn't his favorite pastime. This was different, though. These people were important to Bray, and therefore, they would become important to him and Jordan, too.

As he went about making drinks, he considered how easily they had fallen into their relationship. Although they hadn't strictly taken things to the last level as a triad, everything else had slipped into place as if they were made for it. Everyone's support was amazing, but he knew it wouldn't last. There were going to be several people within their community—and their families—that would not take too kindly to them being together. They were not the "norm," and therefore, they shouldn't happen.

Despite Mattie's misgivings about that part of their future, he was, by no means, ready to call things off. Especially not after the other night. If it was that hot between the two of them with the third on the phone, they would be combustible together.

And he couldn't fucking wait.

He placed the six mugs on a tray and carried it to the living room, where Freer had hold of Ama. Putting the tray on the coffee table, he knelt beside it to hand out the drinks and then slipped to the floor in a cross-legged position. He wouldn't be able to stay that way for long, but there weren't any other spaces at that moment. He'd have to look into buying another sofa or something because their numbers had just grown exponentially, what with family and friends added together.

With his friends distracted by Jordan, Bray nudged Mattie's shoulder and tapped his leg, but Mattie shook his head as his cheeks heated. Bray raised his eyebrows and tapped his leg again. Mattie understood what he was saying, but he wasn't sure if he was confident enough to sit on Bray's lap when everyone was there. Bray waited, staring at him. Not forcing him to do it, but giving him time to think it through. If Mattie chose not to, Bray wouldn't push it, but Mattie wanted to. What would everyone think? There was only one way to find out. It's not like they were in the middle of a cafe or anything.

Mattie rose and moved closer to him. Bray grabbed his hips, turned him forcefully and settled him on his lap to one side so they could both see his friends. Mattie tensed, his cheeks warmed, and he watched everyone for their response to his new position. No one batted an eyelid. No one even looked over at them, though they had to know he'd moved. Mattie's back and shoulders relaxed, and he melted into Bray, resting his head back against his shoulder.

"Are you tired?" Bray murmured into his ear, and Mattie closed his eyes.

"Mmhmm."

"Why don't you get some sleep, and I'll take the night shift again?"

Mattie forced his eyelids open. "No. But will you...?" His

heart pounded so hard he was sure Bray could feel it. "Will you stay tonight? Just to sleep."

Bray pressed his lips to Mattie's temple, and his eyes fell shut again. "I'd love to."

"How will they get back?" He nodded towards Bray's friends.

"They can drive my car back to fetch their own and then drop it back again after. It's no problem."

"Hey, Pack, what was it that you called Captain Roth?" Freer asked.

Bray's huff of laughter vibrated through to Mattie's body. "A penguin wannabe who is heading towards becoming a dodo instead."

They laughed, and Ama's arms and legs jerked from where she'd fallen asleep in Dante's arms. When he and Freer had swapped, Mattie didn't know.

"Oh, sorry, sweetie," Dante said.

Mattie's heart swelled at the care and consideration Bray's friends gave to her. They would fit perfectly in their group. He turned his head to whisper in Bray's ear. "Are they all single?" Bray raised his eyebrows, and Mattie flushed. "I don't mean for me, silly."

Bray's mouth twitched. "Dante has a boyfriend, but Freer and Radar are single. Why?"

"I can see how nice they are. I wish we could help them find someone. Especially Radar."

Bray nodded, still keeping his voice low. "Radar wants a family desperately. It means a lot to him, and he wants to fill his house with children."

"I told him not to wait. That if he wanted it, to go ahead and start trying. Life's too short."

"I agree." A shadow went across Bray's face, but he smiled it away.

"Bray, why do they call you Pack?" Jordan asked, drawing his attention.

Bray chuckled. "Dante, why don't you tell the story as you elaborate so beautifully?"

As Dante weaved a tale of desert landscapes, hot weather and even more heated exchanges, Bray shuffled Mattie around until both his legs were fully draped across his lap, and Bray wrapped his arms around him. He could easily fall asleep in that position, but he was drawn to Dante's words. A master storyteller, if ever there was one. He'd have to get him to record himself reading books because his voice was perfect for it.

"This pack of dogs—well, originally, we thought they were hyenas—but this pack of dogs came snarling towards us, encircling us until we had no option but to stand back to back and keep an eye on them all." He paused. "Then all of a sudden, Pack came whistling over the hill behind the dogs as if nothing was amiss. We tried to warn him, but several of the dogs turned towards him, their mouths dripping with saliva." He paused again to hand Ama to Radar. "I tried to call to him, but it was too late. The dogs started towards him. My heart skipped several beats as my brain supplied images of him being torn to shreds. So imagine my surprise when Pack sat on the ground and caught both dogs around their necks and fucking cuddled them! Who the fuck does that?"

"Pack does," Freer and Radar said in unison.

They laughed, and Dante continued. "The rest of the dogs were still surrounding us, but they whined more than growled. One after the other, they left us in a sweaty heap and trotted over to Pack, receiving belly rubs from him. After that, he was no longer Bray, he was Pack."

Mattie smiled at the story. "How much of that was true?" he whispered.

"Surprisingly, most of it this time. He usually elaborates a lot more." Bray's phone chimed, and he jostled Mattie to get it from his pocket. Mattie closed his eyes, not wanting to intrude, and Bray chuckled. "Here's my two imbeciles," he said, and Mattie blinked at the photo on his phone screen.

Two guys had each other in a headlock, their curly hair all over the place, and Mattie could see the resemblance immediately.

"Which one is which?"

Bray pointed. "That's Kit, that's Noah."

"Jordan, come see this," Mattie said.

Jordan moved closer, leaning over the back of the chair they were in. "Oh, wow." He chuckled. "They look like they're having fun."

Bray snorted. "Too much fun," he grumbled, swiping to get rid of the picture. Mattie saw his background and gasped.

"You have that picture," he said, grabbing Bray's hand to hold the phone steady. The picture was the one they'd taken earlier that day.

Bray shrugged. "It's a wonderful picture. I'll change it for one of all of us eventually, but for now, this will do fine."

Mattie leaned forward and kissed him, unable to do anything else. Bray tightened his hold with the arm that wasn't holding the phone. The warmth of Bray's breath coasted across Mattie's lips, and he took it into himself, sliding his tongue into Bray's mouth. His eyes drifted closed, and he sank into the kiss, not wanting to let go when his emotions were high. The kiss gentled, and they pulled back, Bray resting their foreheads together.

"Sorry," Mattie murmured, his cheeks heating.

"Don't be sorry for that. You can kiss me anytime."

Mattie tucked his face into Bray's neck, breathing gently as he calmed. It was a stupid thing. Being happy that Bray had a picture of them on his phone was silly, but it made him realise it wasn't all him. At the back of his mind, he'd been wondering if he was imagining it all, and Jordan and Bray were just going along with it, but that was just his nerves talking.

Conversation filtered back into his head, and his cheeks heated even more when he remembered they had visitors, and he'd just kissed Bray within an inch of his life. As if he understood what had flown through his head, Bray rubbed his hand up and down his back.

They talked for a while longer, Ama being passed from person to person, uncaring of who held her. When it got time for her three B's—as Jordan called it—Jordan cradled her against his chest and headed for the kitchen, while Bray pulled Dante aside, murmuring to him. Dante nodded and gestured to the others.

"It was nice to meet you, Mattie," Dante said.

"You, too. You're welcome here anytime."

Freer and Radar thanked him for the drinks, and they all said bye to Jordan and Ama when he returned to the room. Then they were gone. Butterflies fluttered in Mattie's stomach. Although he'd said they wouldn't be doing anything that night, he wanted to. He wanted to feel them both, tie them to him so they couldn't leave him. The thought sent him to the kitchen to tidy up, something he did when he needed to think. He'd been an independent person before he started a relationship with Jordan and Bray, but he'd always had a tendency to cling to his partners. Although maybe cling was the wrong word. He didn't enjoy being alone; he much preferred company. But he needed to remember that each of them was an individual and had their own lives as well as one together.

"What's wrong?" Jordan asked, entering the kitchen when Mattie's hands were elbow-deep in suds.

Mattie smiled over at him. "Nothing. Would you and Bray like to do the nighttime routine today?"

Jordan shook his head. "All three of us are doing it."

"I don't mind—"

"All three of us are doing it," Jordan said more insistently.

Mattie snorted. "Okay." He pulled his hands free and

dried them. "Let's go." He grabbed the bottle Jordan must've made and followed Jordan to the stairs.

"Bray's taken her up to get her ready for her bath," Jordan said, reaching back for Mattie's hand despite the narrowness of the staircase.

Mattie smiled. "He has more experience than we do."

Jordan pulled him to a stop outside the bathroom. "He doesn't really," he said, keeping his voice low. "Remember, he was in the military when Kit and Noah were born? He didn't see them as much when they were younger. He probably knows as much as we do."

Mattie hadn't thought about it like that. All he'd seen was Bray having twenty-year-old kids and being confident about his abilities. It never occurred to him that Bray didn't get to see all of their childhood.

Jordan squeezed his hand and entered the bathroom, stopping just inside the door but leaving enough room for Mattie to look over his shoulder. Bray was crouched beside the bath, gently trickling water over Ama's tummy. Ama's arms and legs were waving as she lay in the bath chair Jordan had bought her, swearing it was needed because they wouldn't break their arms holding her when she got excited whilst she was slippery.

"And here's Daddy," Bray said.

"We'll have to get names for you both," he said without thinking. Bray blinked up at him, and Jordan stared at him. Mattie licked his lips. "Unless you don't want her to call you anything," he said, backtracking.

"Well, you're Daddy. What do your kids call you, Bray?"

"Papa."

"There we go then. You can be Papa, and I'll be Dad. So, Daddy, Papa and Dad," Jordan said with a smile.

Mattie loved the idea, but he could see reservations in Bray's eyes. "There's no rush if you're not comfortable. We can stick with Bray for now." He refocused on Ama. "Hey, sweetpea." He crouched beside Bray and tickled Ama's tummy.

Bray rested his hand on Mattie's arm. "I'd love it," he said, staring into his eyes. "But only if you're sure."

Mattie sent him a smile. "I am." Truly and deeply sure that his life was never going to be the same again.

CHAPTER 17

JORDAN

Jordan could see Mattie was having second thoughts. No, not second thoughts. He was thinking he and Bray were having second thoughts. Jordan understood his hesitation. They would just need to prove to him that they were going to stick around.

Being called Dad by Ama, however, was something he hadn't been sure Mattie would want. Not because he was selfish, because he was far from it. But because Ama wasn't related to him. Children often called step-parents by the moniker, but not always. He would've understood if Mattie wasn't ready, especially as he'd only just found out about Ama to begin with. Or maybe that was the reason it was easier for him. Either way, gratitude overwhelmed him. And it made him want more kids. Plenty more.

"Well, it's time to get out, sweetheart," Mattie said, and Jordan realized how long he'd been wool-gathering.

He grabbed Ama's little towel, the one with tiger ears on the hood, and held it out. Mattie passed her over to him, and he wrapped her tiny body in the fluffy fabric, cradling her against him and smiling down at her. She was beautiful. Just like her father.

Carrying her to the nursery, he laid her on the changing table and dried her off.

When he finished, he picked her up and put her to his shoulder, pressing his lips to her head.

"There we go, princess."

He turned and jumped when he saw Mattie and Bray leaning against the doorjamb, entangled in each other's arms and watching him with identical smiles.

"What?" he asked.

"I love that you love her as much as I do," Mattie said.

"Who couldn't love this little one?" He grinned. "Here you go, Daddy. Time for my bottle." He stopped in front of Mattie, but the man shook his head.

"Bray's turn." He peered up at Bray as if thinking he'd decline, but a smile spread across his face.

"It's been a long time since I've done a bedtime routine, but I'd love to."

He pushed away from the door and took Ama, crossing the room to the bookshelf, plucking a book from its quickly growing pile, and settled in the chair next to where the bottle waited. Jordan took Bray's space and pulled Mattie into his arms as Bray started reading while feeding the little girl.

"How does he turn the page without dropping the bottle?" Mattie whispered. "I don't have enough dexterity to do that."

Jordan chuckled softly. "It's a gift. Though if you look at those arms, they're twice as long as ours."

Mattie hummed. "Well, when I look at those arms, I don't think anything but what I shouldn't."

Jordan froze and stared down at him. "Mattie Evans!" he whispered mock scandalously.

Mattie turned his face into Jordan's chest, probably hiding his embarrassment. Bray glanced up from his seat, and Jordan smiled across at him, waggling his eyebrows. Bray's mouth twitched, and he returned to reading the final pages. When he closed the book, he pulled the bottle from Ama's slack mouth and gently manoeuvred her to his shoulder where he winded her. After she let out a very un-ladylike burp, Bray chuckled and stood, crossing the space to her cot. He cradled her as he laid her down and brushed his finger over her head before heading towards them. Stopping in front of them, Bray tilted his head.

"Time for bed," he whispered.

It was far too early for bed, but Jordan wanted the experience of holding and being held by them as much as they did. He stepped back, letting Mattie pull away from his arms. He moved into the room, leaning down over Ama and kissing her forehead before coming back and leading the way. Bray brushed past him, and Jordan watched as they disappeared. When they entered Mattie's—their—room, Jordan glanced back at Ama, following in Mattie's footsteps to say goodnight to the little girl.

Entering the bedroom a few minutes later, he found Mattie and Bray with their arms wrapped around each other. Just holding each other. Jordan smiled and stepped over to them, sliding his arms around them both. He pressed his lips to their cheeks in turn.

"Time for sleep," he said.

They all pulled apart but didn't step back. Jordan lifted his hands to the hem of Mattie's T-shirt. As he slowly undressed Mattie, Bray closed in behind him, doing the same to Jordan, his hands sliding over his fabric-covered body. It was a slow, seductive undressing, and when they were down to their underwear, Jordan having undressed Bray, too, he led them to the bed. He pulled the covers back, gesturing for them to climb in. No words were needed as they situated themselves. Mattie was in the middle with Jordan to his back and Bray to his front.

Jordan's sigh was loud, and they chuckled. "Sorry," he said. "That was a good sigh. I promise."

Mattie glanced over his shoulder at him. "I know how you feel."

Bray tightened his hold, his arm stretching across Mattie's hips to rest on Jordan's. "As much as I was unsure about this, to begin with, the feeling of…ease and rightness right now shows I've—we've—made the right choice."

Jordan's heart skipped a beat and restarted with a faster rhythm. "We have."

Mattie sighed, and they chuckled again. "Let's sleep. I want to wake up with you tomorrow."

Jordan kissed Mattie's jaw and leaned forward to kiss Bray, and then settled his head on the pillow, enjoying the scent and sound of his men. He stayed awake for a short time, and when their breathing changed into that of the deep inhales and exhales of sleep, he allowed himself to follow.

Ama's cries woke him, and he rubbed his eyes, sliding from the bed. Bray and Mattie stirred.

"It's okay. I'll get her. Sleep," he said. He pulled on a T-shirt while he walked the short distance to the nursery and cooed to her. "It's okay, sweetie. I'm here. You hungry?"

He picked her up and rested her against his shoulder, wandering down the stairs to the kitchen. It was a little chilly, so he grabbed a little fleece blanket and tucked it around Ama while he worked to get her bottle ready. He loved these moments with her. The quiet of the night. The soft sounds of her breathing and babbling. The lack of rushing around that daytime brought.

While the bottle warmed, he changed her diaper and dressed her again. He settled into the armchair and held the bottle to her lips. She latched on immediately, and he smiled down at her.

"You look so much like your father," he murmured. He studied her face, seeing the features that would eventually lose their babyish looks and turn into a knockout. If she grew up as gorgeous as her dad was, they'd have their work cut out for them, keeping her safe from boys who'd want more than they were allowed.

She drained the bottle and fell asleep as he winded her, and then he replaced her in bed. Jordan wandered back to the bedroom, and as he rounded the bed, four hands grabbed at him and pulled him between two hard bodies.

He laughed. "You were supposed to go back to sleep." He peered up at Mattie and Bray, who were leaning above him with identical smiles. "Aren't you tired?"

"Not anymore," Mattie said. He glanced at Bray and then back at Jordan. "You were very kind by letting us sleep…even though we didn't…so we discussed…" He eyed Bray again.

"Giving you a reward," Bray finished.

Jordan raised his eyebrows as a smile curved his lips. "A reward? Maybe I should take the night shift more often."

Bray chuckled. "Let's see if you like the reward first."

He slid down the bed until his head was level with Jordan's hips, and Jordan's cock responded immediately. "I thought we were just sleeping tonight?" he whispered hoarsely.

"We will. After," Mattie said, following Bray's lead and sliding down.

Bray hooked his fingers into one side of his briefs, and Mattie did the same. Together, they dragged the briefs over his straining cock and freeing it to the cool air. Jordan hissed when warm air flowed over it, a gust of breath from either side. Staring down at the dual heads of sable and blond hair, his lungs constricted with how much he felt for them. And not just because their tongues were licking up his dick, tangling together over the head as he leaked.

"Fuck," he breathed. "You have no idea how arousing this is."

Mattie grinned at him. "I think I can guess."

Jordan gripped the sheets beneath him as Mattie and Bray took him to new heights. Their tongues, their hands, their lips sending electricity down his spine and pooling in his groin, making his cock harder and leak even more.

Bray cupped his balls, pulling and rolling them in his hand. Jordan's eyes wanted to close, but he was also unable to look away. His breathing increased, and he licked his dry lips. Mattie's fingers slid underneath Bray's hand and massaged his pucker. It was almost enough to send him over.

"Oh, fucking hell. Ah." He gasped when Bray's mouth sank down on his cock completely, taking him into the back of his mouth. He fisted the sheets as heat flowed through him. "Oh, god, please!"

They kept him right on the edge until Mattie pressed harder against his entrance, and it was game over. His eyelids dropped without consent, and he flew. Tremors wracked him as his body clenched and unclenched, pleasure suffusing every inch of him. His brain misfired, unable to think of anything but the contractions.

When his body finally relaxed, it ached, but the pleasure still thrummed through him. He couldn't open his eyes, but he swallowed and said, "Wow."

Mattie chuckled and rested his head on Jordan's chest without him having even realized he'd moved. Bray pressed his lips to Jordan's temple and pried his fingers from the sheets, rubbing his hands over his knuckles, and Jordan finally opened his eyes.

"That was…"

Mattie kissed his jaw. "Tasty."

"Filling," Bray added.

Jordan's mind supplied images from their words, and his dick tried valiantly to rise to the challenge, but it was a losing battle.

"Tomorrow I will do something about the images in my head. I promise it," he said.

"Sleep," Bray said. "Sleep."

Jordan's eyelids fell again, and he didn't wake until a warm bundle was placed beside him. He blinked and smiled when he saw Ama kicking away, arms waving just as excitedly.

He rubbed her stomach. "Hello, princess. I like you being my alarm clock."

The bed depressed behind him, and an arm came around his waist. "Good morning," a rough voice said, and Jordan linked his fingers with Bray's hand.

"Morning. How long have you been up?"

"Only half an hour or so. Mattie's cooking breakfast before you both have to go to work."

Ama ate her fists, pumping her legs and drooling everywhere.

"I could get used to this," Jordan murmured.

"A baby waking you up?" Bray joked.

Jordan snorted. "Yes. That, too."

Bray nuzzled the back of his neck, and Jordan sighed. All that was missing was Mattie, but it wasn't that he was far away. He was still with them. Still inside Jordan's heart. A relationship that had once been a wonderful friendship had morphed into something more. Something deeper. Something he had never expected to come from that friendship. And he loved it. He loved them.

His heart thumped. Them. He loved *them*.

He must be wrong. How could he have fallen in love in a week? It wasn't possible. Yes, they were both amazing men, who were kind, generous, loving, but there was no way he knew Bray well enough to love him, surely?

"What's wrong?" Bray asked.

"Nothing." He sighed. He needed to be sure. He didn't want to hurt any of them, and rushing into things was the worst thing he could do. But his feelings didn't feel different when he thought of Mattie than when he thought of Bray, so there must be something there.

"Shall we get dressed and take Ama down for breakfast?" Bray said, pressing a kiss to his nape.

"Sure. I think I need a quick shower, though. Oh, could I ask you to help me grab my stuff from the apartment soon?"

"Of course! Just tell me when. Okay. I'll take the little one down and you grab a shower. We'll keep your breakfast warm for you."

"Thanks." He leaned down and kissed Ama's cheek before Bray lifted her to his chest.

Bray cupped his cheek. "Whatever it is, we'll figure it out." He kissed Jordan and disappeared out of the room.

Jordan slumped back on the bed, staring at the ceiling. Whenever he thought about Mattie and Bray, his heart pumped faster. He understood the phrase "a heart expanding with love." He wanted what he was feeling to be true. He wanted to believe that he could fall in love in a week. He wanted to trust in his head and his heart, but he wouldn't do anything that could hurt them. So, while he wanted to exclaim his love to the world, he'd keep it quiet for now. He'd double-check he was all in, and then, when the time was right, he would give them the words they deserved.

Because they deserved all the love in the world.

CHAPTER 18

BRAY

As Bray carried Ama down the stairs to her daddy, his heart felt raw. Seeing the little girl with Jordan and how careful and loving he was to her was the end to any questions Bray had about his feelings towards the men. He loved them. How the hell that had happened so quickly he didn't know, but he was used to making split-second decisions in the military, and that meant he was all in. He couldn't tell them yet because it was far too early, but he could show them.

"Hey, you," Mattie said when he entered the kitchen. "And you, sweetpea."

Bray leaned down and kissed him. "Jordan will be down in a few minutes. He's just having a shower."

Mattie smiled up at him. "Good timing. The omelette will be ready in a few minutes." He dropped a kiss on Bray's mouth and reached for Ama. "And for you, little miss, you have a yummy bottle."

Bray watched him with her, remembering when he did similar things for his sons when they were little. He didn't get a huge amount of time with them growing up, but he had some. And feeding them was always something he enjoyed. It made him feel closer to them and allowed him to spend time with them one-on-one.

"Let me finish this while you feed her," he said, grabbing Mattie's hips and moving him away from the stove.

Mattie settled into the chair by the table and cradled Ama while teasing her lips with the teat. When she latched on, he smiled, and Bray returned his focus to breakfast.

"Are you sure you're okay with taking her again today?" Mattie asked.

"Of course. I have the day spare, and I'd love to. I was planning on taking her into town to fetch a few things I need."

"Only if you're sure. I'm going to speak to Corey today to sort out what hours I need."

"Sounds good. You've got it all sorted."

Mattie huffed a laugh. "I wouldn't say that. I don't know how much I'd be able to do without you, Jordan, Mama, and everyone. I'm going to advertise for help at the store, too. I work far too many hours to have a baby at home."

Bray smiled. "These things happen, but you're working to sort it out. It's not like she's missing out on anything or being neglected. You're doing an amazing job, Mattie." Mattie put Ama on his shoulder and patted her back. "Don't sell yourself short. You've been dropped into a life you weren't expecting, but you're figuring it out. Give yourself a break."

"Yeah, what he said," Jordan added as he entered the room.

Mattie snorted, and Bray plated the food. "Easier said than done."

Internalised failings were always a bugger to get rid of when they were so deep-rooted. Bray silently promised to make Mattie feel better about what he was capable of. He was a damn good businessman and now had a baby to look after, too. He was doing amazingly well for such a short time to get used to the idea.

They ate breakfast together before Mattie and Jordan headed off to work. Once Bray had closed the door, he lay Ama in her playpen and grabbed the things he needed to take with them. Piling it all into the car, he strapped Ama into the car seat and climbed in. The drive to town didn't take long, and when he parked, he grabbed the stroller and placed Ama in it. It had been a long time since he'd experienced pushing a stroller around, but he was a little excited, too. He wanted to show Ama off, which made him a little like Mattie's mother, but he could deal with that.

Locking the car, he started off. He needed to hit the hardware store to grab some more glue and nails for the wooden toys, and a few little pots of paint for the decoration, and he also needed to grab some more wrapping paper. He always wrapped the toys for the kids because who didn't enjoy getting presents?

Entering the store, he grabbed a basket and steered the stroller one-handed while he picked up the things he needed.

"—can't believe he has the audacity to be seen when he's *involved* with two other men."

The not-so-whispered words met his ears, and heat built inside him. There was no disguising who they were talking about, and though he'd expected it, he'd also expected them to be a little more discreet about it. He rubbed his forehead and continued through the store, ignoring the looks he received when he passed by customers. When he reached the till, he placed the items on the counter and smiled at the man behind it.

"Good morning, Gerald. How are the wife and kids?" he asked.

Gerald pursed his lips. "Good, thank you."

His politeness was inbred. The need to keep customers happy instead of disapproving was something he wouldn't be able to ignore, and Bray relied on that knowledge to keep things civil.

"Anything else for you today?" Gerald asked.

"No, thank you. I'm visiting the hospital again soon, so I need to stock up."

"He needs to stay away from children. What was Anthony thinking, allowing them to keep the baby?" a voice said from behind him.

He glared over his shoulder as he paid, and the woman's eyes widened, and she scuttled away. He collected the bags in one hand and pushed the stroller out of the store with the other.

"Bray?" Gerald called, and he turned around. "It's not true, is it?"

Bray's blood boiled. "What would that be, Gerald?" He'd make them voice it.

"You're not in a relationship with Mattie *and* Jordan, are you?"

Fury hit him, though he tempered his response. "I am. And I'm telling you right now, our kids couldn't want for a better life. Nothing we do in our personal relationship has an effect on how capable we are of looking after them," he snapped.

Gasps sounded, but he ignored them and exited, heading back to his car to put the bags away before resuming his stroll down the streets. He would grab a couple of tacos from Let's Talk Tacos and take one to Mattie in time for lunch. But for now, he'd do what he usually did, and visit local shops to support them as best he could.

He waved to several people he knew and bought small trinkets from different shops, but each time he heard someone whispering behind his back, he got angrier. He'd just about had enough when he was stopped by Anthony. Bray knew him in passing—a friend of a friend kind of thing—and Mattie had told him that was who was dealing with Ama's case. He only hoped Anthony didn't have something to say about him looking after Ama.

"Hey, Bray. How're things?"

Bray nodded. "Not bad, thanks. How are you and Scott and the twins?"

Anthony's face lit up. "We're doing good, thanks." He glanced at the stroller and leaned down. "Hi, Ama." He straightened again and met Bray's gaze, and Bray expected to hear something he didn't want to. "I'm glad Mattie has people in his corner. It'll help a lot with the process."

"I wish others thought the same," he muttered, glancing behind Anthony to the people staring his way.

"Ignore them. Everyone gets talked about at some point or another. It'll pass. Stand strong—which I know you'll do anyway—and everything will blow over soon."

"I just wish I could protect them all from it."

Anthony nodded. "I know. But people will talk. They always do. The main thing I want to see is that Ama is being looked after, and I know she is. The rest is a formality."

Bray sighed. "Thanks."

"Take care." He wandered off, and Bray resumed his walk. It was only eleven o'clock, but he decided to grab the tacos and take them before he ended up saying something to someone that he'd regret. Well, maybe he wouldn't regret it, but he'd certainly wish he'd kept it to himself.

When he entered Let's Talk Tacos, Nico bellowed his name. "Bray! Lovely to see you. Do you want your usual?"

"Hey, Nico. Yes, but also add another two, please. I'm feeding someone else today as well."

"Consider it done." He glanced at Ama. "Ooh, is she awake?"

Bray chuckled and freed Ama from the stroller, holding her against his chest so she could see around, and Nico could see her.

"Ah, she's a beauty."

"She takes after her father," Bray said with a smile.

Nico called his order through to the kitchen and then

returned to him. It wasn't very busy, so Bray settled at the counter to wait.

"There are lots of rumours going around, Bray."

Bray sighed and shook his head. "I know. I'm not going to deny it. I'm with Mattie and Jordan, Nico. It's new. We don't know where we'll end up, but we're going to try. What harm can it cause?"

Nico held up his hands. "I'm happy for you. I really am. I just wasn't sure if you knew."

"It's hard not to when people are less than covert as they talk about us behind my back."

Nico raised an eyebrow. "It's juicy stuff." He grinned, and Bray raked his fingers through his hair, barely concealing his eye roll.

Ama started complaining, and Bray rocked her, pressing his lips to her head. She was getting tired. He'd have to get her to Mattie before she fell asleep, or he'd miss it.

"You're a natural," Nico said as he placed the bags of food on the counter.

Bray chuckled and put Ama back into the stroller, much to her displeasure. "Out of practice, you mean."

"Doesn't look like it from here." Nico winked, and Bray paid and left, heading straight for Lovely in Lace.

The bell tinkled when he entered, and Mattie's face lit up when he saw them. He was talking to a customer, so Bray pushed the stroller back and forth while he waited for him to finish. When he had, Bray fit the stroller behind the counter, and Mattie picked Ama up.

"Hey, sweetpea." Ama grumbled. "Aww, are you tired or hungry?" he asked, looking at Bray.

"More than likely, both."

"I'll get her bottle in the warmer, and then I'll feed her," Mattie said.

"No, you eat while it's hot. I'll sort her bottle."

He moved into the small kitchen area at the back of the

building and set Ama's milk to heat. It wouldn't take long, and he leaned against the counter listening to Mattie talk to Ama about a fussy customer he'd had earlier that morning.

"Tut, tut, tut, Mattie Evans. What's this I hear about you colluding with Jordan and someone else? Are you not content with Jordan?"

Bray tensed and grabbed the bottle from the warmer. He refused to let Mattie fight this battle alone.

"Mrs James, I can assure you that what I do is best for me and my family," Mattie replied as Bray stepped up behind him.

Mrs James, who Bray didn't recognise, glared at him and then refocused on Mattie. "I don't think that having a relationship with *two* people is a good example, young man."

Bray hated when older people used the "young man" phrase. It rankled, making him feel like he was immature. He had no idea what Mattie thought about it, but it couldn't be good.

"I give as good an example as anyone can," Mattie argued. "Is there anything I can help you purchase today, Mrs. James?"

She looked scandalised. "Certainly not."

"Then I wish you a good day."

Mattie effectively dismissed her, and unless she wanted to come across as even more rude than she had already been, she couldn't do much but leave. And there was Bray worrying about how he'd deal with it.

"Are you okay?" he asked once she'd left.

Mattie sighed. "Yes, it's not the first comment I've received, and I doubt it will be the last either." He took the bottle from him. "Let me feed her."

"You haven't eaten," Bray said.

"I don't mind eating it cold." He settled into his chair and fed Ama while staring down at her with a small smile curving his mouth.

Bray ate his taco while watching Mattie and Ama. "I saw Anthony today," he said when he'd finished.

Mattie raised his eyebrows. "Everything okay?"

Bray nodded. "He was fine with everything. He wasn't even really checking on us. He was just passing by." He cleared his throat and stared down at the wrapper in his hand. "I did, however, confirm our relationship with a couple of people." He looked up at him. "I should've asked first, sorry."

Mattie smiled down at Ama. "You hear what Papa said, Ama? He's telling everyone. How wonderful is that?" He met Bray's gaze, his eyes shining, and Bray's heart sped up at the name he used. "It's fine by me. And I know it will be fine with Jordan, too." He picked Ama up. "Oh, I spoke to Corey. There's space for Ama when I need her to be there. I'm going to take her tomorrow morning for a session to see how she gets on."

"Sounds good." Bray would've loved to look after her full time, but he knew socializing with other children was important. It would help her immensely with her social skills as she grew.

Mattie held Ama out to him, and Bray took her, holding her close. "What are your plans for the rest of the day?" He grabbed his taco.

Bray shrugged. "I don't really have one. I'm going to see what Ama wants to do." He grinned.

Mattie chuckled and put his taco down again. He leaned forward, sliding his arm around Bray's shoulders. "I'd love to hear what she has to say about it when I get home."

"I'm sure she'll tell you all about it."

They finished their lunch, and Bray took Ama home. They still garnered stares as he walked to the car, but he was more easily able to ignore them. People could be so unfair at times. As if what other people did in the comforts of their own home was something that grievously affected them. They'd get over it, but he wished they'd just leave them in peace.

They would. Eventually.

But in the meantime, Bray wouldn't falter. He knew what Mattie and Jordan meant to him, and he wouldn't do anything to mess that up. Everyone else could get lost.

CHAPTER 19

MATTIE

After telling Bray about putting in the advert for someone to help him, Mattie spent a few hours sifting through applicants the following morning. There was a surprising number considering what products he sold. When he'd first opened the store, there had been a lot of pushback about the items, but the public had soon turned around and started visiting. He'd expected the same kind of resistance when advertising for help, but over twenty people had applied.

Looking through their information, he narrowed it down to those who actually seemed like they wanted the job, rather than the titillating idea of working in such a niche industry. When he narrowed it further to those who had experience in retail, he had four people to interview. He sent emails to those four applicants, requesting a suitable time for them to come into the shop. He wouldn't do the interviews somewhere else because he wanted to see how comfortable they were in the environment they would work in. Plus, he had no one who could take over if he was indisposed. The applicants would also get first-hand experience of what happened should he get customers during their interview.

By the time he had confirmed their interviews, surprisingly quickly and that same day, he was ready for a break. He'd been on the go for hours after dropping Ama at Charmers Day Care with Corey. Corey had eased his fears about leaving her, which had left him free to get his work done, but she was always at the back of his mind. He'd called the daycare once to check on her, and Corey had reassured him that she was fine.

The first applicant arrived on time, which was a bonus in their favour, to begin with.

"It's nice to meet you, Kris. Come on around the counter. The interview is rather unorthodox in that if customers come in, I will have to serve them. This is just one reason why I need some help here."

Kris smiled and settled into a chair behind the counter next to Mattie. "That's not a problem. I can understand how running your own business leaves less time for all the things that need to be done."

"Okay, so let me tell you a little about the position first, and then we'll look at your experience and if you think it's something you could and would want to do."

Mattie explained what he did, what he would expect of someone working there, and the responsibilities involved, including opening and locking up and cashing the till at the end of the day. There was a lot, but Mattie had provided a more than generous payment package to go with the role. He was only looking for two or three days of cover so he could spend more time with his new family. He wouldn't abandon the store completely.

During the interview, Mattie had to serve several people, but Kris watched and asked questions after each one had left. All in all, Mattie had a good feeling about the guy, and when he left, Mattie wrote down his initial thoughts about him before the next applicant arrived. He went through the process with the other people and ruled out two of them as soon as their interview had been over. They just weren't suitable for the role.

Locking up, he caught the bus to the daycare and picked up Ama before heading home with her. When he got there, Jordan was already making dinner, and the scent of lasagne filled the house.

"You'll be so happy when you can have food, sweetpea. Their cooking is to die for," he murmured, kicking off his shoes and pulling her free from the stroller.

He entered the kitchen, a smile spreading across his face when he saw Bray at the stove and Jordan chopping vegetables. "Hey. I wasn't expecting to see you so soon," he said to Bray, lifting his chin to kiss him. He moved over to Jordan and kissed him, too.

"I finished what I needed to, so thought I'd come over."

"You know you're welcome to come and go as you please," Mattie said. He settled into a chair and bounced Ama on his knee.

"How did the interviews go?" Jordan asked.

Mattie had sent messages to Jordan throughout the day. "Really well. I've narrowed it down to two people. I just need to decide which one fits best."

"We can have a look at your notes after dinner if you like. Maybe we can see something you haven't."

Mattie grinned. "That would be great, thanks."

"I won't be able to stay over tonight, though. I have to help Mom tonight," Bray said.

Though Mattie was sad, he understood. "That's okay. You do what you need to. We'll get other chances."

Bray smiled at him. "Definitely."

Dinner was a relaxed affair, and while Jordan played with Ama on the floor of the living room, Bray settled beside Mattie and they worked through the applicants.

"I think you know which one fits best," Bray said.

"Why do you say that?"

"Because you've pointed out his abilities more than once."

Mattie nodded slowly. "Yeah. I guess I have." He sighed. "I'll call them tomorrow."

Bray didn't stay for much longer after that, and they enjoyed a leisurely kiss before he left.

"Is it weird I miss him already?" Jordan said as they snuggled on the sofa after they'd put Ama to bed.

"If it is, I'm weird, too."

They watched a movie and went to bed, wrapping their bodies around each other as they drifted off, and when Mattie woke the next morning, it was with a start because he hadn't heard Ama. He scrambled out of bed—out of Jordan's arms—and raced to her bedroom. She was gurgling and kicking her legs and arms, but she wasn't crying. It seemed like she had slept through the night for the first time. He knew it wouldn't last, but as his heart calmed, he smiled down at her.

"Hey, sweetpea. I bet you're hungry right now, aren't you?" He picked her up. "Come on. Let's get some breakfast."

He carried her down the stairs and bounced her against his chest as he made her bottle. Arms slid around his waist and a chin rested on his shoulder.

"Morning," Jordan said groggily. "Is she okay?"

"Yes. She worried me because she didn't wake up in the night. Did she wake you?" he asked.

"No. She slept through?" Jordan said, lifting his head and leaning against the counter.

Mattie nodded. "Scared ten years off my life."

Jordan chuckled and made some coffee. "It won't be the only time that happens."

"I can imagine."

By the time Mattie's mother arrived to look after Ama for the morning, he was ready to make the calls to the applicants and get the ball rolling. It would be a sad phone call to the unsuccessful one, but Kris would get the pleasant call. Mattie hoped he would be able to start straight away. He had mentioned being available immediately, and Mattie would like it if he could start the next day.

As it happened, Kris was available straight away. As in that day. So Mattie invited him in to complete the paperwork he needed to get him set up and began his training. The afternoon slipped by quickly, and Mattie was heading home before he knew it. Things with Kris turned out well, and they had become friends. If everything continued on the path Mattie wanted it to, Kris would be trained in a couple of weeks, and Mattie would be able to take some time off for his family.

Home called his name, and he entered the house to squeals and laughter. "I'm home."

Cody came barrelling around the corner and skidded to a stop in front of him. "Can I call you Daddy, too?"

Mattie's mouth gaped, his mind trying to catch up with a conversation he'd not been part of. "Um…sure."

Cody fist-bumped the air and shouted, "Yeah!" and raced out of sight. "He said yes!"

Jordan's laughter floated out of the living room, and Mattie's body followed the sound. "Hey," he said, meeting Jordan's bright-eyed gaze.

"Afternoon. How was your day?"

"Busy. Kris started. He was as eager to start as I was to have him start." He moved over to Ama, who was busily kicking and batting at the toys hanging above her where she lay on the padded floor mat. "Hey, I'm home," he whispered.

"It's great that he seems eager. What do you think of him now he's started? Do you still have the same good feeling about him?"

"I do," Mattie said, leaving Ama where she was happy and snuggling into Jordan's side. "He's going to fit in well, I think." He glanced at Cody, who was sitting near Ama but on his tablet. "What's this about Daddy?" he murmured.

Jordan pressed his lips to Mattie's head, whispering in his ear. "He asked what Ama was going to call you, and then randomly asked if he could call you that, too. Not sure if it will extend to Bray, but I couldn't deny him. I did tell him he had to ask you first, though."

Mattie's heart thumped. "I'd love it if he called me Daddy, but what about Ash?"

Jordan shook his head. "He won't mind. We might have an issue with Bray, what with Cody calling Ash Papa, but we can figure something out if he wants to include him, too. I'm leaving that up to Cody, though."

"Understandable. I honestly thought it would take more for him to be used to the three of us, but I suppose what they say about kids is true. They're more willing to go with the flow because they don't have the hang-ups that adults do."

"That's definitely true."

"Is Bray coming tonight, do you know?" Mattie asked.

"He is," Jordan said. "He's also bringing takeaway." Mattie's stomach rumbled, and Jordan laughed. "And he should be here soon."

"Dad, can I help bathe Ama tonight?"

Jordan shook his head. "You can't tonight, bud. Papa's picking you up straight after dinner, remember? But maybe this weekend? You'll be with us all weekend."

Cody's face fell and then brightened with Jordan's words, and Mattie smiled. He was such a good big brother. Mattie stood. "Coffee?"

"I'll get it. You rest."

They swapped positions, and Cody came and sat beside Mattie. "Uncle..." He glanced at Mattie and smiled. "Daddy, can you help me with this? I can't get past this level."

Mattie inhaled and stared down at the screen. "I'm not

very good at these things, but I can give it a try. What do we have to do?"

Cody explained the rules of the game, and Mattie tried to complete the level. Jordan brought his drink in, and they were still trying when Bray entered the room, the scent of takeaway preceding him. As if he was the magic they needed, Mattie took one last go at it and completed it.

"Yes! Thanks, Daddy!" Cody said, smiling down at the screen he'd taken back from Mattie.

Bray raised his eyebrows, and Mattie grinned. Ash picked Cody up after they'd finished eating, and though he grumbled about it, Cody said goodbye to them all. Ash's only response to Cody calling Mattie Daddy was a small smile and a twinkle in his eye. As much as Mattie had withheld his judgement about Ash when they'd first met, he'd come to be a good friend, too. Jordan saw them to the door, and Bray slipped his arm around Mattie's shoulders.

"Daddy, huh?"

Mattie chuckled. "Yeah. He threw it at me the moment I stepped in the door today."

"He just asked what he could call you, Bray," Jordan said, entering the room again. "Ash suggested Pops, but I said I'd ask you."

Bray's mouth fell open. "What?"

Jordan settled on Bray's other side. "He wants to include you in the family. He can't call you Papa because he calls Ash that and it'd get confusing. So would Pops be okay, or would you prefer something else?"

Bray cleared his throat. "He can call me whatever he wants to."

Jordan leaned his head against Bray's shoulder, and Mattie did the same on the other side. "I'll let him know."

Ama let out a squeal, and they laughed. Mattie slid to the floor, laying on his stomach beside her. "And what's so funny, madam?" He nuzzled her cheek. "I think it's time for a diaper change as well as bedtime." He picked her up.

"We'll clean up and then join you," Jordan said, stacking the plates.

Mattie carried Ama to the nursery, cleaning her diaper before wrapping her in a towel and carrying her to the bathroom. The routine was calming for him, and he loved spending time with her. Nothing had prepared him for having a child, but it was something he'd always wanted. He'd wished it wasn't at the expense of Dionne's life. She might not have been the person he wanted to spend his life with, but she had been a nice person all the same. He'd need to find some pictures of her so he could keep them around for Ama as she grew. He'd make sure she knew who she was, and even who Rhia was. It wasn't Ama's fault that Rhia couldn't cope. It was understandable.

Jordan brought a bottle up with them when they came, and Mattie dried, dressed, and fed her before they all said goodnight. Mattie aimed for the stairs, but Jordan grabbed his hand to stay him.

"It's bedtime."

Mattie's throat dried, but he dutifully followed them to the bedroom, placing the monitor on the bedside table. Jordan dragged him to the bed and slid his arms around him. His mouth descended, and Mattie lost himself in the kiss. A warmth encased his back, and Jordan's hands moved to his hips as Bray joined them. They undressed him, dragging it out and sending tingles of arousal through his body. He needed them with a force he'd never experienced before. He wanted them. Fully.

"I need you," he whimpered as Bray's lips found where his neck joined his shoulder, and Jordan's mouth found his earlobe.

"We know," Bray said. "We'll take care of you, don't worry."

Mattie's breath left him when their fingers deftly yanked his shirt over his head and unfastened his jeans, pulling them down his legs. When he was left in his briefs, he turned the tables on Jordan, grappling at his T-shirt to get rid of it. Once he was semi-naked, he pressed his chest to Jordan's, moaning at the feel of his slightly hairy chest resting against Jordan's smooth one. Their lips joined again, and Bray's cheek rested against Mattie's, their breathing synchronising.

"Please," Mattie begged when he pulled his mouth away, dropping his head back against Bray's shoulder.

"We'll make you feel good, don't worry," Jordan said with a chuckle.

"Get on the bed, Mattie," Bray said.

Mattie disentangled himself from their arms and crawled into the middle of the bed. He watched as Bray took Jordan's mouth, his hands divesting him of the rest of his clothes. Jordan returned the favour, and before Mattie could blink, they were all down to their underwear.

Jordan turned his focus on Mattie, and Bray's gaze heated him from inside.

"I'm done with going slow. I want you both now," Mattie said. "Please. Will you..." His courage failed him, and he licked his lips instead.

Jordan smirked and glanced at Bray. "I think that's something we can all get on board with, don't you, Bray?"

"Without a doubt."

Mattie swallowed. "How is this going to work?"

Jordan crawled up the bed, his legs on either side of Mattie's thighs. "I'm sure we can figure this out, but I love the idea of sinking inside you while Bray fucks your mouth. What do you think, Bray?"

Bray rubbed his chin. "I can think of something better. You inside Mattie, while I'm inside you. How does that sound?"

Jordan's and Mattie's moans joined in the air, and Bray chuckled. "I think you like that idea. Jordan, kiss him. I intend to get you both ready before we finally get what we want. I'm going to prep you good. Real good."

Mattie wasn't sure that was a good thing because it meant Bray was going to take his time, and Mattie wasn't sure how long he would last. But he would do whatever Bray asked him to. And whatever Jordan wanted him to. He was at their mercy, and he wouldn't have it any other way.

CHAPTER 20

JORDAN

Bray's chuckle reverberated through Jordan, and he shivered from above Mattie. Their cocks rubbed against each other, and Jordan lowered his head for a kiss. It wasn't the deep, uncontrolled kiss they sometimes shared, but this one was just as soul-destroying. Mattie's hand slipped into his hair, scratching at his scalp as sounds of Bray moving around behind him reached his ears.

He trembled when Bray's hand rested against his lower back, rubbing up and down for a few seconds before disappearing again. With his lips joined with Mattie's, all he could do was whimper. Bray didn't keep him waiting long.

"Mattie, spread your legs around Jordan's. I need room to work."

Their mouths separated, eyes glassy, but they did as Bray asked. If Jordan lowered himself enough, he could slide right into him, but that wasn't what Bray wanted. Jordan glanced over his shoulder when he heard a click, and Bray squeezed lube onto his fingers, putting the tube on the bed within reach. He caught Jordan's gaze and smirked, and Jordan's heart melted at the tenderness in his eyes.

Bray knelt behind them, and Jordan turned back to Mattie

in time to see his eyes widen and catch the gasp with his mouth. He leisurely kissed, licked and nipped at Mattie's mouth, lips and neck as Mattie's fingers dug into his arms. He took a moment to watch Bray between their legs, and though he couldn't see a lot, it was enough to know he was prepping Mattie.

What he wasn't expecting was a warm, wet tongue to lick a stripe up his crack and flick against his pucker. He gasped against Mattie's neck as Bray's tongue massaged him and pushed against him. Jordan bore down and inhaled shakily when it slipped inside him. He couldn't help bucking his hips, to get away or to move closer, he wasn't sure. It had the unexpected reward of rubbing his cock with Mattie's, so he did it again. And again.

Mattie picked up his rhythm, and Bray thrust his tongue in time with their movements. Then, his tongue was gone, and his fingers replaced them.

"Jesus, fuck," Jordan breathed. "I'm not going to last."

"Yes, you will," Bray said, his tone brooked no argument.

Jordan had the feeling he was going to disappoint them both, but he inhaled and exhaled carefully, trying to push back the tingling in his spine as it snaked towards his groin. It didn't help when Bray slipped three fingers inside him. The stretch was immense, the bite of burning as his body accommodated him breath-taking, but he wanted more.

Bray's fingers disappeared—from them both, if Mattie's whimper was any indication. Jordan groaned when Bray's hand encircled his cock, slicking it with lube and stroking several times.

"Bray…stop. I'm too…close," Jordan muttered, squeezing his eyes closed and fisting the bed covers.

Bray chuckled and let go, and Jordan blew out a breath, meeting Mattie's glazed eyes. "Are you okay?" he murmured, brushing his lips across Mattie's mouth.

"Huh?" Mattie blinked, and Jordan snorted, his inhale

shaky when Bray's body braced over his back and his hand wrapped around his dick again.

"Fuck, Bray. I won't last two seconds at this rate," Jordan complained, though there was no heat with his words.

"Slide inside him, J," Bray murmured into his ear.

Bray pushed against his hips, moving Jordan closer to Mattie's waiting hole. Having no control over his cock—what with Bray's hand moving him where he wanted him—he shivered when his head pressed against the pucker. Bray held onto him until he pushed past the ring of muscles, and Mattie's eyelids fluttered closed on a sigh.

"Work your way deep. Then I want you to stop."

Jordan clenched his teeth against the need to rut into him and take his pleasure. It wouldn't take long; he hadn't been exaggerating. But the need to follow Bray's order was a heady thing, and once he was as deep as he could go, Mattie's ass squeezing him tightly, he wrapped his arms around Mattie's back, breathed into his neck and stopped. They both moaned, and it took every ounce of restraint to keep himself still.

"Good," Bray praised.

Jordan inhaled and exhaled Mattie's scent, closing his eyes and focusing on the sensations bombarding him. The sounds, the smells, the taste of Mattie whenever he licked the sweat away. The heat kindling between them. And the remembered vision of Bray's hand around his cock as he guided it into Mattie. Everything was overwhelming, but he refused to come until Bray said he could.

A blunt head pressed against Jordan's pucker, and he instinctively clenched before inhaling and relaxing, bearing down so Bray could push forward. The burn was back, but it held something more with it. A sting of pleasure pooled around his cock and balls. His dick pulsed inside Mattie, and Mattie moaned into Jordan's skin.

"Please."

"Not long now," Bray said, pushing further and further, sending more and more darts of pleasure through Jordan.

When he finally rested his groin against Jordan's ass, he lowered himself to his hands beside them and kissed Jordan's shoulder.

"You ready?" he murmured. All Jordan could manage was a hum of acknowledgement, and the warmth of Bray left his back again. "Hold tight."

Mattie's arms slid around Jordan's waist and tightened. Bray withdrew from Jordan's ass and slid back in again. He did it twice and then slammed forward on the third. Jordan didn't need to move inside Mattie because, with every movement Bray made, his hips copied. He wasn't fully withdrawing each time, but he didn't need to. Mattie's groans filled the air, and Jordan couldn't keep his own from joining him.

The slide of Bray's cock in his channel, nudging his prostate with each withdrawal and thrust, was more than Jordan could cope with, and he put a bit of space between him and Mattie before wrapping his hand around Mattie's cock.

Mattie cursed and clamped down on Jordan's dick as his release poured over his hand. Trembles wracked him as Bray's speed increased.

"Fuck, fuck, fuck!" he said as his orgasm crashed over him. Waves and waves of pleasure flowed through him, and he lost track of everything.

When he came back to himself, Bray's grip on his hips was bruising, and Jordan glanced behind him, watching Bray's expression as he came while holding himself deep. His head thrown back, sweat streaking down his neck, and his entire body clenched hard enough that he could've been made from stone. And then he relaxed, tightening his hold on Jordan's hips so he didn't slip free.

Bray gave one more half-hearted roll of his hips, wincing,

and pulled free. Jordan pulled out of Mattie, though he'd almost slid out anyway, and rolled to the side, breathing heavily.

"Wow," Mattie said, staring at the ceiling.

Jordan found that hilarious and burst out laughing. "Wow, indeed." He glanced at Bray, who stood beside the bed. "Joining us?"

Bray snapped out of wherever his brain had gone and said, "In a minute." He disappeared, returning a few seconds later with a cloth. He wiped Mattie clean, then Jordan, and then himself before throwing it in the washing basket and putting his hands on his hips as he stared at them.

"Bedtime," he said.

"Definitely," Jordan said, yawning. "You've worn me out."

Mattie dragged himself to a pillow and closed his eyes. "I'm tired, too."

Jordan waited until Bray joined them in the not-big-enough bed before wrapping his arm around Mattie's waist and snuggling back into Bray. Bray's hand covered his on Mattie's stomach and then fell silent.

After a few minutes, Jordan said, "That went well, if I do say so myself. I don't think we have anything to worry about regarding compatibility."

Bray's laughter warmed Jordan's neck, and he got nothing from Mattie apart from a soft snore. Jordan fell asleep easily, surrounded by warmth, and to thoughts of sunny days surrounded by his men and their complete family.

———

"You're seeing them both?" Helen asked as they scanned the shore for any problems two days later.

Jordan crossed his arms over his chest and leaned his hip against the deck. "Yes. There's no cheating involved. We're all seeing each other. Individually and together." Her mouth twisted, and Jordan sighed. "We're not hurting anyone, Helen. It's not anyone's business but our own."

She glanced at him, biting her bottom lip, and then nodded. "You're right. I'm just not…used to it."

Jordan snorted. "We're not, either. It takes work. Compromise. Hell, we've only been together a week, but it feels…" He stopped, not wanting to voice his feelings when it was so new.

"It feels…?" Helen prompted.

Jordan turned to the ocean, staring out across the vast undulating water. "I love them," he whispered. He exhaled. "I'm in love with them, Helen. How the hell does that happen in a week?"

She laughed. "Love doesn't have a timescale, Jordan. It is what it is." She sighed. "I can't begin to understand your relationship with them, but I don't have to understand it. It's your choice. If you're happy, I'm happy."

He turned to her and saw the truth on her face. He hugged her. "Thanks. That means a lot."

"You'll have to invite them to our house one day. We can get to know them."

Jordan huffed a laugh. "You already know Mattie."

"Yeah, but not as your boyfriend."

"Hey, Jordan!"

Jordan glanced down from the tower and saw Dante holding a surfboard. "Hey, Dante. How're things?" He squeezed Helen's shoulder. "I'll be back in a minute." He stepped down the ramp and stopped before Bray's friend.

"I'm good, thanks. How're things with you?"

"Great. You just starting or just finished?" He gestured to the board.

"Just starting. Making the most of the less busy time." Dante ran a hand through his hair.

"Don't blame you. This weekend will be rammed. As usual." Jordan scanned the beach.

"Are you working?"

Jordan shook his head. "Not this weekend. Cody's staying with me…us."

Dante smiled. "Oh, it's great that they'll get to see Cody as well."

Jordan frowned. "Who?"

"Kit and Noah." Jordan stared at him, and Dante froze. "Shit. Bray hasn't told you?" Dante raked his fingers through his hair again. "Crap. He has only just told me, so maybe he was going to tell you when you finished work."

"Tell me what?"

"Kit and Noah are visiting this weekend. Bray told them about you both, and they want to meet you."

Jordan's throat dried up at the thought of meeting Bray's kids. Not because he didn't want to. He wanted to give a good impression to them. Would they approve of their father's choices?

Dante clapped his shoulder. "I'm sorry. I should've kept my mouth shut."

"It's fine. I just wasn't expecting it. I saw him yesterday for Cody's lesson, but he didn't mention it, but maybe he's only just found out. It's all good."

Dante exhaled. "On that note, I'm going to drown myself in the ocean. Before Bray does it for me."

Jordan threw back his head and laughed. "I won't let him."

"I'll hold you to that."

Dante waved and headed down the beach, undoubtedly going to the area where the least amount of people were settled. Jordan shook his head and tried to ignore the butter-flies in his stomach. Kit and Noah were important to Bray, and Jordan didn't want to do anything to mess with that. Family was everything.

When he got home after finishing his shift, Bray and

Mattie were cuddled on the sofa with Ama. He smiled and leaned down for a kiss, pressing his lips to Ama's head.

"Everything okay?" Mattie asked.

Jordan nodded. "No casualties, so we're good. I saw Dante."

Bray smiled. "He's going to turn into a fish if he's not careful." Jordan chuckled and opened his mouth, but Bray beat him to it. "My kids are visiting this weekend. Would it be okay if they met you?"

Jordan's heart raced, but he nodded. "Of course." He glanced at Mattie.

Mattie's cheeks heated. "He asked me earlier today when he found out. He didn't want to interrupt your shift to tell you, though I told him it would've been fine."

Jordan smirked. "Dante beat you to the punch," he admitted. "Though he has my solemn promise that I'll stop you from drowning him for the slip." He grinned.

Bray rolled his shoulders. "Asshole. Sorry. If I'd known he was going to tell you, I would've called or texted you to let you know. I wasn't keeping it a secret from you."

Jordan waved him away. "I know. But feel free to call me anytime. You don't have to worry about waiting."

Bray nodded. "I'll remember that."

"When are they coming?"

Bray checked his watch. "An hour? Maybe two, depending on how slow Noah is at getting ready. He drives Kit up the wall." Jordan chuckled. "I'll be staying at my house this weekend. I hope you don't mind."

"I'm happy for everyone to be here. I know there's not enough room for them to sleep here unless they want to sleep on the sofas, but they can stay here the rest of the time," Mattie said. "I want them to feel like this is home to them, too."

Bray kissed his cheek. "Thank you. I'll see what they want

to do, but I know spending time with you both is what they want. We will visit Mom at some point, too."

"Well, Cody should be here soon. There'll be plenty of kids around," Jordan said.

"A house full," Mattie said and smiled, his eyes twinkling. He'd always loved the idea of having lots of kids around him.

If any more kids were in their future, they'd need to look for a bigger house. Jordan blinked as images of lots of kids running around filled his head. He'd love it.

"Okay. I'm going for a shower before everyone gets here. Do you want me to cook dinner?" Jordan asked as he stood.

Bray shook his head. "I'm going to get takeaway for us all tonight. It'll give us a break from cooking and give us the chance to talk."

Jordan nodded, though the butterflies were back in his stomach. "Sounds good."

And it did. Although he was nervous, he was also excited about meeting the two men whom Bray had a hand in creating. He'd seen pictures of them and saw how alike they were, both to each other and to Bray. It would be fun.

He hoped.

CHAPTER 21

BRAY

When Bray had told his kids about his relationship with Jordan and Mattie, he hadn't expected them to drop their weekend plans and travel back to see him. They'd want to meet them, granted, but he hadn't thought they'd do it there and then. But he couldn't say no when they'd asked. Rather than meet them at Bray's house and drive back to Mattie's, he gave them directions so they could come straight there. Kit had been giving him text updates, and when they were half an hour away, he ordered the takeaway, knowing they would be famished.

Ash had just dropped off Cody when the doorbell rang. Bray opened the door, and something settled inside him when his kids grinned in identical expressions from the other. He loved them so much, and though he agreed with their choices of location, it didn't stop him from hating them being so far away.

He dragged them both into a hug in the hallway. He couldn't help himself. Most military men he knew wouldn't show much emotion around anyone, but he threw that on the bonfire the moment he had kids. He wouldn't let them think he was a stuck-up, indifferent father. He would be the one they were willing to turn to, no matter what issues they had.

"Hey, Papa," Kit said, pulling back.

Bray cupped his cheek and smiled. "Hey, Kit." He glanced at his hair. "Nice colour."

Kit chuckled and slid his hands through his chin-length, blue hair. "Something different."

"Looks good." Bray turned to Noah and cupped his nape. "How are you, No?" There was something different about him, but he couldn't place it.

"Good, thanks." And then Bray saw it. The happiness in his eyes.

"Have you met someone?" Bray asked, and Noah blushed, something his kids were prone to do, even with their tanned skin.

"Yeah. It's still fairly early, but it's going well," Noah said.

"Well, if you're vetting my relationship, I have to vet yours." Bray raised his eyebrows and barely withheld his laughter when Noah's eyes widened. "I'm joking. Partly."

Noah exhaled. "You can meet her, just not yet."

Bray nodded. "Okay." He let them go. "Are you ready?"

His kids smiled and nodded. "Hell, yes," they said in unison. It was something Jordan and Mattie would have to get used to. Although his kids weren't identical twins, they were close enough, and whoever said there was a psychic bond between twins was being truthful. He swore it. The number of times they spoke together or finished each other's sentences was immeasurable.

He guided them into the living room, where everyone waited. Jordan sat on the sofa next to Cody, who held Ama, and Mattie sat on the floor in front of them. They all looked in their direction when they entered. Bray smiled at them.

"Kit, Noah, I'd like you to meet Jordan," Jordan waved, "Mattie," Mattie held up his hand, "Cody and Ama."

Cody grinned at them and returned his focus to Ama. Kit stepped forward, holding his hand out to Mattie.

"It's nice to meet you," he said, shaking Mattie's hand and then Jordan's.

Noah moved further into the room and leaned over Cody, looking at Ama. "She's a beauty," Noah said, brushing his finger over her cheek.

"She's my little sister," Cody said. He looked up at Noah. "And you're my big brother. So is Kit."

Oh, the innocence of children.

Noah grinned. "We are, yes. Do you like having siblings?"

Cody nodded, his hair waving all over the place with his exuberance. "I love it."

Jordan ruffled his hair. "You want a football team, don't you?"

Cody frowned. "No, I want more siblings, not a football team."

Jordan chuckled and shook his head, meeting Bray's gaze. "Yeah, I hear you."

The doorbell rang again, and as Bray was closest, he answered it. He took the takeaway into the kitchen after popping his head into the living room to tell them it was there. He emptied the bags onto the dining table and set them in the center. He'd bought a variety of items so they could choose what they wanted or if they wanted to try something new. He had no idea what Cody would eat, and he hoped he'd got at least one thing he would like.

Kit came in first with Cody, and Jordan followed, settling his son at the table and pointing out the different dishes. Bray retrieved plates and put them down, only just realising they didn't have enough chairs. He grabbed a stool and put it at the corner of the table. He'd use that one.

Mattie entered with Noah following, holding Ama close to his chest, a serene smile on his face. Noah had always been one to want kids, even from a young age, and if he wasn't mistaken, Cody appeared to be the same way. It wouldn't surprise Bray if Noah had kids earlier rather than later, whereas Kit probably would abstain, either completely or until later in life.

"Eat up," Bray said, and they settled in.

The conversation wasn't remotely strained, and Kit and Noah regaled them all with the trials and tribulations of university life, keeping it cleaner than they ever had before.

"I thought we could go to the beach tomorrow," Bray said when there was a slight lull. "With Mattie being at work, we can manage four kids between us, can't we, Jordan?"

Jordan nodded and mumbled around his food. "Definitely. Not sure if I have enough rubber rings for Kit and Noah, though." He winked in their direction, and Kit threw a napkin at him.

"I'll have you know…I have my own ring." Kit stuck his nose in the air and spoiled it by laughing.

"Well, I'm a lifeguard, so I suppose I can save you if there are problems," Jordan said.

They all laughed, and Mattie rose to get Ama's bottle when she started fussing. When they finished eating and everyone helped to clean up—much to Mattie's uneasiness— he helped get Ama ready for bed. Cody wanted to bathe her, so Jordan helped him. Mattie got her bed ready, and Bray set up Cody's bed. Cody and Ama would be sleeping in the same room, but Cody wouldn't be going to bed at the same time as Ama.

Kit and Noah sat at the top of the stairs, talking while everyone busied around, and when Ama was settled, they said goodbye to Jordan, Mattie, and Cody. Bray kissed his boyfriends in full view of his sons, hugged Cody, and then they headed out. He would've taken Mattie up on his offer of having them stay, but he had a feeling his kids wanted to talk to him about something, so he made excuses for them. They could maybe sort out a sleepover for Saturday night instead.

Bray drove himself, while Noah drove him and Kit to Bray's house. Kit folded himself into his favorite armchair, and Noah settled on the floor at his feet. Same as usual. Bray grabbed some drinks and handed them out.

"So…" he said. "What have you got to tell me?"

Kit chuckled. "Nothing really. We just wanted you to know that we love them. They're so perfect for you. You're perfect together. It's nauseating." He laughed again when Noah slapped his leg.

"What he meant to say was it's beautiful, and you deserve it."

Bray felt his cheeks heating. "Thanks. That means a lot."

"Has Grandma met them yet?"

Bray shook his head. "She has a cough. She's waiting until it's cleared before she comes over."

Noah frowned. "Is she okay?"

Bray sighed, deciding to go for honesty. "I don't know. She won't go to the doctor. I'm going to give her a couple of weeks to see if this cough goes, and if it doesn't, I'm physically dragging her there."

"Do you think it's something else?" Kit asked.

Bray rubbed his hand over his head. "I'm not sure. I hope not."

They fell into silence for a few minutes, and then Kit fidgeted. "I like them, Papa. You did well."

"Thanks, Kit."

"I can't wait for the beach tomorrow. All those lifeguards." Kit winked.

Bray laughed. "I'll let Jordan know you're interested. He can tell you which ones are decent. And single." Kit winced. It wouldn't be the first time Kit had started something with someone who had hidden that they were already with someone. Poor guy had bad luck when it came to relationships.

They spoke long into the night and finally succumbed to sleep in the early hours of the morning. Bray fought to pull himself from sleep the next day, having not set his alarm. Whenever he slept longer than usual, he felt worse than if he'd had less sleep. It was something that had always buggered him up when he was in the Army.

He stumbled from bed and showered in the coldest water he could stand, and then dressed and made breakfast. The scents would bring his kids from their room before long.

Noah was the first to appear with dishevelled hair and creases on his cheeks. He slumped into a chair at the table and put his forehead in his hands, groaning. "I really shouldn't go to bed so late."

Bray snorted. "I'm sure you go to bed so early at university."

Noah glared at him. "I do. If I don't, I can't concentrate the next day." He rubbed his face. "I need coffee."

Bray filled him a cup and handed it to him, and Noah cradled it to his face, inhaling and closing his eyes. Kit entered the kitchen just as Bray was plating the food. He looked completely put together and awake, which was surprising. Kit was usually the one to stumble in at the last minute, looking like he'd fought with a hedge and lost during his sleep.

They ate, and Bray drove them back to Mattie's once they were all dressed and ready to go. They'd made it just in time to see Mattie off to work. Bray helped to corral the kids while Jordan sorted Ama for the beach, and they packed the car with buckets, spades, suncream, hats, and all manner of para-phernalia. Bray had no idea where most of it had come from.

He found a parking space close to their destination, and they grabbed everything they could. Bray carried Ama—there was no point using the stroller—and Cody carried the buckets and spades. The beach was already busy, but Jordan pointed them towards a gap near to one of the towers. They spread out blankets and dug an enormous umbrella into the sand to protect them from the sun. Cody was chomping to get into the water, and Kit offered to take him. Jordan didn't hesitate in saying yes, which was more than Bray had been expecting. After all, he'd only met them the previous evening.

His thoughts must've been showing on his face because Jordan chuckled and dropped beside him, pressing his lips to Bray's cheek.

"They're your kids, Bray. I don't need to grow to trust them. You trust them; therefore, I trust them."

Bray caught his chin in his hand and kissed him, tilting his head to deepen it when Jordan opened for him. Ama was pulled from his arms, and he yanked his mouth away, ready to fight whoever had tried to take her, when he saw Noah.

"Now, now. Ama doesn't want to see you two kissing face all the time. Do you, sweetheart? You want to feel the sand between your toes."

Bray wrapped his arm around Jordan, who melted into him as they watched Noah with Ama. He was a natural.

"He's a natural," Jordan whispered, echoing his thoughts.

"He is."

"Don't they want to surf?"

Bray smiled. "They'll probably do it later once they've tried to exhaust Cody."

Jordan chuckled. "Good luck with that."

They spent a wonderful few hours with the scent of the ocean in their nostrils until too many stomachs began to rumble.

"Let's get all this stuff back to the car, and we can get some food while we're here," Bray said.

When they were finally seated at a table in Let's Talk Tacos, the scent of spices in the air, Bray realized how much he missed Mattie. Yes, they'd had fun, but it felt like part of him was missing whenever they were apart. Kit and Noah settled Cody between them, who preened from all the attention his "big brothers" were paying to him. Jordan and Bray sat on the other side of the table, holding Ama. They would have to think about bigger tables and stuff like that when they went out and about.

Jordan pulled his phone out once they'd ordered and smiled down at it. He typed something and put it back in his pocket.

"Everything okay?" Bray asked.

Jordan nodded. "Yep."

Bray glanced around the restaurant, meeting the gazes of several customers. Mixed expressions covered their faces, some disgusted, some kind, but he tried not to let it bother him. It was hard, especially with some comments they overheard. And it wasn't difficult to hear them. No one was being particularly quiet about their opinions. Bray could feel himself getting more and more angry as they waited for their food, and only Jordan's hand on his arm stopped him from blowing up. Even Kit and Noah could see he was reaching boiling point.

He inhaled and let it out, focusing solely on his family and trying to push away the voices. At least until one particular voice reached his ears.

"Fancy seeing you here," Mattie said, dragging a chair from a nearby table to settle at the end. "Hey, sweetpea. Have you had a good day?"

Mattie reached for Ama, who kicked her arms and legs as if she'd not seen him for days instead of hours, and if Bray was being honest, he felt like doing the same.

"I wasn't expecting to see you," he said instead of tackling him to the floor like he wanted.

"Jordan told me where you were, so I decided to leave the store in Kris's hands for a short time. See how he does without me." He bounced Ama on his lap.

"I've ordered for you," Jordan said. Bray frowned. When had he done that? "You don't really think all that food I ordered was just for me, did you?"

Bray shrugged. "I thought you were hungry."

Jordan laughed and kissed his cheek. "I am, but I couldn't eat that much."

They ate in relative peace, none of them able to completely ignore the comments and looks thrown their way. Nico came over and loudly apologised for people's behaviours, but it didn't stop it. In the end, Bray had enough.

"Enough," he muttered, pushing at Jordan so he could leave the booth.

Jordan rested a hand on his arm. "Wait." He glanced at Kit and Noah, who nodded.

Kit smiled at Cody. "Shall we get some ice cream?"

Cody's face lit up. "Yes, please!"

Kit slid out of the seat, Cody and Noah following, the latter reaching for Ama as they went.

"We'll be outside."

Jordan reached into Bray's pocket and retrieved his keys, handing them to Noah. "Thanks."

Noah glanced at him, but he was too angry to do anything other than vibrate and clench his fists.

"They have no right," Bray said.

Jordan cupped his cheeks, forcibly turning him to look at him. "They don't, but don't let them win, Bray. They want a reaction. They want something to gossip about. They want to see bad in us. Don't let them. We're better than that."

Bray inhaled and closed his eyes, letting Jordan's words reach deep inside him. Mattie's hand rested on his shoulder. He hated the idea of leaving things as they were, but Jordan was right. They'd only cause more gossip if he reacted.

"Let's go."

It took all of his control to get them out of the doors without responding to those comments, but it wouldn't be the last time. He was sure there would be more. He'd have to use his military-trained control to keep from blowing up at anyone because no one hurt his family. No one.

CHAPTER 22

MATTIE

MATTIE HADN'T MEANT TO LEAVE KRIS FOR AS LONG AS HE HAD, but when he'd heard the comments in the restaurant, he couldn't leave them. Bray, especially, needed him. Them. It wasn't fair to leave them to deal with it alone.

When they reached the car, Mattie slid his arms around Bray's waist, resting his head against his chest. "We're okay, Bray. It's just words."

Bray shuddered and exhaled into Mattie's hair. "It just pisses me off. They think they have the right to voice their opinions right to our faces, and it stinks."

"It does. But we're better than they are." Mattie lifted his head. "We know how we feel. How we want to live. Who we want to…" he swallowed, "love."

Bray's eyes widened as he looked down at Mattie, but there was no disgust or denial in his expression. Banked heat rose instead, and Mattie licked his lips. The words were on the tip of his tongue, but was now the right time?

"It doesn't matter what anyone else thinks," Jordan said, stopping beside them. "We're not hurting anyone."

Mattie slid one arm around Jordan, pulling him closer. He took a breath. "I love you," he whispered, making sure to look at them both. They stilled, staring at him. "I love you," he said again.

Jordan tucked his face into Mattie's neck, sniffing against his skin, and Bray stared at him. "How are you so brave?" he murmured, brushing his finger across Mattie's cheek. "I wish I had as much strength as you do."

Mattie's cheeks heated, but his brain didn't miss the fact that neither had said it back. He shoved down his disappointment. "I'm not brave. You have more strength than I do. There's no competition."

Bray shook his head. "I've wanted to say those words, but I kept thinking it was too soon. That there was no way I could feel that way about you both after such a short time. I was scared you'd reject me. So I kept the words inside." Bray shook his head again. "I love you, Mattie." He tugged at Jordan, whose face was red from his tears. "I love you, Jordan."

More tears flowed down Jordan's cheeks, and Mattie smiled so widely his jaw cracked.

"How can this be my life?" Jordan hiccupped. "You're both bloody amazing." He sniffed and wiped his face. "I love you both. We're all the same, you know. We all felt it but were too scared to say it. You, Mattie Evans, are the bravest man among us."

Mattie ducked his head, but Bray lifted his chin again. They shared a three-way kiss, and whistles sounded. Mattie chuckled and pulled away, his cheeks as hot as an oven. He glanced at Kit and Noah, who were jumping Cody and Ama up and down as they grinned. Whether they'd heard their declarations, Mattie didn't know, but they were happy all the same. And that was all that mattered.

"Now we have that out of the way, I have to get back to work. If I have a place to get back to," he muttered.

Dropping another kiss on each of their lips, he kissed Ama and said goodbye to everyone else. The walk worked off his leftover anger at the restaurant situation and he focused solely on their words. They loved him!

He entered the store with a skip in his step, bracing himself for disaster, but Kris was standing behind the counter, talking to a customer. Mattie smiled as he slipped to the back, letting Kris finish his conversation, though he couldn't help but overhear it.

"Personally, the satin is more comfortable, but some people like the feel of lace. It really is a personal preference. If you don't want to ask, I would go with the satin in the first instance." Kris glanced at him. "Do you agree?"

Mattie discussed the merits of the fabrics with the woman, and after she'd paid for the items she'd decided on and left, he turned to Kris.

"Sorry for taking so long. There was an…issue we had to deal with."

"It's okay." He gestured to the notepad beside the till. "I jotted down everything I sold just in case I did something wrong with the till. Hopefully, it all matches up."

"That's great. Thanks, Kris. You're doing brilliantly. You'll be running the place in no time."

Kris laughed. "That is the point, isn't it?"

Mattie joined him, laughing. "It is. I'm looking forward to having some extra time with my kids."

"I don't know how you do it," Kris said, reaching for his drink. "Small kids and running your own business. It's a lot."

"I wouldn't have it any other way, though. Not now."

The afternoon went quickly, and Mattie locked up, eager to get home to his family. Having three adults and four kids under one roof was chaotic, but he loved it. One day, they might have to consider moving to a bigger place. A two-bedroom house was not sufficient for the number of kids they had, even if they didn't stay with them all the time. The bus took its time, but eventually, he was on his way. He put his headphones on and closed his eyes, counting the stops so he knew when to get off without having to open them.

His eyes lit up when Jordan stood at the bus stop, waiting for him. He hadn't changed his clothes, even though a blob of meat juice had dropped onto his T-shirt at lunchtime.

"Hey. I wasn't expecting to see you."

Jordan slid his arms around him and kissed him. "I thought you'd want an update on Bray before we get home."

Mattie's heart jumped. "Is he okay?"

Jordan nodded. "He's calmed down a lot since lunch, but he's still angry."

Mattie sighed and snuggled into Jordan's side as they headed towards home. "I can understand it. It's never nice having people talk about us as if we're not there, but we can't stop them, as much as we might want to."

"One day, they'll find something else to talk about. It'll just take time until something else grabs their interest. I wish Bray could ignore it, but I suppose it's the same for us. If something upsets one of us, especially the kids, then the others will fight tooth and nail to make it better."

Mattie chuckled. "Papa Bear style."

"Without a doubt."

They dropped into silence until they reached the house, and Mattie went first, hearing laughter and conversation, and his heart exploded with joy. This was what he'd always dreamed of. This was what he wanted. A house full of people. Laughter, smiles, love. Everything that makes life worth living. He couldn't believe this was his life now. Even though Kit and Noah were short-term visitors, and Cody only came a few times a week, it was perfection, and Mattie didn't want anything to change it.

Jordan slipped past where he'd frozen with undoubtedly a sappy smile on his face and headed into the living room. Mattie slipped off his shoes, dropped his bag, and followed.

There was nothing that was more important than his family right now. Nothing.

"Ah, there he is," Kit said. "We wanted to know if you'd like us to babysit tonight so you three can go out for a bit?"

Mattie glanced at Bray and Jordan, who shrugged. "We said we'd leave it up to you," Bray said.

Looking around the living room, he inhaled and shook his head. "What I'd like is to spend the evening with you all. Together."

Kit raised his eyebrows, seemingly surprised, but Noah smiled. "Sounds good to me. Movie and popcorn?"

Mattie grinned. "How much are we all going to fight over what we're watching?" he asked Noah.

Noah snorted. "I guarantee it'll take a good hour or so to decide."

Mattie sighed and put his hands on his hips, faux annoyed. "Well, I'm going to leave that with you to decide. I'll take little madam and get the popcorn started." He stepped towards Bray, leaned down to kiss him before reaching for Ama. "Come on, little miss. You're never too young to learn how to make popcorn."

"Can I help?" Cody asked.

"Of course. The more the merrier."

They traipsed into the kitchen, and Mattie shook his head when voices raised almost immediately as they fought over what film they'd watch. He glanced at Cody, who frowned at the sound.

Mattie touched his shoulder. "They're not really mad, you know."

"No?" Cody peered up at him with wide eyes.

Mattie shook his head. "Nope. They're just pretending. When everyone wants to watch something different, it's diffi-cult to come to a compromise."

"What's a compromise?"

Mattie settled into a chair, giving Cody his full attention.

The popcorn could wait. "A compromise is when you decide between you what is the best thing to do. So, they're going to say which films they want to see, and then they'll go through and figure out which ones they definitely won't watch to make it so there are less to choose from. A compromise is someone deciding that maybe they don't mind watching something else because they'll get to watch it another time." It wasn't the best explanation, but Cody nodded, and Mattie hoped it was good enough.

"So it's like a negosh…negot…" Cody grumbled, tilting his head as he thought.

"Negotiation?" Mattie asked.

"Yes. Papa said I'm good at negotiating, which means he says one thing, then I offer a different thing instead."

Mattie chuckled. "Yes, it's similar, but not exactly the same." He side-eyed him. "You're getting good at negotiating, are you? I'm sure your dad loves that."

Cody preened. "He says I'm a live-wire."

Mattie laughed, startling Ama, who cried. He rested her against his shoulder. "Oh, sorry, sweetpea. Shh, shh. It's okay. I didn't mean to make you jump."

Cody stepped around him so he could see Ama's face. "It's okay, Ama. We're not arguing."

Mattie loved this little boy with all his heart. Every person in the house at that moment had taken a piece of the organ beating in his chest. He didn't want anything to change, but he knew it would. Kit and Noah would go back to university, Cody would go back to Ash, and Bray would go home. Only he, Jordan, and Ama would remain, and the house would feel empty. There would still be love surrounding them, but there'd be several pieces of his heart missing until they were all together again.

"Right, shall we get the popcorn started?" he said once Ama had settled again, eating her fist against his chest.

"Yes!" Cody punched the air. "What do we need?"

"First, a bowl. Then, popcorn."

Working together, they got several bags of popcorn popped and into large bowls, and they each carried one into the living room. He handed Ama to Jordan and went back for the other two bowls. It might've seemed like overkill, but he had the feeling every single kernel of corn would be gone before the film ended. Or even before it started, if Kit and Noah's crunching was anything to go by.

"What did you decide on?"

"*The Croods,*" Kit said, grinning.

"Sounds good to me." Mattie settled beside Jordan, who sat next to Bray. It was a bit of a squeeze on the sofa, but they managed. Cody sat beside Kit on the other sofa, and Noah settled on the floor, with his back resting against Kit's sofa, his legs stretched out towards the screen. It seemed he had control of the TV.

As the film started, Mattie watched his family instead of the film—he'd seen it a hundred times, anyway; it was one of Cody's favourites. Despite having only met Kit and Noah the previous evening, they seemed to have settled in with them well enough. Before they left the following day, he would make sure they knew they had a home here as well as with Bray, whenever they needed or wanted it. He intended for them to know they were just as part of the family as everyone else was, even if they were out of reach for most of the year.

Jordan leaned towards him, his mouth grazing Mattie's ear, making him shiver. "Everything okay?" he whispered.

Mattie nodded, meeting his gaze. "Perfect." He smiled, and Jordan kissed his cheek.

There would be plenty of tough times ahead of them, but at that moment in time, nothing else mattered. The outside world would still be there when they ventured away from the comfort of home, but, despite the looks, comments and actions of others, they were doing what was right for them. He hoped it would blow over quickly, mainly for Bray's sake.

He hadn't been the recipient of these types of actions before because he'd never come out before he'd started a relationship with Mattie and Jordan. Though he'd probably witnessed the "isms" of others, it hadn't been aimed his way. It must've come as a shock for it to happen now. But he'd be with him through it all and help him to understand that the best thing he could do was to protect them from inside their circle. Keep being with them. Spending time with them. Loving them.

That's all any of them could do. And when things got difficult, they'd have each other to lean on.

Ama banged her hand against Mattie's bowl, and he laughed.

Yes, he didn't want anything to change.

For the first time in a very long time, he was truly, completely happy.

CHAPTER 23

JORDAN

Jordan sighed, his shoulders lowering when he finally got back home with Ama. He'd had to run some errands that day, and even though it had been over a week, the comments and staring hadn't abated. Being under a microscope was straining, not perfect as Mattie had said. Although everything else about their relationship was.

Some people just couldn't keep their mouths shut, and it rankled.

"Never mind, sweetheart. We have each other. We don't need any nosey busybodies, do we?" He lifted her from the stroller and headed for the kitchen when the doorbell rang. "Well, whoever that is has good timing, don't they?"

He answered the door and hesitated. Anthony stood on the doorstep. "Anthony, hey."

Anthony gave a tight smile. "Good afternoon, Jordan. Can I come in?"

"Sure." He stood back and let Anthony in, closing the door behind him, his stomach churning. The social worker didn't seem happy for some reason. "Shall we go to the kitchen, and I can make us a drink?"

"Thanks."

Jordan wasn't sure what Anthony was there for, but it didn't seem like good news, whatever it was. He busied himself making a drink while Ama played on her playmat, alternately batting the toys hanging down from above her and shoving her fist into her mouth while gurgling happily.

He placed a drink in front of Anthony and settled opposite him. "Is something wrong?"

Anthony sighed. "We've had complaints about your relationship status, and as policy dictates, I have to look into it. I wanted to wait until after Mattie finished work, but I couldn't. Is there any chance you can call Mattie and get him home? Bray, too, please."

Jordan's heart rose to his throat, depriving him of air, but he nodded and reached for his phone. "Can I ask one thing, though?" Anthony nodded. "Are you taking her away?"

Anthony stared at him. "I don't think it'll come to that. I just need to calm people's complaints."

That wasn't exactly reassuring, but he called Mattie. "Hey."

"Hey, you. Everything okay?" Mattie asked.

"Anthony's here, and he needs you to come home."

Mattie was silent for a moment, and Jordan could imagine what was going around his head.

"I can't give her back, Jordan," he said hoarsely, and Jordan's eyes filled.

"I know. Come home, Mattie, and we'll get it squared away."

Mattie sniffed. "On my way."

He ended the call and wiped his face, swallowing hard. He dialled again. "Hey, Bray. Are you busy?"

"I'm just finishing a train for the hospital. Why?"

"Can you come over? We need to talk about Ama. Anthony's here."

Bray paused and sighed. "Sure. I'll be over soon."

"Thanks."

"Are you okay?" Bray asked.

Jordan gave a half-laugh, half-cry. "I will be."

"I'm coming, Jordan. Hold on for me."

He put the phone down and stared at his mug of coffee, suddenly not wanting to touch it.

"Don't be sad, Jordan," Anthony said. "I don't think the complaints have any foundations to them, but I have to look into it. And I can only do that when you're all together."

Jordan huffed a laugh, lacking the humor. "I can only imagine what some people are saying. After the comments and looks we've received this past week, it doesn't take a lot to guess where people's minds have gone."

"While we're waiting, talk to me, Jordan. Tell me about life with Mattie and Ama. And Bray. How does it all work for you?"

"We share everything. The night feeds, the childcare, the chores, the errands. We work around each other's jobs and we can still spend time with Ama. She's not passed from pillar to post without a care for who has her. Mattie's got help at the store now, so he'll be home more once Kris is fully trained. We're doing great, Anthony."

Anthony smiled. "It seems like it." He cradled his mug. "Personally, I can't see anything wrong with your setup, but as I said, I have to check."

They fell into silence while they waited for Mattie and Bray to show up. Jordan excused himself at one point to deal with Ama's dirty diaper, but then he made her a bottle and settled at the table to feed her. And that's where Mattie found them.

"What's wrong?" Mattie said immediately, facing Anthony. "Does Rhia want her back?"

Anthony shook his head and opened his mouth to answer when the door opened again.

"Where are you?" Bray called.

"Kitchen," Jordan answered, smiling down at Ama. "Daddy and Papa are here now."

Bray entered, looking entirely too good, even with the finger-ruffled hair and wide eyes. "What's this about?" he asked Anthony.

"Sit down and I'll go through everything with you."

Mattie settled beside Jordan, and Bray beside Mattie, reaching for his hand. They faced Anthony as one. A unit. Fighting for their family.

"So, I've received a few complaints, which, despite me knowing they won't be true, I still have to be seen to look into them."

"What complaints?" Bray asked.

Anthony sighed. "The main issues seem to center around your relationship rather than you being capable of looking after Ama. They're worried it's not a good environment for her."

"It's because we're a triad, isn't it? I'll stay away. I won't be the reason she's taken away from Mattie," Bray said.

Jordan's heart stopped and restarted at twice the speed. "No!" He glared at Bray. "That's not happening, Bray." He turned to Anthony. "What more could any child want than a good, healthy relationship to grow up with? We're in love, Anthony. What child wouldn't benefit from a loving family caring for them?"

"I agree. So now we need to get it on paper so we have proof. I'll be able to refute their claims with facts, since their issues are unfounded. I'm sorry to have worried you, but I needed to know. I'm certain your relationship is not going to harm her in any way. I know it, but I have to follow the law."

Mattie let out a big sigh. "I understand. You're just doing your job and looking after Ama's well-being. I would've preferred a little more information rather than having a heart attack on the journey home, but it's fine."

"You're sure it won't cause problems?" Bray asked, and

Jordan could feel his need to protect them coming to the forefront.

"It won't. People might not like it, but as long as I can prove that you're taking care of her and she's not in any danger, it doesn't matter what they think." He pulled a notepad from his bag. "Let's get it done, and we can get back to the things that matter most. Our kids."

They spent an hour and a half discussing things with Anthony, explaining every part of their lives, even the uncomfortable bits about their physical relationship. But once it was in writing, Anthony closed his notepad.

"We're done. I'm sorry to put you through this, but in some ways, it's helped tremendously with everything else. It'll help go through the courts quicker because I already have the information ready." He stood. "I'll be in touch if I need anything further, but you have nothing to worry about from the social services side of things."

Mattie exhaled, shoulders lowering. "Thank you. That was exhausting."

Anthony smiled. "I know, but you can spend the rest of your day with your family now, resting and recuperating."

Ama had been passed between the three of them during the talk, and now Bray had her, so Jordan stood to see Anthony out. The social worker said goodbye to them and headed for the door.

"I truly am sorry for the upset. If I could've done it any other way, I would've. Unfortunately, impromptu visits are a must."

Jordan nodded, though his heart still hadn't returned to its original, natural rhythm. "I understand. Maybe give us a couple of weeks before you do that again, though? Please." He was only half-joking.

"Understood. I'll talk to you soon."

Jordan closed the door behind him and rested his forehead against the door, needing a minute to get his equilibrium back. None of them had ever had to go through that situation before. The chance of having a child taken away was terrifying, and even though Ama wasn't his, it still hurt. He wasn't sure how Mattie had kept himself together during the conversation.

He turned around and slid down the door to the floor, bending his knees to rest his arms on. He stared ahead of him, not seeing anything, as tears tracked down his cheeks. He couldn't bear it if their relationship was the reason Mattie lost Ama. What Bray had offered was understandable, but they wouldn't cope without each other. Not now. He had to admit, though, that if that was the reason, Jordan would've offered the same. It was so unfair that people got to dictate what was right and wrong in the world. It burned that a triad was viewed as being less capable than a couple. Where was the logic in that?

"Jordan?" Mattie's voice broke through his thoughts, and he blinked at him as his best friend and boyfriend crouched beside him. "Are you okay?"

Jordan nodded. "I think it's the release of stress." He gripped Mattie's hand. "I was so scared for you."

Mattie gave a small smile. "I was, too. But Anthony is fair, and he works to the law instead of his opinions. Not many people can say that, I think."

Jordan blew out a breath. "God, I'm so tired."

"Come on." Mattie stood, gripping Jordan's hands. "Let's see what Bray's doing. I have an unexpected afternoon off, so I'm planning on making it worthwhile."

"You don't need to get back?" he asked as they headed down the hallway.

"Nope. I told Kris to do what he could and to call if he had any questions or problems. If he does call, I might need to go back, but I think he'll do fine. He's doing a great job so far."

When they entered the kitchen, Bray was holding Ama to

his shoulder with his lips against her head and tears in his eyes.

"Oh, Bray," Mattie said, tugging Jordan over to him. "Everything will be fine. Anthony will see to it."

"I wish I had your faith," Bray muttered.

Mattie straightened. "You said I was the brave one of us, so I'm being brave now. Everything will be fine. I promise."

Jordan knew he shouldn't promise things he had no control over, but it seemed to help Bray's mindset. They stuck close to home and cooked dinner together before getting Ama to bed. Instead of going back downstairs, they snuggled together in bed and put a movie on.

He hadn't thought he'd be able to sleep after everything that had happened, but he woke to gentle hands running across his skin. Somehow, he'd ended up in the center of them instead of to the side where he'd begun earlier that night. Two vastly different-sized hands slid up and down his chest, getting closer to his groin with each pass. They rubbed or flicked over his nipples each time they got near, sending arrows of heat to his groin. His cock filled, but he tried to keep his body relaxed. He enjoyed the sensations, the soft, slow rise of arousal that heated his blood and made his head spin.

It became too much when both bypassed his cock and moved onto his legs. He groaned, shifting his position to keep the slowly encroaching orgasm at bay. He'd never before believed he could climax without having had his cock touched or his ass reamed, but he could believe it was a possibility with what they were doing.

"Please," he whispered.

A soft, gentle hand wrapped around his cock, and Jordan's hips bucked of their own accord. He gasped into the dark room, wanting to hold on to both of his men, but unable to unclench his hands from the covers beneath him.

Mattie worked his shaft, stroking with a slight twist when

he reached the head and then back down again, making sure to brush his balls before repeating the action. Bray's hand slipped between his legs, leisurely smoothing against his taint before retreating.

The bed moved and warm, wet lips sucked both his nipples at the same time as they stroked and massaged him, and Jordan's orgasm rose.

"I'm so close," he muttered. "So close. So close." He couldn't help the chant. The heat built and built, pooling in his groin until Mattie flicked his tongue over his nipple, and Jordan crested, falling over the edge while contractions wracked his body. His mind blanked, his entire focus on his cock and the overwhelming climax tearing through him.

By the time he floated back to the bed, he was sure hours had passed. The sound of kissing met his ears, and he blinked, eyes immediately latching onto the vision before him. Bray and Mattie kissed as if their lives depended on it, but that wasn't all.

Their hands encircled each other's cocks, pumping frantically as they reached for what Jordan had already experienced. Deciding to help, he slid down the bed until his mouth was level with them, and he licked them both at the same time. They moaned into the other's mouth, and Jordan did it again, focusing on the sensitive bundle of nerves beneath the heads, and swiping his tongue over the slits to catch the precome leaking. They tasted divine. Not because the precome tasted nice—it didn't—but because it was his men.

Surprisingly, Bray was the first to break, his release flowing from his cock like a volcano. Mattie didn't take much longer, and his orgasm coated Bray's lower stomach. Jordan caught as much of each release as he could, licking off whatever he could reach. When they appeared like they were going to collapse, Jordan encouraged them to lie down. He wrapped them in his arms, their heads on his chest, and he sighed.

"Perfect," he whispered, echoing Mattie's words from the previous week.

If they were together, there was nothing they couldn't achieve. He was sure of that. No matter what was thrown their way, they would fight and survive. After all, if they didn't fight for their family and their relationship, who would?

No words were needed as they lay content after their releases, and Jordan listened until their breathing fell into the deep inhales and exhales of sleep. Then he followed them.

CHAPTER 24

BRAY

The concerns that Anthony had brought to their attention stayed in the back of Bray's mind, though he pretended it wasn't a big deal. It was easier to shove it all down and forget about it. Which was exactly what he did when he visited the hospital the following day.

He had a box full of wooden toys to hand out, and though he usually dropped them off with the child and then headed straight home, he found himself lingering with each child, talking about their favorite things.

"And superheroes are the coolest. Do you think they'd fit on the train?" the boy, Kevin, said as he ran his fingers over the wooden train Bray had made for him.

"I'm sure they'd be able to. They'd probably bring all their superhero friends and have a party," Bray said.

"That would be so cool."

Kids said what they meant, and it was why he was struggling with his thoughts. He'd been so annoyed that everyone was making comments about their triad relationship, but when he thought about it, wasn't that what everyone always encouraged? Telling the truth? Yeah, okay, adults learned tact —most of the time—as they grew older, but truth was something to be praised not beaten down. But there was a fine line between voicing their truthful opinions and being mean, and some adults just didn't get it.

But Bray needed to rethink things, too. He'd been so mad, trying to get them to be quiet because they deserved to live as they wanted to, that he'd forgotten people could say whatever they wanted because that was their right. Despite it being on that fine line, it was still their truth. At least until there could be some teaching about it. Bray couldn't do that, though. He didn't have the personality for it.

He pushed those thoughts aside again and focused on the children. The parents were overwhelmed with Bray's generosity, and he received more thanks than he needed. The children were as inquisitive as ever. A little girl had asked him what it was like to be strong. Another girl asked him what it was like to be a soldier. A little one asked him if he could sing. One child didn't say a word, and Bray found himself reading to them. Another wanted help with a jigsaw.

All in all, it was an adventure he'd never properly taken part in before, but he decided on his way home that he would do it more often. He dropped off his box of bits and checked the house. He hadn't been home as much as he usually would, opting to spend the nights with Jordan and Mattie, and he wanted to make sure everything was still secure. Once he was happy, he climbed back into his car and headed for Mattie's house—or Mattie and Jordan's house, now that Jordan had moved in.

Jordan was looking after Ama that day, and Bray dropped into Nice Buns to grab some goodies before he went to see them. He'd forgotten how much he loved babies, and he couldn't get enough of the little one. He also loved the time he got to spend with Cody, teaching him his woodwork. It was a precious time for him.

Jordan opened the door and grinned. "Look who's here, Ama. It's Papa." Ama reached her soggy hand forward, having just taken it from her drooling mouth, and Bray let her grab his finger as he stepped across the threshold and leaned down to kiss Jordan.

"Everything okay?"

Jordan smiled. "Everything's perfect."

"I brought treats for after dinner. I thought I'd cook lasagne tonight."

"Oh, be still my heart, a man who can cook." Bray raked his fingers through his hair, and Jordan chuckled. "As much as I love cooking, I'm happy for you to take over today. I'm tired, for some reason." He looked at Bray from the corner of his eye, a slight smirk on his face.

Playful Jordan was a handful—Mattie had warned him—but Bray loved it. Loved him.

"I can't begin to understand why you might be tired." He feigned ignorance and brushed past him to the kitchen. There were only a couple of hours before Mattie would be home, and Bray wanted the food ready to go.

He'd just put the lasagne in the oven for the last leg of its cooking journey when Mattie came in the door.

"Honeys, I'm home!"

Bray chuckled. Sometimes, Mattie was as bad as Jordan. He headed to the hallway, watching Jordan shove Mattie against the wall and *devour* him. Bray adjusted himself as he watched from beside the open living room door, so he could watch Ama, who was on her mat.

Mattie's phone interrupted them, and he pushed Jordan away so he could pull it from his pocket. He frowned. "Hello. Oh, hey, Anthony." He met Bray's gaze, worry bleeding into his eyes. "Yeah, I'm home now." He paused. "Okay, hold on." He pulled it from his ear and pressed the screen. "You're on speaker."

Anthony's voice came through loud and clear. "Okay, I wanted to let you all know the result of the investigation."

"You've finished already?" Mattie asked. "I thought it would take a lot longer."

"This is just the results of the complaints we received. The courts still have to confirm everything with Ama. I just thought we'd fast track the complaint so we don't have more worry on your plate than you need."

"Oh, okay." Mattie's forehead tightened.

"I'm pleased to say that we've found the complaints unfounded, and we won't be taking things any further. Mr Winters agreed with me when I met and discussed it with him this morning. We're putting everything through to the courts tomorrow, and then we just have to wait until they confirm everything. Once that's done, Ama is yours, free and clear."

"Any idea how long that could take?" Bray asked.

"It's really hard to say. They're pretty backed up, but we might get lucky. Anywhere from a couple of months to six months or more. I really couldn't even hazard a guess."

"Okay, thanks."

"On that note, I'm going to leave you to your evening, and I'm going to get to mine. I just wanted to let you know as soon as possible so you weren't stressing too much."

"Thanks, Anthony. We appreciate it," Jordan said.

They ended the call and stared at each other for a long moment before Mattie gave an enormous sigh. "It won't stop them talking," he said.

Bray shook his head and gave a small smile. "It won't, but I realized today that it didn't matter what they said. They only speak their truth, not ours. We live how we want to. That's all that matters now."

Jordan raised his eyebrows. "When did you get so wise?"

Bray chuckled. "The children at the hospital had a lot to say."

Mattie and Jordan frowned at him as if waiting for him to explain, but he shook his head, smiled and headed to Ama.

Dinner would be ready soon, and although Ama was too small to eat it just yet, she could join them at the table. It was never too early to instil routines. Jordan and Mattie were still in the same positions when he exited the living room, and he chuckled.

"Come on. Food's nearly ready."

———

"Please, Daddy! Please come with us. It'll be awesome. I promise. I'll do any of the chores you don't want to do. I promise. Please?"

Bray covered his mouth with his hand to hide his smile at Cody's begging for Mattie to come camping with them. He doubted even Cody could change Mattie's mind, but if anyone would be able to, it was him. Bray zipped up the bag he'd been packing and set it alongside the others in the hallway, ready for their weekend trip. He was going with Jordan and Cody this time, and Kit and Noah had said the next time they were down, they would come with them, too.

"I need to look after Ama, Cody. I can't come with you."

"I'm sure your mom wouldn't mind looking after her," Jordan said as he passed to put another bag with their haul.

Mattie glared at him, but Jordan pretended not to see. Cody, however, jumped on the excuse as Bray—and Jordan—knew he would.

"Yes! Please ask her. I love Ama, but I'd love for you to come with us." He clasped his hands to his chest, and if Bray wasn't already going, he would've caved at that.

Mattie's face was a picture. He could see his tenuous hold on his negative answer waver, and Bray turned away, knowing Mattie's reply before he even said it.

"Okay," he squeaked.

Cody jumped up and down. "Yes! Dad! Mattie's coming with us!" He raced off to the kitchen where Jordan was finishing packing the food. Their conversation was muted by the distance, and Bray crossed his arms over his chest, leaning on the arm of the sofa as he stared at Mattie.

Mattie's cheeks darkened. "I am not good at camping," he muttered.

Bray chuckled and wrapped him in his arms. "You'll be great. You have three pros at your fingertips. We won't leave you alone."

"You better not." Mattie slid his arms around Bray's waist and rested his head on his chest. Bray's arms automatically closed around him and a sigh the size of Gaynor Beach left his body. "Are you okay?" Mattie asked.

"Yeah. Everything's perfect."

Mattie smiled up at him. "I just need to find a babysitter now because I sure as hell don't think we should take Ama with us."

Bray laughed. "I agree, but I'm sure you'll have plenty of offers."

He was right. Mattie had several people who offered to take Ama for the weekend, but he settled on his sister, Lia, because she hadn't had as much time with the little girl as she wanted to because of her work schedule. When they'd packed Ama up and delivered her to Lia, they returned to fill Bray's car with camping essentials. Mattie stared at them open mouthed when he saw certain items, but neither of them told him what they were for. He'd find out when they were there.

As soon as they were ready, they climbed in—Jordan in the back with Cody, and Mattie in the front with Bray driving.

"It's nice to not have to borrow Dad's car all the time," Jordan said as Bray headed off.

"Why have you never got one of your own?" Bray asked.

Jordan glanced at Mattie and they both shrugged. "The bus is just as easy, and I had access to Dad's car when it wasn't. It seemed a pointless expense."

Bray nodded. "Fair enough."

Cody kept them entertained on the brief journey, going quiet when they got closer. Jordan leaned between the seats and whispered, "He likes to look around when he gets here. It's the only time, other than when he's asleep, that he's quiet." He winked, and Bray and Mattie chuckled.

Bray parked where Jordan told him to, and they climbed out. Bray stood, hands on hips, and inhaled, closing his eyes to relish the scent of the forest, the sounds of the animals he could hear, the distant ocean crashing against the cliffs. The difference between camping here and when he'd "camped" in the desert while he was in the military was massive. For one, he wasn't fearing for his life every second of the day.

He opened his eyes, squinting against the sunlight again, and glanced at his companions. His family. When Kit and Noah came, Noah would probably hate every minute, but he would do it for Kit. Had done it for Kit.

"Are we ready to work?" Bray asked.

Cody clapped his hands. "Yeah!"

Jordan ruffled his son's hair, making Cody duck out of reach, and Mattie just sighed and stared at him. "I suppose."

Bray grinned. "Cheer up. You'll be fine."

"Uh-huh."

Chuckling, Bray opened the trunk and started handing out equipment. He gave Mattie the stove and the cooking things because he had a feeling he wouldn't have a clue about setting up a tent. Jordan and Cody took one tent, and Bray took the other. They'd agreed that Cody and Jordan would share one and Mattie and Bray would share the other. They didn't have a big enough one to house the four of them, but Bray would make sure they did the next time. Especially if his sons were coming. There were six-person tents available, so he'd grab one when they got home.

They worked steadily, Bray enlisting Mattie's help with the tent when he stood watching them with wide eyes.

Finally, they were set up with sleeping bags and pillows in the tents, ready for bedtime.

"Right. I think it's time for fishing," Jordan said. "We need to catch our dinner."

Mattie's eyes widened, but he said nothing as he followed them to the place Jordan had always used. Jordan, Cody and Bray settled in with fishing lines, and Mattie stood behind them, staring at the water. Tension held his body still, and Bray wondered what was wrong. He grabbed Mattie's hand and tugged him to him, but Mattie resisted, stepping further away from the edge of the water.

Bray frowned. What was wrong? He pulled his fishing line free and rested it on the ground, moving closer to Mattie.

"What's wrong, sweetheart?" he said, slipping his arms around Mattie's waist. Mattie trembled like a newborn foal, holding Bray in a death grip as his breath sawed in and out of his lungs. "Shh, shh. Talk to me, Mattie."

"I'm not a fan of water. Any expanses of water. If I can't touch the ground, I'm not going near it. I can put my feet in the ocean because I'm still on solid ground, but anything deeper—no way."

"Why didn't you tell me? We could've stayed with the tents." Bray rubbed his hand up and down Mattie's back, trying to soothe him as much as he could.

"I didn't want to ruin things."

Bray tipped Mattie's head until their gazes met. "You'll never ruin anything if you tell us your feelings, Mattie. Does Jordan know?"

Mattie nodded. "He also knows I try to fight it if I can. I won't go in the water, but I won't avoid it completely." He cleared his throat. "Unless it's the pier."

Bray tilted his head. "The pier?"

Mattie's cheeks darkened, and he lowered his eyelids, avoiding Bray's gaze. "You know the ghost stories?" he whispered, and Bray knew it was to stop Cody from hearing. Bray nodded. "I saw something when I was a kid. Something I couldn't explain then and certainly can't explain now." He peered up at him. "It made me leery."

Bray tucked him against his chest. He'd heard the stories. Who hadn't? He'd never experienced anything himself, but Mattie obviously had.

"What did you see?" he couldn't help but ask.

CHAPTER 25

MATTIE

Mattie shuddered. He hated remembering, but he wanted to tell Bray. Explain why he was so scared of the water. He just had to not make himself look like a fool in the process.

"I saw the woman on the rocks," he whispered. "Clear as you are to me now, she was there. At first, I thought it was a parent, and I was about to shout to warn them it was slippery and to be careful." He shook his head. "I don't know why I felt the need to say it because a grown-up would've known that." He sighed. "The next minute, she stared right at me, smiled and disappeared. As I was watching. She disappeared into nothing as I was watching her."

He shivered again, tucking his face back into Bray's solid warmth. Bray's arms tightened around him, and his cheek rested against the top of Mattie's head.

"That must've been scary."

"I've never been in water since. Not fully. I just can't bring myself to do it." He chuckled, though it was without humor. "I'd love to go on a boat, but I can't do it. Something about her made me leery of water and anything on the water from that moment forward."

"Did you tell anyone?"

He shook his head. "Only Jordan. I was sure the other kids would tease me about it, so I kept it quiet."

"Well, if you ever want to try to get rid of that fear of the water, just let me know. We'll all do anything we can to make you feel better about it, okay?"

Mattie lifted to his toes and kissed him. "Thank you."

"I think we have enough now. Even though the slackers over there were too busy chatting to help," Jordan said, and from his tone, he was trying to relax the mood a bit.

"Why do you need us if you've managed so well?" Mattie shot back, mouth twitching.

Jordan squinted at him and huffed. "Come on, Cody. We get to eat first as we did all the hard work."

They picked up their fishing lines, and as Jordan passed Mattie, he brushed his lips against his temple. "I love you, sweetheart."

Mattie grinned. "I love you."

Jordan winked and continued chatting with Cody about school that week. Mattie helped Bray to carry the tackle box, and they followed.

Dinner was a raucous affair. Jordan and Cody told stories about what had happened to them on previous camping trips, and Mattie tried not to be horrified that he hadn't known half of what they'd been up to.

"You left all this out when you told me about camping before!" Mattie said, glaring at Jordan.

"You would've stopped us from coming again." Jordan was unrepentant.

"I would've, yes! For god's sake, Jordan. A wolf?!"

Jordan waved him away. "It's not out of the reach of possibility, but it doesn't happen often. Not here."

Mattie glanced around him, studying the shadows that were lengthening as the sun set. He hated the idea of being out there when unknown things were prowling around. Whoever thought this was fun needed to have a reality check.

After they packed everything away for the night, they said goodnight to Cody and Jordan, and Mattie's body tingled. They'd discussed their sleeping arrangements before they'd left, and Jordan had told them he was fine if they wanted to fool around—quietly—while they were away. Jordan wouldn't join them because he wanted to stay with Cody, but he'd said he was fine with Mattie and Bray being together without him. Bray had whispered in Mattie's ear after that conversation, "We can make it up to him when we get home."

Mattie's body trembled, a low-level buzz with the knowledge he and Bray were going to do something in their tent.

But what?

"Come on, Mattie," Bray said, clasping his hand. "Time for bed."

His voice had lowered to a soft growl, and goosebumps flowed over every inch of Mattie's skin. Tripping over his own feet, he followed Bray into their tent. He settled on the sleeping bag while Bray closed the zip, and then Bray turned, and Mattie bit his lip to stop the moan from escaping at his expression.

"I'm going to make you change your mind about camping," Bray promised, kneeling in front of him.

Mattie opened his mouth to respond, but Bray slammed their mouths together, and he lost himself in the kiss. When they finally pulled apart, Bray rested their foreheads together, and Mattie relished the contact.

"Take your clothes off," Bray murmured, pulling back from him. Their eyes met, and Bray unbuttoned his shirt.

Mattie licked his lips and grabbed the hem of his T-shirt. The fabric made his body sing as it brushed against his sensitive nipples. He wanted to reach across the distance between them and follow the valleys and hills of Bray's abs. He wanted to bite on his full lower lip. He wanted to wrap his hand around his cock and watch as the pleasure became more than his control could handle. But instead, he stripped, his gaze returning to Bray's body every time more skin was exposed.

When they were both naked, chests heaving with the weight of each other's stares, Bray's arms slid around Mattie's waist, drawing an inhale from him, and laid him down. Bray's massive body braced over him, and Mattie had never felt more loved. Both Bray and Jordan looked after him in ways he'd never imagined anyone wanting to do. They loved him, and he loved them. And despite the unusual aspect of their relationship, they were happy, which was all that mattered.

Bray cradled Mattie's face, lowering his head for a kiss. A soft, slow exploration that sent Mattie's head spinning. Luckily, he was already on the ground because, otherwise, his knees wouldn't have held him up. He gripped Bray's wrists, needing something to center him as Bray drove him wild with his lips and tongue.

After a long time, when Mattie's lips had gone past bruised, Bray's hand slipped down Mattie's back to his ass, squeezing the cheek and pulling him closer until their groins met. Both their cocks were straining, and the extra friction brought a moan from Mattie's mouth.

"Shh, sweetheart. We have to be quiet," Bray whispered.

Mattie blinked at him. Quiet? Who the hell could be quiet when they're being touched like that?

Mattie lifted a leg over Bray's hips, thrusting to get more, but Bray stayed his hips with his hand.

"Patience."

Bray kissed him again and then manoeuvred him to his other side, so his back was against Bray's chest. Mattie looked over his shoulder with an eyebrow raised.

Bray's mouth descended to his ear. "This way, I can put my hand over your mouth and stifle your cries."

Mattie's eyelids fluttered closed, and the breath punched

from his lungs. A click brought his attention back, and he glanced at Bray again.

"Just going to get you ready, sweetheart. Relax for me." His voice was still low.

Bray pushed Mattie's upper leg over so he was partially on his front. It exposed his ass, and heat bloomed inside him as being so open. Bray's lips found his shoulder as his finger found his pucker, and Mattie closed his eyes, losing himself in the sensations bombarding him. Bray's finger slipped inside him, stretching him, though he wouldn't need a lot. Another finger slid inside. The burn was welcomed, however brief. He bit his lip, trying to keep the sounds inside.

By the time he was fully stretched, sweat covered his skin that had nothing to do with the temperature of the area and everything to do with Bray's ministrations.

"Please, Bray," he whimpered.

Bray's fingers left him, and cool air replaced Bray's body against Mattie's back for a short time. Then Bray returned, and the head of his cock pressed against Mattie's entrance. He bore down, wanting Bray inside him. *Needing* Bray inside him.

Mattie groaned, and Bray slipped his arm beneath him, sliding his hand over Mattie's mouth.

"Keep quiet. Not one sound. Understand?"

Mattie nodded and breathed through his nose, trying to swallow the sounds he desperately wanted to make. When Bray's groin met his ass, they both sighed. Bray's forehead rested against his shoulder while they paused, Mattie getting accustomed to the welcome intrusion.

Mattie mumbled against Bray's hand, which tightened over his mouth. But Bray understood because he withdrew slowly, dragging his shaft over every nerve ending Mattie had in his channel. He slid deep again, painstakingly slow, but silently. No sound at all. Not even a rustle of the sleeping bags beneath them.

He continued the rhythm, going so slowly that Mattie thought he'd lose his mind. He was ready to combust when Bray pushed him further onto his front and lay on top of Mattie, squashing him, but not in a bad way. Bray's cock slid in and out, in and out, and Mattie buried his face in the fabric of the covers, muffling his sounds. Bray didn't increase his speed, and Mattie knew it was because the sound of slapping skin would carry through the tent to the other one, and Cody might hear. Jordan definitely would. He was probably listening for any sounds. The idea made Mattie impossibly harder.

So Mattie let Bray have his way. The slow build-up to their orgasms was a brutal test of his stamina, and when he finally let his climax claim him, the waves of pleasure cascaded over him like he assumed the waves of the ocean would. The harsh tugging of his endurance. Could he take more, or would he pull away from more? Positioned as he was, there was nothing he could do to stop Bray from taking everything his body could give him. And Mattie loved it.

Bray's release received a quiet growl low in his chest, and Mattie tucked the sound away to remember another time. Bray rested his head against Mattie's back, panting against his skin, and when he finally pulled free, Mattie wanted to drag him back again, but he was pleasantly exhausted.

"Feeling better?" Bray asked when he returned to his side.

"Mmm," Mattie said.

———

Two days later, Mattie could honestly say he was sad they were leaving the campsite. It had proved to be more enjoyable than he'd originally thought, even if he didn't include the sexy nighttime shenanigans he and Bray had. They had plenty of things to tell Jordan when they got home and no little ears were around.

After finally arriving home and unpacking the car, they picked up Ama from Lia's house.

"Hey, sweetpea. Have you been a good girl for Auntie Lia?" Mattie said, cradling his daughter close to his chest while he breathed in her scent.

Lia chuckled. "She's been an angel. A little spoiled, but that's what aunties are supposed to do."

"I didn't expect any different."

"Ama!" Cody said, stopping beside him. He brushed his hand across her head ever so gently, smiling at her like she was the sun and he was a daffodil.

"Thank you again for having her," Mattie said.

"No problem at all. Did you have fun?" Lia raised her eyebrows, no doubt expecting him to say no.

"I actually did. It must've been the company." He met Bray's gaze and felt his cheeks heat, so he turned away again.

"Uh-huh." Lia stared at him, a grin on her face. "I can imagine." She scrunched her face. "Actually, scrap that. I don't want to."

"Yes, please don't."

"Hey, princess. Are you coming to Dad?" Jordan said, holding his hands out to Ama. She kicked her legs, and they laughed, Jordan taking her. "Shall we get you in the car?"

"I'll bring her stuff out in a minute."

"Dad, why do I have to go home now? I've hardly seen Ama," Cody said as they wandered out of the door.

"He adores her, doesn't he?" Lia said.

Mattie nodded. "He truly does."

Lia pulled him in for a hug. "You've never seemed unhappy, but now I can tell the difference in you. You are so in love with them and content, it makes me nauseous." She chuckled as he backhanded her shoulder. "I'm so happy for you."

"Thanks, sis."

The truth was, he was happy for himself, too. Lia had

made a valid point. He'd never been truly unhappy, but he'd always wanted someone to share his life with. Someone to cuddle with on the sofa at night. Someone to share the woes of life. Someone to lean on him if they needed to. And now he had two someones, and he hoped, to the very bottom of his soul, that they would stay together for years to come.

After he'd said goodbye to his sister, he climbed in the car, and Cody grinned. "I'm staying at your house tonight."

Mattie had known Jordan would cave, but he hadn't believed Ash would let him. "I'm glad. You'll get to see Ama in the morning before school."

"I know! I've told all my friends about her."

Mattie's heart expanded just a little more at the acknowledgement, and he smiled at Cody. "I'm glad you're happy, Cody."

He shared a glance with Bray, whose smile stretched across his face. "Ready for fun times tonight?" he murmured.

Mattie coughed, trying to cover the laughter at his words. "As long as we keep quiet, yes."

Jordan leaned between the seats. "What was that about being quiet?"

"Nothing," they both replied, dissolving into chuckles when Jordan cursed at them.

Mattie inhaled and watched the scenery as Bray drove them the short distance home. One day, Bray might want to consider Mattie's home his own, but they'd barely known each other for a month. He would let Bray know he was always welcome by giving him a key so he could come and go as he pleased, but he doubted Bray was ready to move in. And that was okay. They were together a lot of the time, but Bray had his own family, his own house. They had years ahead of them, and nothing needed to be rushed.

Despite Mattie wanting everyone under his roof at once.

"Penny for them?" Bray murmured.

Mattie stared at him. "One day, we're all going to live together, aren't we?"

Bray glanced at him, studying his face for a few seconds before returning to the road. "We are."

That was all the reassurance Mattie needed.

CHAPTER 26

JORDAN

Before they knew it, Halloween had crept up on them. They had gotten themselves into a routine of balancing work life and home life, plus childcare and still having time for themselves as a triad. It wasn't easy, but then Jordan had never thought to do things the easy way. Comments and mutterings had died down to a manageable level, but there was still the odd one who thought they had the right to poke their noses in. They were easily ignored, though. Especially when other residents now came to their defense.

The previous month, they'd attended a kids' get-together, meeting up with other parents and children for fun and games, and it seemed to help other people see them and get to know them better. After that, there were fewer comments, though they were still not completely free and clear.

Ama was five months old and into everything. Jordan thought she'd be walking within the next few months with how fast her crawling was. It wouldn't take her long when Cody was showing her the ropes all the time. On top of all the other things Anthony had helped them with, he'd been in contact with Rhia, Ama's aunt. Rhia had sent some photos to him for Ama, and he'd given them to Mattie at the party. It was way outside of his duties, but he must've known how important it was to them. Ama now had a small photo album with pictures of her mama.

That night, they were all going out trick-or-treating, and they had the cutest outfits to wear. Mattie had persuaded them all to dress up—including Bray—and it was going to be epic. Mattie was a ghost—not much paler than he usually was. Jordan was a vampire because who didn't love them? Bray was the big bad wolf because…muscles. Cody had decided on a monster outfit, though he chose to have a mask instead of face paint because he wanted to take it off if Ama got scared. And little Ama was the devil. The cutest, squishy-ist devil known to mankind, but a devil, none-theless.

Kit and Noah hadn't been able to make it because they had an event to attend, but for their first Halloween together, it was looking good. They were going around to their friends' and families' houses to grab candy. Jordan wasn't sure how Ama was going to react to the decorations and noises, but there were enough of them to take her if she didn't like it.

"Are you ready?" he asked Ama, tickling her tummy. She giggled, and his heart soared.

"Let's go!" Cody said.

Jordan went out first, wanting to see Cody's reaction to what Bray had done to the car, and he wasn't disappointed. Bray had decorated it with skulls and pumpkins and all other kinds of paraphernalia, and Cody's expression was priceless.

"Wow! This is awesome!"

Bray hadn't been sure he would be allowed to drive the car with so many items on it, but he'd checked with a police officer at the station and had been given the go-ahead for a one-off journey to their families' homes.

Piling into the car, they set off for door number one. Jordan's parents were expecting them, of course, but they didn't know what they were dressed as. Jordan tried not to scratch at his face paint, which was itchy as hell, and Cody knocked on the door with Ama beside him in Mattie's arms.

"Trick or treat!" Cody said when the door opened.

"Oh, my!" Ronnie said, covering her heart with her hand. "We've got some scary people at the door, Carl! Whatever will I do?"

Jordan's father came up behind her. "Give them sweets, and they might leave us alone." He held out a bowl full of sweets. "Please don't hurt us, monster," he said, pretending to be scared.

Jordan tried not to smile at the overly fake responses, but Cody grinned and took a handful of sweets.

"You gave us treats, so we won't trick you," Cody said in a low voice.

"Oh, thank you so much!" Ronnie said, wiping her forehead. "I was scared I wouldn't see my grandchildren again."

Cody took off his mask. "It's me, Grandma!"

"Oh my word, Cody. I thought you were a monster." Ronnie tugged him into a hug. "That outfit looks wonderful." She looked around at them. "You all do." She tickled Ama's cheek, making the little girl kick her legs. "You're too adorable to be a devil." She stink-eyed Mattie.

Mattie shook his head. "Wasn't my idea. Blame your son."

Ronnie raised her eyebrows at him. "Really?"

Jordan looked at his nails, avoiding her gaze. "Both outfits are quite apt, thank you."

Ronnie and Carl gasped, and Bray and Mattie withheld their chuckles. Just.

"Anyway, time to go!" Jordan said with fake cheer, turning everyone to face the car. "More people to scare."

"Bye, Grandma, Grandpa. See you at the weekend!" Cody called.

Their next destination was Dante's house. Cody was a little hesitant to knock on this one. He'd met Dante and his boyfriend several times, but they didn't see as much of him as other people. Imposing as he was, Dante filled the doorway when he opened the door, and Cody stepped back.

"Trick or treat!" Bray said.

Dante glanced at his former boss and rubbed his hand over his lips. Jordan thought he saw a smile escape, but he wasn't sure because when Dante removed his hand, his face was straight.

"I think I have just the thing to feed monsters and devils on." He held out a pumpkin full of chocolate. "Eat your fill."

Cody hesitated for a second and then stuck his hand in the pumpkin. He took a couple of chocolates. "Thank you, Dante."

"You're welcome, Mr Monster." Dante flicked his gaze to Bray again, and his mouth twitched. "Have a good evening, guys."

Jordan led the way back to the car, hearing the first part of Bray's conversation with Dante.

"Is there another reason I need to call you Pack?" Dante asked.

"Hey, I do what I'm told. I—"

Jordan couldn't hear anymore, but he laughed, and Mattie frowned at him. So he explained what he'd heard. "I never thought about the werewolf being classed as a dog."

Mattie chuckled. "Me neither."

Their evening continued. They visited Mattie's parents, Lia, Radar and Freer, and then they headed for Bray's house, where his mom was staying for a couple of days. She'd been quite poorly for the past few weeks and had only just started recovering from bronchitis. But she was on the mend and had wanted to make the journey to see the kids on Halloween.

Cody ran to the door, pounding on it. "Trick or treat!"

The door flew open, and two ghosts and a dog stood there. Jordan frowned. The ghosts hadn't been part of their plan.

"Who said you could knock on our door?" they said, and Jordan glanced at Bray, whose mouth gaped.

Cody glanced at Jordan, who recovered and nodded. "I said so. I want candy!"

Laughter beneath the outfits. "You want candy, huh? Well, it just so happens… Come on in. If you dare." Roscoe barked.

Cody hesitated again but then straightened and stalked through the door. They went to follow him, but the ghosts stood in their way. They plucked Ama from Mattie's arms and closed the door, leaving them on the wrong side of it.

"Don't give them too many sweets!" Bray called. He sighed and shook his head. "I wasn't expecting Kit and Noah to be here."

"This was obviously the event they said they had to attend. People sure can keep a secret when they need to," Mattie said. "It's nice of them to make the trip. I know it's not easy for them."

"They'd do anything for their brother and sister," Jordan said. "And you both know it."

The door flung open again, and Cody came barrelling out. "Pops, can Kit and Noah have a sleepover?"

Kit's laughter followed. "Cody, we're having a sleepover with Nana, remember? We'll see you tomorrow after school, though, and for the weekend."

Cody punched the air. "Yes!"

Noah had removed his outfit and was cradling Ama. "We'll take Nana back with us to save you a trip."

"You don't have to. I don't mind."

"We know. But we're going that way, anyway. Seems like a good idea."

"Why are you all standing out there? I want to see what you look like!" Paula shouted, ending her sentence with a cough that rattled the windows.

Bray and Jordan shared a glance. They had all been worried about Paula's health, but she was stubborn and unwilling to accept more help than she already had. At some point, they were going to have to put their foot down about getting her seen by a doctor again. But for the moment, they trudged into the house and sat down with a drink for a quick chat.

When it got closer to bedtime, and even though enough sugar had been consumed by a certain eight-year-old boy that Jordan doubted he would sleep anytime soon, they said goodbye and headed home. Ama fell asleep in the car, and Cody talked a mile a minute, describing all the outfits they'd seen and the differently decorated houses along the streets. Gaynor Beach had plenty of autumn and Halloween events going on, but this year, they'd wanted to keep it to just family. When Ama was a little older, they would venture out further and visit the Fright Night or Oktober-fest, but not yet.

When Cody had finally settled into bed—crashing and burning was a tame word for what he did; it was more like his body shut down mid-sentence—Jordan, Mattie and Bray headed downstairs to watch TV on their new bigger sofa. One that comfortably held the three of them without feeling squashed.

They were in the middle of *The Nightmare Before Christmas* when Mattie suddenly said, "I want to go on a boat."

Jordan stared at him for a long second. "What?"

Mattie pushed himself to a sitting position from where he'd been lying on Bray's thighs. "I want to go on a boat. Maybe not on the ocean. Maybe somewhere a bit calmer, to begin with. It's time I faced my fears. I don't want them to stop me from being able to do something with the kids. They'll want to go in the water. They'll want to go on a boat. Where I am at the minute, I won't be able to take them. I want to be able to."

Jordan pulled him into his arms, pressing his lips to his temple. "You are amazing, Mattie Evans. And yes, I'm sure we can arrange something for you. We know enough people between us."

"Dante has a boat. Maybe we can go over and see it, stand on it, before it even hits the water," Bray added.

Mattie nodded. "Sounds like an idea." He let out a shaky breath.

Jordan chuckled. "How long were you keeping those words inside?"

"Um, a while," Mattie hedged.

"Would it be easier or harder if we took the kids with us?" Bray asked. "I ask because I'm not sure if you would be calmer if they were there or if they weren't."

Mattie shrugged. "I don't really know. I might be more agitated if I thought something would happen to them. But I might also forget about myself because I'm thinking about them. I don't know."

"We can always take them to see the boat while it's not on the water, and then just go with us when we do it on water," Bray said.

"That sounds like a plan." Mattie paused and covered his face with his hands, groaning. "Oh, god. We have a plan."

Jordan laughed and tucked him into his side. "We do, and it'll be great."

And it was. When Mattie first stepped onto the boat while it was still out of the water, he smiled so widely that Jordan thought he'd break his jaw. That smile dimmed a little when he climbed on when it was on the water, but he had been so brave that day. Jordan and Bray had taken him to get ice cream afterwards, and though he'd protested feeling like a kid, Jordan could see he loved it.

It was a different matter when Dante offered to do a short run from the marina to the pier and back.

"I don't think I can," Mattie said, his legs shaking so much they barely kept him upright as he held onto the side of the boat with both hands.

Jordan crouched beside him. "If you're not ready, that's fine, Mattie. We'll try another day."

It was the first clear day they'd had for days, which was why they thought they'd try it. With the days creeping in on Christmas, they wouldn't get as many days where they could go out on the water. But they'd wait if Mattie needed to.

"No, we won't," Bray said. He grasped Mattie to him, dragged him to the seat at the back of the boat, and sat, holding Mattie in a tight grip. "Dante, go."

Jordan opened his mouth, but Bray shook his head slightly. Knowing Bray was doing the right thing made Jordan feel better, but Mattie might not think so.

"No! I'll get off. We can—"

"Dante," Bray said.

The engine roared, and they set off, slowly at first, but Jordan's heart broke as Mattie sobbed into Bray's chest. Most people would think they were cruel to do it to him, but they knew Mattie. They knew what he could cope with, how he would deal with things, and this was the best option to get him outside of his head and in the moment. If left to his own devices, he would never take the step to get them out on the water.

Jordan watched the two of them, ready to jump in should Mattie look like he was about to throw Bray overboard. Bray whispered to Mattie, and Mattie sobbed, but there was no anger between them. Mattie's grip on Bray's T-shirt loosened first, and then his eyes opened. He winced when they went over a wave with a small bump, but he lifted his head from Bray's chest and looked around.

"Keep hold of me," Jordan heard over the wind and engine.

"I'll never let you go."

Jordan moved closer and settled on Mattie's other side, placing a hand on his thigh. "How are you doing, sweetheart?"

Mattie stared around them, a small smile curving the edges of his mouth. "I'm on the ocean. I'm on a boat on the ocean."

Jordan smiled. "You are. What do you think?"

"It's louder than I expected, even though I'd heard the engine before." Mattie let go of Bray, though Bray kept his arm around his back.

The joy on Mattie's face rivaled kids on Christmas Day. When they reached the pier—or level with it—Mattie's joy dimmed a bit, and Jordan realized that was where he'd seen the woman when he was a child. Jordan squeezed his thigh, and Mattie smiled at him, nodding as if replying to an unasked question. Dante turned the boat around in a wide arc, and they headed back to the marina. They didn't talk, just let Mattie experience his first boat ride.

When Dante cut the engine a short time later, he hopped off and waved, giving them the space they needed.

And it was a good job he did. Mattie stood with their help, and when his legs finally held themselves, Mattie punched Bray on the arm.

"Don't do that again, mister!"

Jordan rolled his lips inwards, trying not to laugh, but then Mattie's ire was thrown his way. "And you! You never stopped him! I could've died!"

At that, Jordan couldn't withhold his laughter anymore. "You could not."

"I could've had a heart attack. I was so scared!"

Jordan stepped closer. "But you did it, Mattie. You did it."

Mattie paused and then threw his arms around them both. "Thank you. I don't think I ever would've agreed to go on the water if you hadn't kidnapped me."

They all laughed, and Jordan met Bray's gaze over Mattie's head. "Thank you," he mouthed.

Bray winked.

CHAPTER 27

BRAY

Christmas Day dawned far too early for Bray's new regime. Being out of the Army had made him soft and a sucker for a lie-in despite him trying not to be. Unfortunately, with a house full of kids and presents ready to be opened, an early wake-up call was the least of his worries. Noise, food, sugar rushes, and socializing were the expectations of the day. As long as Bray got coffee along the way, he was all there for it.

Despite it being Mattie's house, both Mattie's and Jordan's moms had decreed they would take over the kitchen to cook dinner. For once, Mattie hadn't minded, even though he loved everything in its place and preferred to keep things just right. Maybe the idea that cooking would take time away from the kids had made him rethink.

"Has Santa been?" Cody whispered in a not-so-whispered way.

Jordan lifted his head and groaned, obviously seeing the five o'clock timestamp. "Cody! You've never woken this early on Christmas Day before," he grumbled, rolling over towards his son.

"But it's different this year! It's Ama's first Christmas!"

Bray's heart expanded for the little boy who had welcomed them all into his life without a care. He was the best big brother anyone could've asked for, but woe betide anyone who upset Ama when she was older. Having three big brothers would be hell for her, not to mention having three dads.

Bray swung his legs over the edge of the bed and rubbed his face. "I'll take him down to get some breakfast while you two get up." He shoved his legs into some joggers and ruffled Cody's head. "Ama's not awake yet, so you get an early breakfast and some TV time until she is. Deal?"

Cody nodded and followed him down the stairs. Cody didn't believe in Santa anymore, but he was happy to pretend for Ama's sake, even though Ama was far too young to understand.

Bray set the coffee machine going and put a pan on the stove. "French toast?"

Cody slid into a chair at the table. They had a small TV installed on the wall near it so the kids could watch a bit of TV with their breakfast in the morning. It seemed the easiest way to get Cody moving on a school day. "Yes, please."

How the kid was not bouncing around the room, wanting to check out his presents, was a mystery to him. He'd always been the first to race into the living room on Christmas morning when he was younger, so Jordan had told him. The boy had made some small wooden animals for both Mattie and Jordan as his projects during his whittling lessons with Bray. And from the latest report from his school, the bullying seemed to have ended. Whether it would stay that way, he wasn't sure, but he hoped so.

Bray got everything ready and had just taken a sip of his coffee when Jordan and Mattie entered, looking far more put together than he was. Jordan slipped his arms around Bray's waist and kissed between his shoulder blades.

"Sorry I was grumpy," he said.

Bray chuckled. "I'll let you off, as it's so early."

"Are Kit and Noah awake?" Mattie asked.

"I've not heard or seen them yet, so I'm not sure."

"I'll check!" Cody said, slipping off the chair and heading for the living room where Bray's sons had slept the previous evening.

Bray paused, waiting for the inevitable sound when Cody saw the mountain of presents, but when it didn't come, he frowned. Moving the pan off the stove, he put down his coffee and went to the living room. Cody stood there with his mouth open, staring at the presents, instead of checking on Kit and Noah. His sons were staring at Cody with identical grins, each already dressed and ready for the day. Unfortunately, Noah's relationship had fizzled out, and he was there alone, but he'd find someone. So would Kit.

"Santa's been," Cody whispered.

Bray chuckled and turned around, smiling at the sight of Mattie and Jordan behind him. "I think he's overwhelmed."

"Yeah, well, everyone went a little overboard this year, I think," Jordan said just as a soft knock sounded at the front door. He frowned. "Who's that?" He headed for the door, and Bray went back to the kitchen to finish breakfast for the masses.

Conversation floated down the hallway and then a squeal from Cody. Mattie entered the kitchen. "Ash and Kevin turned up."

Bray smiled. "I didn't think he'd manage until eight o'clock. Guess I was right. I'm glad Kevin decided to come." Kevin was Ash's boyfriend. Bray pointed to his cup. "Could you be the amazing man I know you are and refill my coffee, please?"

Mattie reached up and kissed him. "Of course I can."

Bray spent the next half an hour cooking French toast for everyone, and then Mattie ran upstairs when Ama started babbling to herself, the sign she was awake. She rarely cried when she woke. She lay there staring, eating her fist and toes and babbling.

"I think it's time to move this into the living room. Cody has been extremely patient," Jordan said.

They filed into the room, not an easy feat when there were so many of them, plus furniture and a mound of presents, but they managed.

"All right, Cody. Tuck in."

Cody grabbed a present, read the label, and handed it to Kit. He did the same until everyone had a present, including himself. Then he tore into the paper, punching a fist in the air when he saw the games console. He already had one at Ash's house, but they'd talked about whether he should have another one at their house for when he stayed over. It wasn't something they wanted to do without Ash's input, and when they'd asked him, he said it was up to them, but they'd insisted on talking it through with him like a family. Because that's what they were. Yes, Ash was Cody's father, but they were all in it together.

Bray helped Ama open her present, a soft plushy duck, which she shoved into her mouth and drool over. He watched Kit and Noah open their first gifts, and then he focused on Mattie and Jordan. The present they were opening wasn't his gift to them. He had something small hidden at the back of the tree for them, but that could wait until the very end.

It was a good hour of opening presents before someone pounded on the door.

Kit stood. "I'll get it."

Laughter sounded, and Mattie's parents entered, bearing more gifts. At this rate, they'd need a bigger house just to fit the presents in.

"Merry Christmas!" everyone said.

More people arrived shortly after. Jordan's parents, Mattie's sister, and then Bray's mom and aunts descended, too. The house wasn't big enough for them all, but they made it work. It was the reason for his last gift. One he hoped Jordan and Mattie would accept, even though they wouldn't have had a say in what it looked like.

Evie and Ronnie started dinner once all the presents were opened. Kit and Noah were setting up the games console for Cody, Ama was being doted on by his mom and aunts—with Lia trying to get her to keep a tiara on her head, though Ama was having none of it—Paul, Carl and Ash were discussing something, and Jordan and Mattie cuddled on the sofa, watching everyone.

Bray moved over to the tree, reaching to the back to retrieve the last gift. He didn't want a huge audience, but he couldn't wait any longer. He handed it to Mattie and Jordan, and then settled on the arm of the sofa, watching them. Mattie frowned up at him.

"What's this?"

Bray smiled. "A gift for you both. Open it."

The small box contained two identical keys, and Jordan smiled. "Keys to your house?"

Bray shook his head. "To a new house. Hopefully, our new home. Though if you don't like it, we can find something else."

Mattie sat forward. "Can we see?"

"If someone doesn't mind watching the kids, I can take you there. It's not far."

They arranged it with everyone, and Bray ushered them into the car. He had secretly been getting information from them over the past weeks to find out what they'd like in their ideal home, and then, when he'd found this place, it had seemed to be made for them. Although he wouldn't usually take the decision out of their hands, he hadn't wanted to miss out on it if someone else tried to buy it. So he'd taken a risk. Now he'd find out if it had paid off.

They peppered him with questions for the ten-minute drive, and when he pulled up in front of a house right between Willis Heights and Conway Heights, he stopped the engine. And waited.

"This?" Mattie asked, staring at the white, two-story building.

"Uh-huh." Bray wasn't sure of their thoughts, but he swallowed and continued. "Let's go inside and see what you think." He climbed out. "Like I said, we can find somewhere else if you don't like it. I saw it come up for sale, and I thought it hit a lot of what we'd said we wanted, so I went for it. I'm sorry for not asking you first."

Mattie threw his arms around Bray's waist. "The outside is lovely. Let's see what you've found, and then we decide together."

Jordan smiled at him over Mattie's head. "Yes, let's see what you've found us."

Bray led the way, unlocking and opening the door for them. He didn't say a word, just followed them around the house as they took everything in. He tried to see it from their point of view. It was empty of furniture, but that was easily remedied. The walls were painted white. There was a living room, a separate dining room, a separate kitchen with all the counter space Mattie could want, a laundry room, a toilet, and decking outside the back of the house. Upstairs, there were four bedrooms, two bathrooms and a closet space, which could be removed to make one of the rooms bigger.

He hadn't started to look for anything until they'd had confirmation of Mattie's custody of Ama, but the moment they'd attended court and received a resounding affirmative, Bray had started searching for their dream home. Knowing Ama wasn't going anywhere made things easier for them all.

By the time they'd looked at everything, Bray was nervous as hell. Mattie and Jordan had barely said a word. They headed back down the stairs to the front door, and he couldn't take it anymore.

"So...?"

Mattie sank onto the steps of the stairs, wringing his hands. "It's…"

Jordan stared at Bray. "It's perfect."

Mattie lifted wet eyes to him and nodded. "Perfect."

Bray exhaled and rubbed a hand over his face. "I'm glad. I hated that I hadn't brought you into this, but there had been little leeway to say yes before someone else snatched it up. If you don't like it, we can find something else. It's not a problem."

"But how…?" Mattie said. "How could you afford this?"

"I had money saved, and I got a good deal for my house."

Jordan gasped. "You sold your house! You love that house!"

Bray smiled, knowing right then and there he'd made the right decision. "I do, but I love you both more."

He was slammed against the front door as two bodies collided with him, and he laughed, holding them close. "I've put your names on the documents, too. This is *our* house, not mine." Tears soaked into his shirt, and he held them tighter. "I love you."

"What about Smudge?"

Bray snorted. "If she's that eager to see me, she'll find her way, I'm sure. But there will be other suckers she'll find to feed her."

They finally headed back home and spent the rest of the day soaking in the family atmosphere. Their new house would make it ten times easier to host family gatherings, and there was an extra room for when Kit and Noah wanted to stay, or anyone else for that matter.

After dinner, the grandparents had taken over. Kit and Noah had guided Paula, Loretta and Maggie out of the house, offering to take them home, so Bray threw his car keys to them. He knew they'd stay the night and visit again the following day. Ama was kidnapped by Mattie's parents, and

Cody was staying with Ronnie and Carl for the night. Both Jordan and Ash got to have a kid-free night.

When everyone had gone, and there was nothing but silence, they stared at each other.

"I don't know whether to sleep or have sex," Jordan said, and they burst into laughter.

"The cleaning up can wait until tomorrow, Mattie," Bray said, steering him to the stairs. "I have plans."

He planned to shower, get naked, and into bed. Lying in bed with his men was the best feeling in the world—except for his kids hugging him.

"Oh, by the way," Jordan said, "I found something…" He reached over to the bedside table and pulled a yellow piece of material from the drawer, holding it up. He raised his eyebrows at Mattie. "I think I found my yellow tank top."

Mattie buried his face in the pillow, and Bray wanted to know why. When he asked, Jordan said, "It went missing a little while ago, and I thought I'd left it somewhere. Couldn't for the life of me find it. Until today. You're a sneaky little man, Mattie Evans." He dropped it back over the edge of the bed and tickled Mattie, who squirmed to get away.

"I'm sorry! I just wanted something of yours!" he panted.

Jordan stopped his attack and slid his arms around them both. "You're welcome to it."

After a few seconds of silence, Mattie said, "I might need you to wear it a bit again, though."

"Why?" Jordan asked.

"It doesn't smell like you anymore." He turned to Bray. "And I want something of yours, too."

He wrapped his arm around them both and kissed whatever skin he could reach. He had designed a plan to seduce his men, but instead, he found he wanted to hold them. So he did.

"Whatever you want."

And as they fell asleep, one by one, despite nothing sexual happening, he was the happiest man alive.

———

WOULD YOU LIKE TO READ MY BOOKS BEFORE ANYONE ELSE? YOU can sign up to Steamy Delights, a membership subscription service, and gain early access to chapters from my work-in-progresses, exclusive bonus content and more. I have four tiers available: Contemporary, Kink & Daddy, Taboo & Dark and Club Royal Bonus. See which one grabs your fancy.

Read on for a teaser of <u>Rogue Royal.</u>

And for a taste of the free short story you get if you sign up to my newsletter…

NEXT IN THE GAYNOR BEACH SERIES

LUCIEN BY ALICE LA ROUX

Lucien

Divorced, with four children, and having to start again with my career – life at almost 40 was nothing like I'd planned.

When my ex-wife leaves our children with me for the summer, it's clear I'm in over my head. It isn't long until daycare worker Oz has me pulling up my socks and seeing what's important.

Oz

The Westlake family need a little more fun and love in their lives. Not my family to fix, that's what I tell myself. But…but what if I want it to be?

What does it matter that Lucien Westlake is thirteen years older than me?

Or that his ex-wife is a model and he's never looked at another guy before?

It's never too late to chase happiness.

Lucien is a bi-awakening, a second chance at life with an age gap, a hippie mother, adorable kids and a whole host of first times as our grumpy MC learns to open up to the sunshine that is Oz Holmes.

The next book is available here:
books2read.com/u/3nGkY8

ALSO SET IN GAYNOR BEACH

Single Dads of Gaynor Beach Series

Jake by Charley Descoteaux

Finn by Jessie G

Wynn by Amelia Hayden

Hugh by Gabbi Grey

Anderson by Foxy Valentine

Alec by Kaje Harper

Demetrius by SA Sway & Zelda Knight

Leo by Meredith Spies

Anthony by Gabbi Grey

Hiroshi by Zelda Knight

Jaime by SA Sway

Nate by Amelia Hayden

Tress by Michele Shriver

Eden by Leona Windwalker

Xavier by Gabbi Grey

Mattie by Elouise East

Lucien by Alice La Roux

Lanyon by TH Compton

Friends of Gaynor Beach Animal Rescue

Love Furever by Gabbi Grey

Iguana You to Want Me by Meredith Spies

Farming for Love by Layla Dorine

Bullying Benjamin by SA Sway

Pugnaciously Yours by Michele Shriver

FREE BOOK!

FREE just go to elouiseeast.com/newsletter

Jason doesn't have the strength to fight his stepfather for a happy life, so, to stop the man from turning his fists and words to his younger siblings, he takes the brunt of his anger himself. He vows to get those children away from him as soon as possible. Then, when there is one bruise too many for his best friend eyes, they come up with a plan for a fake boyfriend for Jason—someone who's really a bodyguard.

Darius doesn't get asked to the royal family's domain often, but he doesn't say no when he is. Being asked to be a fake boyfriend is far from usual, but he's happy to do it if it means he gets to spend time—and protect—the man he can't stop staring at. When things don't quite go the way Jason hopes, Darius offers another option. One that might backfire. But with Darius at his side, Jason finds more strength than he ever thought possible.

And maybe, he might've found the one person who could give him his happily ever after.

This is an MM bodyguard romance that spans both the Club Royal and Guarding Royalty series.

Get this book free at: elouiseeast.com/newsletter

ROGUE ROYAL TEASER

MAVERICK

Mav rubbed at his temple with his fingers and thumb, closing his eyes at the brightness in the room. How he wished he could've retreated to bed and pulled the covers over his head for the next two days.

"What's wrong?"

Douglas's voice was closer than Mav expected it to be, and he startled, nearly dropping the tablet.

"A headache. I'm fine." Mav tried for a smile.

Douglas's eyes narrowed. "Have you taken anything for it?"

Mav's cheeks heated. "Yes, although I have to let it run its course. It won't stop me from doing my job."

Douglas's forehead creased. "I never thought it would, but you also shouldn't be working if it's bad. Why don't you take the rest of the day off?"

"I'm fine, Your Highness."

"I insist. In fact, let me help you. I have experience with head massages. It will help to alleviate some of the pain if you'll allow me."

Mav didn't think he could manage with Douglas touching him. "Honestly, Your Highness, I'm—"

"If you say fine, I won't be pleased because I know you're lying."

Mav closed his eyes and inhaled through his nose to stop from saying something he'd regret. And to stop a shiver running down his spine from becoming visible. That voice. "It will go away on its own."

Douglas worked his jaw from side to side. "It's a migraine, isn't it?"

Mav sighed and gave a dismissive wave of his hand. "Yes, which is why it will go away in time. I'm used to it, Your Highness."

"How often do you get them?"

Mav didn't want any information to get out that would stop him from doing his job, so he remained silent. Douglas narrowed his eyes again.

"Right, come on. Back to your room, and I will give you a head massage. You can sleep for a few hours afterwards."

"Your Highness, please. I promise I'm fine."

"It's not up for debate, Maverick. Lead the way."

The tone brooked no argument, and with a heavy sigh, Mav pivoted so he didn't lose his balance and aimed for his room. He'd never had the prince in his room before; it was kind of surreal. Another bout of nausea hit, and he breathed.

A hand touched his elbow. "Are you all right?"

Mav didn't answer for a few seconds. "Yes. The nausea comes and goes." More information he hadn't meant to give Douglas. With all the issues Mav was exposing, Douglas would have all the evidence he needed to get him fired.

His nerves grew as they approached his door, and he tried again to dissuade Douglas, but it was no good. Mav opened his door and indicated for Douglas to enter.

Douglas glanced around the room, then pointed to a burgundy chaise lounge. "If you sit there with a cushion behind your lower back and rest your head on the cushioned side, I will be able to reach easily."

Mav hesitated but placed the tablet on the table and took the seat, pausing again before moving a cushion as Douglas asked. He had no idea what he was doing, but he couldn't stop. He told himself it was because he wanted the headache to go.

He clenched his jaw and breathed heavily as another roll of sickness washed over him. Laying back, he rested his head on the side of the chaise lounge. Mav stared at the ceiling and waited for further instructions, running his thumbs over the soft fabric beneath him. When none came, he moved his head to watch what Douglas was doing. The prince was returning from the bathroom with a washcloth, and Mav frowned. As Douglas came closer, Mav had trouble breathing.

Douglas picked up a chair and carried it to behind where Mav lay, and Mav returned his head to stare at the ceiling.

"I'm going to place this warm flannel over your eyes. The heat should help, as will the darkness. Then I will massage certain points on your head and your hands."

"This is too much."

"After everything you have put up with from me, this is the least I can do."

That shut Mav up. He'd never expected Douglas to care about how much work he was causing Mav. He lay the flannel over his eyes, leaving his nose and mouth free. Immediately, the heat seeped into his skin, and he felt a loosening in the tension of his body.

"That's it. Relax for me."

Douglas's voice rolled over him, and Mav sighed. He doubted this would work, but if Douglas wanted to try, Mav would let him.

Soft fingers threaded through his hair, pressing mildly into his scalp. He lost track of how long this carried on for before Douglas moved to press against a point in the centre of Mav's forehead. The pressure lasted for several minutes, moving to the corners of his eyebrows, at the top of his nose, on either side. After, Douglas moved to his ears, pressing against different areas.

With every action, Mav relaxed further until he was limp as a noodle, and Douglas was back to massaging his scalp. He didn't know if it was because he couldn't see, but every time Douglas moved his hand, Mav tingled everywhere, and goosebumps skated over his skin.

Douglas removed his hands, and Mav might've whimpered, though he would forever deny it. He heard a soft sound, then a warmth encased his right hand, and he realised it was Douglas's hand. Douglas turned Mav's hand palm up and put pressure between his thumb and forefinger. It continued for several moments, and Mav wouldn't have been able to move if he tried.

His muscles jerked when something began tracing the fingers and palm of his hand. It tickled, but also...didn't. It was as if a small current was trickling along his skin, leaving behind more tingles.

Several minutes later, Douglas replaced his hand on his lap, and his left hand was lifted and subjected to the same ministrations.

When Douglas spoke, he sounded far away, "Let's get you into bed."

Mav felt hands sliding under his body, and he tried to argue, but he was too tired. He could scarcely hold his own head up. The sheets were cool through his clothes, the pillows chilled beneath his head, and he absently noticed Douglas removing his shoes. The flannel was still over his eyes, though it, too, had cooled.

Douglas pulled a cover over him as he sank closer to slumber. He tried to wake up enough to speak to Douglas, but his body was too far gone.

"Sleep. Rest. Relax."

And it was the last thing he remembered.

Grab it here books2read.com/rogueroyal

BOOKS BY ELOUISE EAST

<u>Guarding Royalty</u>

Protecting his Past

Protecting his Heart

Protecting his Secrets

Protecting his Life

<u>Club Royal</u>

Royal Firsts

Rogue Royal

Secretive Royal

Grieving Royal

Disowned Royal

Trained Royal

Awakened Royal

Commanding Royal

<u>Illuminate Matchmaking</u>

Ignite

Blaze

Kindle

Scorch

<u>Boys, Daddies, Snuggles & More</u>

Need Him

Trust Him

<u>Daddy</u>

Love Me, Daddy

Soothe Me, Daddy

Spoil Me, Daddy

The Complete Daddy Series

<u>Love in Flames</u>

Out of the Frying Pan

Smokescreen

Breathing Fire

Love in Flames Collection

<u>Crush</u>

Love Conquers

Instant Desire

Primary Seduction

Deep Down

A Crush for Christmas

Life Support

Covert Strength

Love Scene

Lawful Attraction

Crush Collection Volume 1

Crush Collection Volume 2

Crush Collection Volume 3

<u>Just A Little Crush</u>

First Kiss

He's Behind You

A Special Love

<u>Standalone</u>

Treehouse Whispers

Star-Crossed

Protecting the Thief

Sizzling Chauffeur

A Home for Barney

Mattie

<u>Elouise R East (taboo)</u>

Dark & Divergent

Forbidden Temptation

Too Many Secrets: A Life of Secrets

Too Many Secrets: The Lake House

Collide

When Fantasies Collide

When Dreams Collide

When Pleasures Collide

When Cravings Collide

When Hungers Collide

ABOUT ELOUISE EAST

Elouise East writes sweet and steamy connections in gay romance. She also touches on taboo stories under the name Elouise R East.

Books that tell the stories where friendship and family are the focal point - be it blood family or chosen - are very important to her. That's why she includes a variety of personalities, talents, ages, situations and abilities as she believes a story or character needs. She wants her characters to be real, to be relatable, to be free to have whatever views they tell her they have. And trust her, most of the time, she does not have *any* say in the matter!

Her characters come to life on the page for her as well as her readers. Their stories unfold in front of her as she writes, and she has very little input into how they want to be shown. Just like real life, the lives of her characters change with every choice, every interaction and every conversation. And she wouldn't have it any other way.

She writes books that are emotionally realistic, even if liberties are taken with other aspects of the stories. She doesn't know any other way to write. It comes from deep inside.

Who is she? A single parent to two children living in the UK. An avid reader who still tries to devour every book she can get her hands on. A student of learning about any subject that takes her fancy. An author of books she would read herself. And a romantic at heart who loves anything cheesy.

Who's joining her on her journey?

Stalk her here… ;-)
Website : https://elouiseeast.com
Newsletter : https://elouiseeast.com/newsletter
All links : https://elouiseeast.com/links